I0564214

INTO THE ABYSS

HAYLEY REESE CHOW

Whimsical
Publishing & Illustration

Whimsical Publishing

Copyright © 2025 by Hayley Reese Chow

All rights reserved.

No part of this book may be reproduced in any form or by any electronic or
mechanical means, including information storage and retrieval systems,
without written permission from the author, except for the use of brief
quotations in a book review.

NO AI TRAINING: Without in any way limiting the author's [and
publisher's] exclusive rights under copyright, any use of this publication to
"train" generative artificial intelligence (AI) technologies to generate text is
expressly prohibited.

For information address Whimsical Publishing, whimsicalpublishing.ca

ISBN: 978-1-998195-22-0

Edited by Micheline Ryckman and Deborah O'Carroll
Cover illustration by Gabriella Bujdoso
Cover design by Micheline Ryckman
Map by Micheline Ryckman
First interior illustration by Hunter Ryckman
Middle interior illustration by Micheline Ryckman & Amanda Roberts
Final interior illustration by Ekaterina Vitkovskaya

STAR CV-11
ZAO

CRION
ICY, AIRLESS

24 SPACE
STATIONS

BELETHEA
UNSTABLE ATMOSHERE

CASOLLA SYSTEM

CASOLLA
22 UNINHABITED
MOONS

OBRONE
OCEANIC, EARTH ATMO

WORM GATE
BETA3

DRIETIS
DRY ATMO

To Adeline, and all my other stargazers.

MICAH'S TOP-SECRET RECAP: BEWARE OF SPOILERS!

INTO THE CHURN:

After discovering that Calderon was behind the murder of their teammate, Genevieve Navarro, Sterling/Hart won the BRR and used the spotlight to expose Calderon's crimes.

INTO THE FIRE:

After Calderon was wrongfully exonerated, Sterling/Hart traveled to Otho to save Ezren's dad from Baxter Research. There, they found that Baxter had been trafficking the Casolla system's first complex lifeforms—the luxies—through the system's dark syndicates, and Calderon Industries had been attempting to protect them. Ezren's dad sacrificed himself so Sterling/Hart could save the luxies with help from Calderon's team, though Ambassador York, the syndicate's political front man, escaped.

A CHURN IN THE DARK:

After Calderon was wrongfully exonerated, Sterling/Hart

traveled to Otho to save Ezren's dad from Baxter Research. There, they found that Baxter had been trafficking the Casolla system's first complex lifeforms—the luxies—through the system's dark syndicates, and Calderon Industries had been attempting to protect them. Ezren's dad sacrificed himself so Sterling/Hart could save the luxies with help from Calderon's team, though Ambassador York, the syndicate's political front man, escaped.

CHAPTER 1

4.25.44B: T-minus 9 days until the BRR

A YEAR AGO, Ezren never would've dreamed she'd be sitting at a table with Belethea's most powerful leaders, and yet somehow this had become her new normal. The Belethea Race Royale council meetings weren't exactly her favorite pastime in the 'verse, but to her own shock, she didn't hate them either. To be fair, her standards had dropped drastically since her second near-death experience—the one that claimed her father's life on Otho. Here, seated in a plush chair at a broad synwood table surrounded by familiar faces in the high-collared, long jackets of Belethean business wear with Foster beside her, they were relatively safe.

And that was enough.

She'd even gotten used to the weight of the gun pressed against her thigh and the sight of its duplicate on Foster's waist —a requirement levied by Shiro after one too many death threats. Between the hardware and Shiro's omnipresence outside the council door, they were always ready for the syndicates to deliver on their promise of retribution after Ezren and Foster had shut down their illegal luxie trade, but so far they'd been all bark and no bite.

Drawing her thoughts away from that dark spiral, Ezren forced her attention back to the meeting. The council only had ten core Belethean members, but their biweekly holocons often included ambassadors from the other twenty-seven Casollan stations and planets as topics were brought to their attention and resolved. They discussed the organization of the royale season, which events were held where, potential cheating accusations, the legality of cybernetic enhancements, disciplinary actions, outdated rules, waivers, safety, suit technology... the list went on. Though most of the other attendees were present as holopros, she, Foster, Villegas, and Calderon always attended in the flesh with the roiling Belethean sky projected on the domed ceiling above them.

As the Obronian ambassador argued to change team size requirements, Ezren cut a glance to Calderon where he sat on Foster's left. While Calderon was certainly the black mark on the proceedings, his knowledge and authority were impossible to refute.

Even as the high-status Dreitian and Obronian officials challenged them on every level, happily contradicting Villegas and the other Beletheans at every turn, they fell quiet when Calderon spoke. They listened. They respected him.

And it was infuriating.

Worse was the way he patiently took the time to lean over and explain every nuance of the discussion to her and Foster, including the questions they didn't know to ask. The other council members, Belethea's foremost political and industry leaders, had been downright glacial the first time she and Foster had walked into the boardroom at the top of Calderon's headquarters in Petraskis. It was only after Calderon gave a flowery speech about them being the face of the future—of their hands guiding Casolla through the turbulence rocking its present— that the others thawed. It also didn't hurt that he'd almost snapped Villegas's head off when she'd muttered some comment about their place being in the BRR.

Villegas hadn't said a word about it since. In fact, after seven months of these conferences, she and the other Belethean council members regarded them with something akin to acceptance. The ten of them functioned more or less as a coherent team, connected by the stacked powers against them, their dedication to Belethea, and the race royale that captured Casolla's entire attention once a year.

Which was crazy. Because Calderon—the de facto council leader in everything but name—was a chaffing murderer.

But now Ezren understood how he'd miraculously dodged the lambast of public opinion. It was almost impossible to reconcile this patient, measured man in his perfectly tailored teal suit with Vieve's murderer. After all, this was the same man dubbed by VSoc as the grandfather of Belethea for the last fifty years. The man who'd intervened to save the first sentient species in Casolla. And yet he'd also tried to murder her teammates. Tried to murder *her*.

His mask was perfect—an incongruity which just made him more dangerous.

Calderon ended the call, and the holos of the other attendees winked out of sight before he turned to where Foster sat massaging his hand, expression inscrutable.

"The Obronians lobby to adjust team size for population every year, but precedent is on our side. Never waver on equal representation from all entities."

Foster nodded, but he crossed his arms, his jaw ticking in the way it did every time Calderon addressed him. Which was weirdly often. Despite Foster's stormy visage and rebellious reticence, when he did speak up in these meetings—almost always to contradict Calderon—it was more than evident that he was paying close attention.

While Ezren mostly stuck to advising on terraforming and scientific funding, Foster's focus had been cutting through the corruption that had marred the BRR for decades—from gambling to spectator extortion, to the buying and selling of the royalers themselves. He'd pushed so hard on those issues that *The Royaler Review*, of all hololiogs, had called him "as cutthroat a champion in the council as he was in the race."

His latest idea, to stonewall all companies with syndicate affiliations from profiting in any way from the BRR, had been particularly popular. With Calderon's vocal support, the decision had passed through the Belethean Chamber unanimously and was actually set to go into effect—she checked her goggs—tomorrow. With any luck, it would be overshadowed by the BRR hype, but she sent a mental reminder to Sylvia to be ready for yet another landslide of death threats just in case.

Across the broad table, Villegas tapped her celestial-painted fingernails on the polished wood, her shrewd gaze on Ezren. "Everything is set for the BRR qualifier in two days, and we'll have one meeting with all the attending ambassadors between the qualifier and the final race."

"We'll be there." Ezren leaned forward, nerves tingling through her chest at the thought of the BRR. "And many of the ambassadors have also requested one-on-one meetings during that week as well."

"Good." Calderon's flinty stare turned toward her, the navy clouds in the holopro above reflected in his dark pupils. "An opportunity to meet is an opportunity to influence. The deeper your ties, the easier it will be to sort out future conflicts." His attention swiveled to Foster. "I know Coach Long has an excellent archive of pertinent information, so be sure you use it to your advantage."

Villegas rapped her knuckles on the table in agreement. "This is Belethea's time to shine, so make sure you're hammering home the message about unity and ethical leadership."

"*Ethical.*" Foster snorted. "What a load of shaft." He rose and offered Ezren his hand. "All I know is in nine days, my contract is up, and you'll have to get another puppet to jerk around on a string."

Ezren suppressed a sigh. Despite her obvious reservations, she appreciated the immense opportunity their council appointment brought. Foster, meanwhile, had a harder time looking past the required proximity to Calderon.

Villegas and Calderon shared a knowing look, and Ezren wondered about their relationship for perhaps the hundredth time. Though they were never friendly, per se, they did seem to be in sync on a deep level. Had Calderon once mentored Villegas like he was doing for her and Foster now? In fact, she realized, at 103, Calderon had probably been behind every appointment to this council since he first founded the BRR eighty years ago—had probably mentored every sitting member.

The sheer power and influence of the notion sent a chill through her.

"Don't be ridiculous, Sterling." Villegas adjusted the gold goggs in her jet-black hair.

"There's no running from this." She rose from her seat, the two columns of brass buttons on her long, sleek jacket gleaming under a flash of lightning from the holo above. "Besides, we all know that you're not going to leave Hart to shoulder the burden alone."

Her hard gaze flicked from Ezren to Calderon meaningfully, and Ezren had to admit, she wasn't wrong. Though Ezren often argued with Foster that she was quite comfortable sitting on the council while he pursued his own path, he refused to even consider it.

Foster's hard façade cracked as he glanced at Ezren, his hand spasming in her grasp.

She offered him a reassuring smile and gave his fingers a

hard squeeze. "There's no use deciding anything now. We'll continue to consider the options during our break in the off-season."

"As is customary and earned." Calderon picked up his black cane from where it stood perfectly balanced, waiting for him. His stare, however, never left Foster's. "But please don't forget that since you've joined the council, we've had three successful organized crime raids, you've ensured system-wide protection for the luxopodos, shut down their illegal trade, ensured smooth planning of the BRR, raised your Belethea team to the third-most lucrative in the system, and decreased Casolla-wide tensions three-fold."

"And we also made Crion into a livable space and increased terraforming conditions outside the churn belt by 250%," Ezren chimed in with a sweet smile.

While the BRR may have been their shared aim, she never missed a chance to press her own dream of a livable surface for Belethea. That was why she had originally started down this path almost two years ago, after all.

Calderon cut her a cool glare, but she couldn't help but note the glint of begrudging admiration there and allowed herself a twinge of satisfaction. While Calderon would never get behind her terraforming measures, there was no denying they both shared a unique tenacity that was impossible to ignore.

Calderon tapped his cane on the tile floor with a smooth click. "Yes, well, I suppose we have to pick our battles, don't we?"

"What Calderon is saying," Villegas cut in, "is that Sterling/Hart's success in the actual BRR is now only rivaled by your success on the interplanetary stage. And..." She sucked in a deep breath, and her face softened, making her already diminutive stature seem even smaller. "We are getting old. If you want these changes to be permanent, we will need your young voices to lead the future." She ran a knobby finger over the glossy table. "Which is all to say, you would be welcome and appreciated here in a long-term role, should you choose it."

Foster's jaw flexed, and Ezren quickly bobbed her head. Though she, Sylvia, and Foster had suspected this offer, it was the first time Villegas had officially proposed it. "We have so appreciated your counsel and wisdom; thank you for helping us fit into these new roles. We're still processing these opportunities, but we're proud to be part of Belethea's hope." Ezren glanced at Foster again, but he looked away. "It's been a long year though, and I think we will take the off-season to consider what the future will look like for us."

"An ambassador's answer." Villegas raised her chin, her sharp features practically glowing with a pride that heated Ezren's chest. Villegas strode to Calderon's side, the two of them looking nearly the same age despite Calderon's silver hair and their forty-year gap. "In the meantime, we will, of course, continue your education in the next year. I trust as you learn, your decision will become clear."

"And should you decide to leave anyway"—Calderon's face darkened into a thunderhead that matched the squalls above—"know that you'd be leaving a power vacuum in your wake."

Foster met his stare, their stony countenances reflecting one another. "I don't want power."

"And that is why Casolla trusts you with so much of it." The steel in Calderon's regard eased into something like regret as he shifted the old-fashioned brass goggs around his neck. "Should you give it away, know that the greedy hands snatching it from the bowels of the system would be more than capable of undoing all the good you have accomplished." He tapped his cane against the mirror-like floor again, his dark velvet voice low and earnest—almost kind. "I know you didn't ask for this, but sometimes opportunity chooses us, instead of the other way around."

The ensuing silence tightened the tension in the air to a snapping point. Ezren stepped forward, trying to find the words to defuse the fraught circle threatening to strangle her. "So far, I think most would agree that Foster and I have risen to every challenge. This seems like a lot of stress over concerns still far off in the future. With the BRR pressing down on us, I think this could at least wait until next season." She pressed closer to Foster, and his expression warmed ever so slightly. "If you can forgive my confidence, I think between the two of us, we'll find our way."

Calderon smiled at her, his face creasing in a hundred wrinkles as he exposed his sharp canines. "Indeed. It's that confidence that I hope—"

The chime of the room's central holopro interrupted him, and Belethea's storm clouds disappeared from the ceiling.

"What?" Villegas blinked at the holo in her goggs. "This is a secure line, who is—"

Another, deeper notification, like that of the single toll of a sonorous bell, interrupted her. The room fell into darkness, and the holo of a lone silver bird glided across the black ceiling. Foster's grip tightened on Ezren's hand, and her fingers moved to brush the stock of her pistol as the projected creature alighted on a rotting tree—one of what must've been a hundred birds perched on the skeletal branches. A mournful, hoarse caw cracked the silence before Calderon connected to the center control and dismissed the holo with a curt wave of his hand.

The lights flashed on, and Ezren blinked the dying tree from her vision, foreboding crawling over her skin. "What was that?" she whispered.

But Calderon's and Villegas's features had turned to stone, and from their locked stares, she knew the chip messages were flying between them. Ezren looked at Foster, but his lips pressed into a firm line. They'd sat in dozens of meetings in this room, and never once had anything remotely like that happened.

EZREN: THAT WAS ODD, RIGHT?

FOSTER: YES.

Finally, Villegas frowned, and Calderon shook his head, clearing his throat. "Nothing important. A mistake. Nothing more." He turned back to them, his ruddy skin a shade paler than before. "As I was saying, it's best to always be prepared, as we never know when"—he paused, his lips twitching as if weighing his words—"*opportunities* might befall us." He picked up his bowler hat from the table, tipping it upside down in farewell while he edged toward the door. "Until we next meet, Sterling/Hart, it has been my pleasure."

"The next two weeks will be chaotic, so be sure to look after one another." Villegas dipped her chin at them as she walked after Calderon, the door hissing open. "I'll follow you out, Warner."

Shiro peeked in on them from his post before the door slid shut again, leaving Ezren and Foster in silence in the empty room.

Foster braced himself against his chair, the muscles in his back bunching beneath his long dark coat as his words slipped out between clenched teeth. "What a chaffing hypocrite."

Ezren leaned back against the table, looking up at the now blank white ceiling. "What do you mean?"

"The message, Ezren—those birds were *crows*."

Ezren's stomach flipped at the insinuation. "You're not saying..."

Ezren trailed off, thinking back three months to when York's body had been found on Crion as a "gift" to them from a man known only as "the Crow." Though Shiro had warned them of his reputation, they'd heard nothing more from him since the incident, and Ezren had tucked the threat away in the back of her mind with all the others.

"That one of the most powerful men in the system is working with the dark syndicate king?" Foster swiped a hand down his clean-shaven jaw. "Well, Calderon certainly had no love for Ambassador York, and the Crow dumped his body on the ice. I'll be curious to see what Shiro thinks of it."

Ezren chewed the inside of her cheek, trying to make the pieces fit. "But... Calderon has been pushing so hard for the crackdown on the syndicates' illegal trade. Not just of luxies, but everything."

"He's a lying murderer with a million secrets." Foster winced, and his left hand moved to massage the other. "I don't know what he's planning, but we have to be on our guard and get out of this place as soon as possible. Villegas even said to take care of each other. I think she was trying to warn us."

"But if we give up our positions in the council, then we'd be leaving Calderon to run it uncontested, Foster. Is that really better?" Ezren took his hand in hers and gently kneaded out the spasms that always seemed to attack in these meetings.

"Surely there must be someone else." Foster's shoulders relaxed as Ezren dug her fingers higher into his wrist. "Villegas or... I don't know—someone."

"Okay, when you think of that someone, you let me know." She pressed a quick kiss to his knuckles and shot him a perceptive smile. "And also, you don't have to come back when your eligibility is up. I really could handle it on my own."

"I know you could." He turned her hand in his, his expression softening as he threaded his fingers with hers. "But there is nowhere I'd rather be than at your side. Always."

"Even if Calderon is on the other one?"

He gave Calderon's seat a flat glare. "Seriously, why does he always sit beside *me*?"

Ezren laughed—a real, ringing laugh that echoed through the room, and finally the furrow in Foster's brow eased with a smile. "I know it's trying." Ezren grinned, tugging him toward the door. "But I think it will be easier once you, Simon, and Bex age out this year, and we have a successful, drama-free BRR. Then, everything will finally calm down."

Foster let her tow him around the table toward the door. "And then we're going to have a nice long vacation, just like over New Year."

"Longer." Ezren raised her eyebrows. "I'm thinking we run away and don't come back until the start of next season."

Foster's grin widened, his eyes falling closed as if in bliss. "And this is why I love you." The door hissed open before them. "Let's go home."

And when he said it, the word was always so much sweeter. The stress and the fear all melted away, and Ezren let herself fall into the daydream of the two of them relaxed and peaceful under an open teal sky.

But as the door closed, Ezren swore the image of the crow tree flickered across the dome ceiling again, and a prickle along her spine warned her the dream was somehow farther than it had ever been before.

CHAPTER 2

4.29.44B T-minus 5 days until the BRR

OVER THE FOLLOWING DAYS, all thoughts of Calderon's usual cryptic shaft evaporated from Foster's mind under the absolute insanity that was BRR hype week. Although he'd reported his suspicions to Shiro, he didn't have time to ruminate over possible ties between Calderon and the Crow as he and Ezren ran—sometimes literally—from interview to meeting to appearance.

Not to mention the nailbiter of a qualifier, where Belethea had managed to qualify two doubles teams for the first time in BRR history. Grady/Guns had snagged fourth with the rookie Amaral siblings tagging along in nineteenth, even after Dean broke his ankle in a bad scrap during the brawl.

But unlike the last two years, all of the Belethean royalers had survived without ending up in intensive care—the knot of fear in Foster's chest only unraveling when the last racer limped across the finish line.

So, it was with a long sigh of relief that he now stepped into the entertaining hall of his father's mansion with Ezren on his arm, the post-qualifier party already in full swing in the early afternoon. The Naris and Belethean teams filled the space with silver and teal, talking and dancing among the waist-high serving bots. Long couches had been pushed to the side of the room, his dad's band played one of their pulsing hit songs from a low stage in the corner, and plates of colorful appetizers spread across sleek tables lining the back.

Foster's mouth quirked up with the heartening realization that the giant, long-empty Yunin compound was finally being put to good use. Since his dad had taken up full-time residence there, he'd hosted at least a half dozen events for the Belethea BRR team in the last eight months. And sometimes, Ezren and Foster stayed the weekend just to get away from the madness of Carmella Hall. Although the Yunin Compound was only thirty miles away from the Petraskis dome, the respite from the insanity of the team's constant training and VSoc stunts was always welcome.

"Okay." Sylvia pushed her curls behind her shoulders with a deep breath as she sidled in beside them, the engagement ring glinting on her finger. The sight of it made Foster's gaze dart to Ezren, his pulse thudding for reasons he couldn't quite name. "This is your break," Sylvia continued, Turnip winding around her ankle with all six tails flicking. "We've got hovercams collecting candid clips for VSoc, but your next appearance isn't until 0800 tomorrow, and we're all staying the night here, so relax and enjoy yourselves before the whirlwind continues in the morning." She pushed up her long, teal-laced sleeves, harried lines etching her face as she glanced at something in her goggs.

Shiro wrapped his arms around her from behind. "Does this mean we get a break too?"

The Sylvia of four months ago would've broken into hives over the word "break," but today, she let herself relax into her fiancé. With Micah taking lead on VSoc and Foster's mom accepting Belethea's head coach position after the BRR, it seemed like a weight had been lifted from Sylvia's shoulders. Even if she was still their general manager.

"Yes, thank the suns. With Gerard covering security and Jabari running the VSoc shift, we get nineteen hours off, so you'd better—" Sylvia straightened as her gaze alighted on something across the room. "Is that my sister? And my parents?"

Shiro smiled down at her as she turned in his arms. "Since Petraskis is on holiday for hype week, I asked Gerard if we could invite them."

"*You*"—Sylvia's eyes filled, and she planted a quick kiss full on his lips—"are my *favorite* human being." Sylvia's grin turned to Ezren and Foster one more time. "Be ready tomorrow at 0800. Till then, no working!" With that, she ran to where her family laughed on a pair of red couches in the corner, tugging the smug Shiro along behind her.

Ezren turned to Foster, delighted mischief dancing across her face. "Nineteen whole hours?" She tugged on his lapels as she bounced on her toes, both of them still in their long, buttoned coats after their meeting with Uvis Station's ambassadors. "Whatever shall we do?"

And as much as Foster wanted to throw her over his shoulder and have her all to himself, it was even rarer that they got to spend time with their families—all of whom he could see dotted across the raucous crowd.

Well, except for Ezren's father—he would forever be missing.

Foster's brows shot up as he saw a pigtail-bunned tornado hurtling in their direction. He tucked a magenta strand behind Ezren's ear. "First, I think there's a few people here who've been waiting for you."

Ezren followed his gaze just as Micah glommed onto her with a flying leap. "Ezzy! We were so worried you weren't going to make it."

Ezren's mother trailed behind Micah with her own genial

smile, waiting her turn to wrap Ezren in a hug. Foster moved behind them to where Davis and Sam's heads bent together, laughing about something as Waffle snuffled between them. At fourteen, Sam was now only a few inches shorter than Davis, his body increasingly stocky like his father's had been.

"Davis." Foster extended his forearm, and Davis knocked his own against it before coming in for a hug.

"Foster, it's been too long, kin." He patted his back with two solid thumps before stepping away.

A genuine smile curved Foster's lips. "What're you talking about, I saw you last week." Though technically, Davis was Ezren's ex, after he'd flown Foster and Grady to the mouth of hell at a moment's notice last year and risked everything to save Foster's life, he now only thought of Davis as a friend. And even though Davis was still completing his studies at Petraskis University, he seemed to hang out at Carmella now just as much as the rest of their team.

Foster turned to Sam, his spherical hummingbot, Giles, perched on his shoulder. "Now, Sam, I haven't seen you in an age, and it looks like you've already grown half a foot."

Sam's bright blue gaze narrowed. "Yeah, well, I'm busy, and you're busy; what do you expect?" Beside him, Turnip mewed at Waffle curiously, but if the capybog acknowledged the pink cat, she gave no sign.

Right. Foster blew out a quiet breath. Sam had been slightly suspicious of him from the beginning, and the story of Sam's dad sacrificing himself for Foster had done him no favors. "Yeah, but the off-season is coming up, and you'll be out of school. Maybe we can all go on a holiday somewhere."

Sam rolled his eyes. "Yeah, like that'll ever happen."

"C'mon, Sam," Davis said, running a hand through his styled sweep of dark hair. "Sometimes we've got to believe the best."

"Sure, I'll believe it when I see it." With that, Sam moved off to where his sister had opened her arms for him. A solid four inches taller than her 5' 2", the youngest member of the Hart family had officially become the tallest—and *not* a fan of Foster's.

Davis clapped a hand on Foster's shoulder with an apologetic smile, his voice low. "It's just a weird age, you know? He'll come around."

Foster was saved from a response as Micah threw her arms around his neck with a happy squeal. "Foster Yunin-Sterling! Did you know the whole 'verse is still holding out hope that you're going to make a surprise run at the BRR?"

"Did you tell them they're going to be disappointed?"

She reached up to muss his mousy brown hair, and he sidestepped her. "Um, excuse you, *I* do not disappoint my Belroy boys and babes." She wiggled a finger in his direction with a teasing grin. "That's what *you* do."

Foster waved her off, tuning in to Ezren and Sam's conversation instead.

"But Sam"—Ezren squeezed his shoulders, her smile strained—"I see you way more than I did when we were training last year. Besides, you used to think the BRR was like the best thing ever." She reached in to tickle his ribs, and he stepped back, his expression empty as he batted her hands away.

"Yeah, well it gets old fast when the only thing anyone wants to talk about is your sister's politics." He made a face. "And it's not just me, it's Mom too, you know."

"Oh, Sam." Dr. Evangeline Hart put an arm around her youngest, her smile edged with worn sorrow. "You know I'm just as busy as the rest of you with the lab." She rubbed his arms as if it would warm his chilly countenance. "It's just a hectic season of life, but it's not forever."

"Speaking of seasons of life," Davis intervened with a diplomatic smile, craning his neck to where Sylvia sat in a circle of her very large extended family. "I got a save-the-date for a December wedding? What's the holdup?"

And again, Foster's chest squeezed at the word *wedding*.

Ezren laughed. "Well, Sylvia and Shiro want to do it the old-fashioned way with a big party and ceremony and everything. She wants her whole family to be there, but they don't even have time to plan it until the off-season."

"Suns, it's been an age since I've been to a traditional ceremony." Dr. Evangeline smiled as she slung one arm each around Sam and Ezren. "Your dad and I ran off to get married the day he proposed—on a ship, just the two of us and a captain on the Obronian sea." She winked at Sam, and he feigned a grimace that didn't quite hide his smile. "I'm telling you, it was romantic."

Foster glanced at her left hand, and noted the thin black line drawn around the ring finger in nanite ink—the traditional mark of marriage after old-world rings had been banned on FOD-sensitive ark ships. His heated gaze moved to meet Ezren's crinkled one, and his pulse kicked.

Ezren's cheeks pinked as she turned back to her mom. "Well, it'll sure be weird when they move out of Carmella. Turnip's practically the team mascot."

Foster looked to where the cat pranced around Waffle, her nub of a tail wagging ever so slightly and her pricked, half-flopped ears at odds with her resting bored expression.

"And Foster will be moving out too, won't he?" Micah smoothed her teal pigtail buns, her eyes—also teal today—flicking between Foster and Ezren with way too much innocence.

Foster opened his mouth to respond when he was attacked from behind.

"We're all moving out!" Grady shouted from where he'd jumped onto Foster's back. "We're going to move into the apartment building next door and call it Carmella Two."

"Don't make me hurt you before the BRR," Foster said, struggling to keep a straight face as he wrestled Grady off of him.

Grady skipped away, lifting his fists and feinting a punch to his ribs. "Bring it, kin. I could take you this year."

Bex shook her head next to him, her white hair falling across one eye and the rare hint of a smile in the tilt of her pale mouth. "Ignore him; he's impossible today."

"Well, yeah, in five days, we're going to win." Grady moved to put Ezren in a headlock, but she spun out of his grasp, hiding behind Micah. Micah reached out grabby hands, baring a manic fangirl smile that even Grady backed away from.

"Wait, someone's talking about us? The next BRR champs?" Kit and Dean, the tall, lavender-haired Amaral siblings, emerged from the crowd as if summoned, any trace of their qualifier injuries already healed after a few hours in Carmella's med tank. Off to one side, Kit's boyfriend, Jabari, shot her a grin as he orchestrated six different holos and over a dozen hovercams.

Grady burst into condescending laughter, dramatically falling onto Bex's shoulder. "The nerve of rookies these days."

Foster resisted the urge to roll his eyes as the two doubles continued their good-natured bickering to the delight of the circle of fans and other royalers. He caught Ezren's attention where Micah was whispering something in her ear.

Foster: I'm going to go find my parents. Need anything?

Ezren smiled, her gaze skimming to Micah, and then down to where Waffle was trying to wedge herself between Ezren's calves with Turnip now sitting atop her wide, brown back.

EZREN: No, I'm good for now. I'll catch up in a minute.

With his own grin, Foster quietly edged away from the growing knot of boasting royalers. Most of the band had dispersed on their break with a lone pianist playing a jazzy beat on the enormously expensive grand piano. Behind him, huge windows showcased Belethea's wind-swept landscape and a legion of dark clouds curling on the mountainous horizon.

Foster continued his scan of the party, still very much in its early stages, until he found his parents together in an armchair tucked into the corner. They both had glasses in their hands, his long-haired father gesturing animatedly from the seat, while his mother, in her silver Naris spacer's jumpsuit, laughed from her perch on the arm.

For a moment, Foster watched them. His parents had never been married, and their relationship seemed to have waxed and waned over the years—both of them more committed to their careers than each other. But even when separated, they'd always seemed in tune. Now with his father staying on Belethea for the foreseeable future and his mother returning to Petraskis, he wondered if they would find their way back to each other. Or maybe they already had.

As one, his parents burst into laughter again, his mom falling into his dad's lap as she wiped tears of mirth from her cheeks. He didn't miss how his dad looked at her—the affection and joy lighting his face. In many ways, they seemed like different people than he'd known when he was younger. But then again, it was only this past year that he'd started spending quality time with them both. Had they been like this all along, and he just hadn't known?

His lips tugged upward as his mom said something, and his dad brushed her hair from her forehead with a thoughtful hum.

Whatever the reason, he was glad to see them happy and doubly glad to be in a place to appreciate their bond.

He looked back to where Ezren stood amidst her own court with Sam and their team, her eyes shining as her words held them rapt. Everything that had happened to him in the last two years... it was all because of one girl running late to a starting line.

One girl who had changed his life.

"Hey!" His dad finally noticed him with a wave.

Torn from his thoughts, Foster raised his chin and ambled closer.

"Foster." His mom rose and wrapped her powerful arms around him. "We're so glad you could make it."

His dad came next with his own embrace. Two hugs that would've seemed unthinkable a year ago now warmed his chest. "Yeah, hope you don't mind the band took the opportunity to practice with an appreciative audience."

"Nah, I caught the tail end of it. You sounded good." And he meant it. For years, he'd avoided his dad's music out of resentment. With their relationship repaired, Foster had rediscovered the songs that all of Casolla was obsessed with, and found, to his surprise, that a fair number of them referenced a lost boy running too fast.

His dad rubbed the back of his neck. "Well, you know, it's been good to take it easy this year. To get back into writing. I think it's made a huge difference."

"I agree. This next album is shaping up to be the best yet." His mom gave his dad a warm smile, and he wrapped an arm around her shoulders.

Foster smirked—turned out the VSoc rumors were right for once. Then again, they were probably coming from Micah. He cleared his throat, gesturing to the Naris royalers now engaged in some kind of extreme food-catching game with the Beletheans. "How're your qualifiers feeling this year?"

"They're good. Experienced." A cocky grin bowed his mom's lips. "In fact, with our alliance with Belethea, I'm thinking we might even have a chance at a top-ten finish, especially if Grady/Guns medal."

Foster couldn't suppress his own grin—because they were *his* royalers. After Sylvia had nearly drowned in team manager duties, he'd unofficially taken on the lead coaching role this year with Ezren as his unofficial assistant. Together they'd trained every one of their ten rookies and sharpened Grady/Guns into a frontrunning contender. "Well, it'll be the first time Belethea's had two doubles running, much less an alliance. It's a whole new world."

"And the first time they've had a champion coach to guide them," his mother added, pride coating every word. "I think we've all noticed the difference."

"What are you going to do next year once you're officially off the roster, and your mom takes over the coaching scene?" His dad lifted his drink, a teasing smirk toggling between both of them. "You'll finally be free."

His mom elbowed him in the ribs with a good-natured roll of her eyes.

"I won't be free yet," Foster muttered, leaning against the enforced windowpanes. "I'll be staying on the chaffing BRR council for another year until Ezren doesn't have to sit next to that fodding murderer."

The good cheer fell from his parents' faces as they exchanged a weighted look.

"I understand the concern, but don't forget, the luxie situation brought Casolla to the brink of war last year. If it wasn't for you and Ezren stepping into the full diplomatic duties at the summit, who knows where we'd be now? And hasn't Ezren also said you've done a lot of good on the council?" His mom folded her arms. "I saw the anti-syndicate measure go through—the one that you proposed—they say it's going to make a huge impact."

His dad swirled the fizzing amber liquid in his glass with a low chuckle. "Yeah, who would've thought you'd be as good as an ambassador as you were in the royale?"

Foster ran a hand through his hair, his usual conflicting feelings putting him off-balance with his parents' praise. He'd been adamant on his uncompromising stance on corruption from the start, thinking he would use his position to undermine Calderon. So it had confused the chaff out of him when Calderon had been the largest proponent of every one of his ideas, and arguably the reason they'd been successful.

The only plausible explanation he could think of was that Calderon had aligned himself with Foster and Ezren to revive his own rep through their association. To be seen as forgiven.

From a quick glance at any VSoc headline showcasing the "productive partnership" of Sterling/Hart and Calderon, it had worked.

Which meant that, unconsciously, Foster had helped the shafting murderer. And he fodding hated it.

"Is the good we've done worth the price of rubbing shoulders with the guy who tried to kill us?" he asked, jaw flexing.

"I'm not saying I don't hate him too," his mom said, her tone carefully neutral. "But if you want to be in a position to oppose him at all, then you have to be on the council, right?"

Keep your enemies close. Calderon's words rattled in Foster's head, and he scowled, wishing for all the world he could scrape the man's influence from his brain with a scalpel. "Look, we've done that. For the last year, we did our part. But is that really our burden to carry for the rest of our lives?"

His dad grimaced, and his mom's lips tightened, her hackles

visibly rising. But then, just when Foster thought she was about to unload, his dad put a hand on her shoulder, and the breath whooshed out of her.

"No one's telling you what choices to make, Foster." His dad's voice was almost gentle. "But I would be careful trading a royal flush for a two pair. Do you have more to lose? Yeah. But you also have more to gain."

"And although you've been quick to reject, well, *any* expectations"—his mom raised a judgmental brow—"just understand, Foster, the world has had them for you because you've lived up to them at every turn. You were a BRR prodigy, and you delivered. You became an ambassador, and you literally changed Casolla for the better. You may underestimate what you're capable of, but don't be surprised when the rest of us don't."

Foster opened his mouth, but no words came out. He'd always felt like he was skating on the edge of failure... But was it possible that everyone else only saw the victories?

"Besides"—his dad smiled, looping his arm around his mom's shoulders once more—"that influence is also what helps you protect your friends, your family, and even Belethea itself. It doesn't have to be a bad thing."

"What doesn't have to be a bad thing?" Ezren bounced into their circle, her pale cheeks practically glowing.

His mom smiled at her as if she'd hung the moon. "Oh, nothing, just talking about the future." She reached out her arms, and Ezren flew in, while his dad stretched his embrace to hug them both at once.

"Ah yes, Grady was just saying all the age-outs were going to move across the street from Carmella." Ezren pulled away, her eyes glinting. "So it sounds like Foster won't be going far."

Foster's lips twisted. With everything going on, he'd barely had time to consider the options once his contract was up. "I guess that depends on if you'll be staying at Carmella or if Villegas will let you move out too this year."

"Well *I'm* on her good side lately." Ezren gave his parents a conspiratorial smile. "Maybe I'll get to move into Carmella 2.0 too."

Foster glanced to where Sam laughed with Micah and Dr. Evangeline. "You wouldn't want to move to be closer to Sam? Or back to Tuzuno?"

Ezren turned her coffee-brown gaze out the window at the rain blowing sideways onto the mauve peaks in the distance. "I don't know if I'd really fit there anymore. We could always visit, but I like talking to the other ambassadors when they come through Petraskis, and I feel like we do more good work here than we could anywhere else."

Foster cocked his head as it truly sank in for the first time how much Ezren had grown from the no-name terraforming intern he'd met almost two years ago. The one who'd wanted to stay in Tuzuno and never leave. The one who'd shied away from the reporters and VSoc. As she'd grown faster and stronger, her drive and passion had grown right along with her. He'd once described her as a chaffing force of nature, but even he couldn't have predicted how unstoppable she would become.

He'd thought when Calderon introduced them to the council as the future, he'd just been buttering them up. But now he realized that the old asschaff had been right. Casolla's future was standing right in front of him, and his jaw went slack in awe.

His mom's I-told-you-so smile stretched across her face. "One head in the stars and the other on the ground. I think that's why you make the best—"

"Foster! We need to talk to you." Micah skidded into their circle, the blood drained from her cheeks as she grabbed his arm. She turned to his parents. "Please excuse us." She yanked him toward a door in the corner. "In here."

The door opened before them, and in three huge steps Micah wrenched him into the small study with lavish furniture, holopros of bookcases lining the room, a holo fireplace in the corner, and a huge window taking up the far wall.

Micah flapped an impatient hand. "Ezren, you get in here too."

Scarcely had Ezren walked inside than Sylvia charged past her, hair wild, and Shiro followed, the door slicing shut behind him. The click of the door seal silenced the noise of the party, the sudden hush unnatural and strangely juxtaposed with the jubilant atmosphere on the other side.

Foster looked from the matching expressions of anxiety stretching from Micah to Sylvia to Shiro. A concern now spreading across Ezren's features in taut lines. Moving to Ezren's side, Foster put a reassuring arm around her shoulders.

Was someone hurt? Who could it be that wasn't at the party? "What's going on?"

Micah turned her wild eyes to Sylvia, who then turned to Shiro, and he huffed out a sigh, his face the kind of grave Foster had only seen on Otho. "You said that a few days ago, you got a holopro warning of crows, right?"

Ezren and Foster exchanged a glance before Ezren spoke. "Well, it was at the council meeting, so we don't know exactly who it was for. Whoever it was hacked into the room itself."

Shiro's features darkened. "There was no indication that it was for someone in particular?"

"No. Just the crows in the tree." Foster racked his brain for the possible consequences Shiro might've dug up. "Why? Were you able to connect the Crow and Calderon? Anything new we could charge him with?"

Shiro's chin dipped as he rubbed his forehead, his tangled

dark hair sticking out under his goggs. "They certainly won't be charging him."

"Of fodding course not." Foster's hands fisted with the need to hit something. "The chaffer always gets away with everything." As if echoing his thoughts, lightning flashed in a web across the sky outside, a funnel cloud swirling above it.

"Foster..." Sylvia whispered, her face creased with some blend of emotion too tangled for him to decipher.

He dragged a frustrated hand through his hair. "What?"

But it was Micah who spoke, her own voice barely louder than the tapping rain on the dome. "Foster, it's all over VSoc." She swallowed, her words vibrating with intensity.

"Calderon's dead."

CHAPTER 3

4.29.44B T-minus 5 days until the BRR

DEAD.

The word rang in Ezren's ears with a shrill, reverberating whine.

"But," she whispered, the word almost hoarse with disbelief. "We just saw him four days ago." She looked at Foster for confirmation, but his face had frozen into a sheet of ice. "How'd he die?"

A herd of wild holos flashed in front of Sylvia, Micah, and Shiro. Sylvia tugged on her curls, holopros darting in and out of her goggs as she shook her head in consternation. "It says they're presuming natural causes."

"So what will happen to the team now since Calderon technically still owned it?" Micah asked from where she chewed on one end of her long sleeve, her teal eyes darting across her holos as she searched for the answer.

"Not just Belethea's BRR team, what will happen to Calderon Industries as a whole?" Sylvia continued, her gaze still on her holos. "Calderon's terranium business touches everything from cargo ships to stations to terraforming—this could affect the whole system."

"Right!" Micah swirled through what looked like ten different news holologs—*The Royaler Review* displayed most prominently in the center. "VSoc is going wild with rumors already because apparently he has no surviving family."

But Ezren could only think of the council meetings. How despite his schedule, Calderon had never missed a single one. Chaff, he'd never even been late. Now there would just be an empty chair there. A voice forever silenced. A murderer finally brought to justice by nature itself. The last of the original Belethean royalers passing on the planet to the next generation. The secret protector of Casolla's newly discovered life. A villain. A legend. The conflicting thoughts bubbled through her chest.

Foster crossed his arms, brows knitting. "But... presumed natural causes... is that what they usually say when someone dies of old age?"

"Calderon has survived more assassination attempts than anyone in Casolla's history." Shiro's dark gaze lifted from his own holo to meet Foster. "And you witnessed the murder tree yourself. What does your gut tell you?"

Micah flinched back as if Shiro had threatened her specifically. "Um, *murder tree?*"

"On ancient earth, a flock of crows was once called a murder." Tension rippled along Shiro's shoulders through his well-fitted CIF uniform. "It's the Crow's warning sign."

A chill raced along Ezren's scalp. "Why didn't you tell us that?"

"We adjusted your security accordingly," Shiro said, his voice resounding with an authority that brooked no argument.

Sylvia gave them an apologetic frown that said she had been in on this secret too. "It would've done no good to scare you."

Foster swiveled to face the storm raging outside the reinforced viewing window. "Could've been a deal that went wrong. If you're working with snakes, you're bound to get bit."

"We've found no evidence that they've been working together," Shiro countered. "However, there are records of intermittent friction between Calderon Industries and the syndicates—the Crow specifically—dating back decades."

The room fell silent, and Ezren could've sworn she heard the word "*murder*" ricochet across the walls underneath the crackling of the holopro fire. There was an irony to it, but one that weighed on her with a heavy fatigue. "So what does this mean for us?" she finally whispered.

"It means you need to be extra careful." Shiro dismissed his holo and leaned against one of the projected bookcases. "If you were in the room, we don't know if that warning was for Calderon or for all of you. I'll contact Villagas again as well to make sure she's taking the right measures. With the whole system in town for the BRR, there is, unfortunately, a high likelihood for unrest."

"Okay, but what do we all do right now?" Sylvia's weight shifted from one foot to the other and back, her skirts ruffling.

"For now, we all go back to the party." Shiro ran an agitated hand through his hair, making it stand on end—any vestige of style destroyed in an unapologetic muss. "And be at ease that there's at least one less murderer in the 'verse."

"Right." Sylvia's still-wild gaze darted from Ezren to Foster. "But before that... I think we'll give you two some time to process." Moving toward the door, she grabbed the holoensconced Micah and beckoned to Shiro. The door hissed open, and Sylvia's face softened as she looked over her shoulder at them. "Don't take too long though or people will start to wonder."

Micah tried for a mischievous grin, but it came out halfhearted. "We'll just tell everyone they're steaming up the—"

The door closed on them, leaving Ezren and Foster in silence once again. Beside her, Foster seemed to deflate as he sank into a soft couch. "At least this will give the Navarros some peace."

"Honestly, I thought I would be happier, but..." Ezren perched on the arm of the couch next to him. "It still just feels sad."

"Does it? He was a hundred years old, and he was... well, he was *Calderon*, Ezren." The shadows of the holopro fire flickered across Foster's face, his expression unreadable.

"Yeah he was old"—Ezren slid from the arm to the cushions next to him—"and he did some really terrible things, but he also built Belethea from the ground up. I just can't stop thinking of that power void he was talking about." She let herself sink further until her head rested on Foster's lap, staring up at the ceiling as he stroked the escaped wisps away from her cheeks. "I guess I'm worried about what's going to come next." Her stomach twisted at the image of the dead Ambassador York sitting down in Calderon's seat with a rotting smile and a hulking syndicate shadow over his shoulder. "Better the evil you know and all that."

"Hmm." For a moment, the drum of the rain filled the silence, Foster's soft gaze lingering on her as his fingers smoothed the furrows from her brow. Ezren let her lashes fall under his attentions, and when he finally spoke, his voice was as quiet as the distant thunder. "Are you scared?"

Ezren swallowed as his fingers tunneled through her hair, massaging her scalp. But even as her muscles relaxed, it didn't relieve the ice coating her spine. "I guess I am."

His hands stilled, his words soft but weighted. "It's going to be okay, Ezren." His hand skated down her arm to squeeze her fingers. "I promise I won't let anything happen to you."

Ezren opened her eyes and reached up to trace his jaw. "I know." He leaned into her palm as she stroked her thumb reassuringly along his cheekbone. "But this is a big deal, Foster. I don't know what comes after this, but whatever it is, I think it's going to change everything. I just don't know if it'll be for better or for worse."

Calderon's words echoed through her thoughts: *Sterling/Hart is the face of the future. It will be their hands guiding the course...* If Calderon had been right, then it would be up to them to make sure that all the changes on terraforming and corruption and everything else they'd worked on for the last year weathered the storm.

She breathed out a long sigh. Just when she thought they'd started to find the balance of the load on their shoulders, it seemed like the eager 'verse only had more to pile on. Like the reward for good work was just more work.

Foster pulled her hand from his cheek and kissed her fingers. "Maybe you're right, but I think whatever is coming for us can wait until tomorrow. Tonight, we still have eighteen hours off, and I don't want to spend it on... *that.*"

Foster was right, there was no use worrying about trouble until it came knocking on their door. Casolla knew they had enough as it was. Ezren smiled as she sat up and faced him. "Oh yeah? Then what do you want to spend it on?"

"Hmm..." He caught her about the waist and shifted her into his lap with a roguish smile. "I could think of a couple things."

A fire curled in Ezren's belly with a breathy laugh, her hands on his shoulders as she bent to brush her lips against his. "I mean... if this is what everyone thinks we're doing anyway, we wouldn't want to disappoint them."

Their mouths met again a slow, languorous dance that set her body alight, their lips and tongues quickening as they sank into the moment. Forgetting about death and threats and the future. Here, with the storm rumbling in the distance, it could be just the two of them, their bodies pressing together as their breaths became ragged in the quiet—her hands raking through Foster's hair while his hands skated along her thighs.

With a low sound in the back of his throat, he flipped her onto her back on the cushions, his body lying over hers with a pleasant weight. And Ezren was lost, every inch of her skin sizzling as his kisses slowly slipped down her neck. *Suns, he knew how to set her ablaze.* Finally, he drew back, his hair tousled and his dark pupils huge. "Ezren... what I feel for you... I can't even find the words to describe it. More than love. More than everything."

Ezren smiled as she cupped his jaw with her hands, the lights of a thousand stars flashing in her chest. A feeling too big to ever get used to. "Like the ties of the galaxies run between us."

"Exactly." He kissed her palm and smiled at her in the way he did only when they were alone. A thoughtfulness warmed his gaze as he regarded her. "You know I was thinking—"

The chime of his goggs interrupted him, and an urgent red holopro popped into the air.

Foster scowled at it. "What the fod—"

The words died on his lips as he read the message, his face blanching, and an icy bucket of fear doused the fire in Ezren's body. "What? What is it?"

Foster slowly sat up, rubbing a hand across his pale features, but still he didn't speak.

"Foster." Ezren squeezed his arm, her voice pitching with fear. Was it Villegas? Could she be dead too? "Wh-what happened?"

"I..." Foster put a hand over hers and squeezed, the uncertainty naked in his gray-green eyes. "I've been summoned immediately to the office of Calderon's lawyer."

Ezren's stomach dropped to the soles of her feet.

It seemed like trouble was knocking on their door after all.

CHAPTER 4

4.29.44B T-minus 5 days until the BRR

A SHORT FIFTY-FOUR minutes later found Foster in an opulent office in Calderon Industries' central building in Petraskis. Shiro waited just inside the closed door and Calderon's personal lawyer sat across a grand obsidian desk. In the tense silence, Foster's gaze strayed to a holo on the bookshelf showing a young Calderon with Carmella at his side—the same photo they showed in every BRR history holo. Except now, they both stared at him from beyond the grave. The young Calderon stood with his usual stony expression, and Carmella speared him with wide, almost mournful eyes, a brown birthmark in the shape of a tear staining her pale cheek.

The pair brought his thoughts back to Ezren, and his nerves buzzed, off-balance without her at his side. But the invitation had been disconcertingly clear that he was to come alone, and when Shiro had mentioned the possibility of a trap, Foster had been happy to leave Ezren safe at the party with his dad's full security team. Even if she was less than thrilled about staying behind.

He was glad though that Shiro had managed to convince the lawyer that security members didn't count as attendees in any situation, so Foster wasn't completely alone in enemy territory. Perched on the tenth floor, the office held a large desk facing two thickly cushioned armchairs and an exceptional view of downtown Petraskis yawning from the floor-to-ceiling window. Over the desk, a stack of holos lit up the air before a round, grim-faced woman who would almost certainly be the bearer of bad news.

"All right." The lawyer dismissed the holos with a curt wave of her hand, her impossibly long white hair piled in a mountain atop her head. "We are now in a secure room, but please know whatever decisions are made here will eventually become public." Her tone was clipped, and judging from the shadows hollowing her cheeks, Foster was willing to bet she'd been working nonstop since Calderon was officially declared dead sixteen hours ago.

"How did this happen so fast?" Foster asked, shifting in the velvety seat. "I thought he died unexpectedly."

"Warner was old and very aware of his mortality. So his affairs were in impeccable order, and his desire for an efficient execution was clearly prioritized." The lawyer leaned back in her chair, steepling her fingers. "And he documented a credible death threat four days ago, so perhaps unexpectedly is too strong of a word."

"But death threats were common for Calderon. There was even an attempt on his life last year at the expo." Though that one had been orchestrated by the now-disbanded Baxter Research Corp. Foster glanced at Shiro for confirmation, but although Foster knew Shiro was listening, his expression remained as blank as if he hadn't heard.

"Indeed, but this was only one of perhaps a dozen across his lifetime that he's deemed credible. The other eleven were all actualized in attempts on his life that were neutralized."

Foster's eyes widened, thinking of the dozens of death threats Shiro sifted through on his and Ezren's behalf. How would Calderon be able to tell which were empty and which were dangerous? Unless... all the credible ones were from the same person. Thinking back, Calderon hadn't seemed exactly surprised to see the murder holo. Was that because he'd seen it before?

"In any event," the woman continued, "though the authorities' full investigation could take weeks, it will not impact our decisions here." She cocked a thick white eyebrow. "Unless you killed him."

Adrenaline ripped through Foster's veins. "Am I a suspect?"

"He has twenty-four-seven security," Shiro cut in. "His whereabouts are never undocumented, and he hasn't had contact with Calderon for ninety-six hours."

"Oh, relax." The woman chuckled as she waved a hand. "I wasn't accusing Sterling, here, I was merely stating a fact. Casolla law forbids an inheritance moving to anyone even suspected of murdering their benefactor." Her tired smile creased the wrinkles around her eyes. "As there are solid records of your whereabouts that indicate innocence, that shouldn't be an issue."

In the corner, Shiro relaxed, but Foster's brain had gotten stuck. "Inheritance? But I'm not related to Calderon." Suns, Calderon better not be his lost great-uncle or something. He racked his brain for the notion of a family tree.

"No, you're not." She leaned forward, lacing her fingers on the table. "But you don't have to be."

"This is ridiculous." Foster pressed back in the soft chair, scrambling for a moment to process. This was all too much; it couldn't possibly be real. "How do I know he's dead and this isn't some game?"

"Not exactly the most trusting type, are we?" Amusement darted across the lawyer's swarthy features as she straightened the lapels of her long business jacket. "I can see why he liked you. But if you're unsure..." A holo popped up of Calderon staggering and falling to the ground on a dark street in Petraskis. The feed fast-forwarded as his security clustered around him, as they began emergency treatment... and as they gave up. The feed flickered out as they pulled a sheet over Calderon's face. "It was a public security cam, so the footage is already being picked apart on VSoc for authenticity if you'd like a second opinion."

"No." Foster clenched and unclenched his fists, his palms gone clammy.

So, Calderon was really dead. And yet somehow, that didn't make Foster feel better. His mouth tightened into a flat line with the distinct feeling that he didn't want to be here. That he didn't want to hear what happened next. His gaze slewed to the window that overlooked Petraskis as if he could escape out of it.

"Okay, so what did he leave me?" Some sick, twisted memento? His murder trophies? Suns, this was chaffed up.

"Oh, my dear boy." The lawyer took in a deep breath, her hands spreading flat on the table as she gave him an apologetic frown. "He left you everything."

Foster blinked. And blinked again. Even Shiro staggered in the corner.

Foster forced his tongue to work as a dry panic desiccated his mouth. "What do you mean, *everything?*"

The lawyer pulled up a holo and read from a list. "His ownership of the Belethea Race Royale team, his seat on the Belethea Council, Calderon Industries, which also encompasses over a hundred child companies, his monetary—"

"H-how can he do that?" Foster spluttered. "Doesn't Calderon Industries have some kind of stakeholders board or something to decide who it should go to?"

"You already have their approval," the lawyer said, her gold eyes calm. "Like I said, his affairs were in perfect order, and he planned everything well in advance." She enlarged the wall of text so he could see. "I'll, of course, send you a copy once we're through here, but you will find detailed instructions, assigned mentors, actions, schedules, recommendations... Rest assured, he has everything here." Her smile widened with something like wry humor. "And if you have any questions, I'm actually on retainer as your personal attorney for the next thirty years."

Foster couldn't breathe—the anxiety like a vice on his chest. This was a joke. It had to be. Was this Calderon's way of continuing to shaft him after death? What other motive did he have for giving his legacy to a guy who *hated* him?

"What happens if I say no?" Foster managed, voice rough.

A shadow passed across her face. "Then, Calderon indicated it would go to public auction to be sold to the highest bidder."

Fodding chaff. The highest bidder would be, without a doubt, a syndicate-appointed front man. After all, Calderon had warned them of the greedy hands waiting in the darkness. Foster rubbed his fingers across the ache of rage building between his temples. "Of course, that motherfodder set up his shafting will to force my hand."

"You'll have a week to decide." The lawyer rose from her seat and straightened her long black jacket. "Simply let me know when you're ready to accept or decline, and we'll meet again to finalize the transfer." She touched a holopro mounted to the table. "And lastly, he also left you this message. I'll leave you to listen to it in peace, but until I see you next, please take care, Foster Sterling." Her eyes crinkled in her first real smile. "I know this is a lot to process, but I just want you to know, I hope you'll do me the honor of working with you. I truly could think of no better candidate to carry Belethea forward." With that, the lawyer nodded to Shiro and left with a hiss of the door.

No sooner had the door slid shut than the holopro began, the uncanny image of Warner Calderon sitting across from Foster in the exact chair the lawyer had just vacated. Even from the grave, the man's icy gaze seemed to pierce Foster through time and space. When he spoke, his voice was the calm, authoritative rumble Foster had become accustomed to over the course of uncountable council meetings.

"Foster, I know this comes as a shock, but it's a decision I made ever since I saw you cross the finish line. Ever since you bested me in the churn belt, you have won this. I know you are young, and you have reservations, but as you have proved yourself a better, stronger person than myself, I have every confidence that you will make the right decision.

"I only caution that although I give this to you freely, it will not come without a struggle, and if the Crow is involved as I suspect, it will not be a fair fight. So, keep watch over your shoulder and keep your doubles partner closer than a shadow. There was a time that I did not, and I paid a price that stole the soul from my bones. I know you think me an evil man, and perhaps I am, but believe me when I say I don't wish you to make the same mistake.

"As strong as Carmella and I were, I know she would agree that you and your Hart outshine us. While Hart and I have our disagreements, I cannot fault her for her tenacity, courage, and unfailing optimism. I must admit there were times I found myself wishing I could believe in humanity as she does. However, though she may inspire, it is your ruthlessness and practicality that will keep you alive and moving forward. She may be the face of Belethea, but I need the fist of Casolla.

"Even now, as you are surely thinking you can't do this, I believe Hart will know that you can, as do I. Although I cannot guarantee your success, just as I couldn't avoid my own failures, I believe the two of you have a better chance than anyone to bring light to a place of darkness. While I have witnessed firsthand your capacity to create and build, I must advise you not to underestimate the capacity for others to destroy and corrupt. Perhaps the scars you bear from my own hand will serve to ground you in this stark reality we face.

"With that, I leave Belethea in your care." His eyes glinted with an intensity that could've cut diamonds. "Give my regards to Hart, and may you match each other step for step to the end of days, the storm winds ever at your back." He straightened, a single flash of sorrow shadowing his features. "Good luck, Sterling."

Warner Calderon winked out of existence as suddenly as he had come into it, leaving Foster staring at an empty chair and the holopro of a bookcase behind it. Head spinning, he sucked in a ragged breath, propping his elbows on his knees as his head dipped. Motherfodding suns.

"I think I'm going to be sick," he choked out.

"Well, I'm pretty sure this office belongs to you now, so feel free to hurl in it if you want." Shiro's hands knotted behind him as he walked up to the window with slow steps, his expression grave.

Sweat broke out on Foster's forehead while he tried to wrestle the shock threatening to turn him inside out. "I didn't want this."

"You're saying you didn't want Calderon dead?" Shiro asked, his calm gaze still on the shorter buildings of Petraskis and the cloudy holos streaking across the dome.

"I'm not saying that." Foster had never been quiet about his hatred of Calderon, and he wouldn't deny he'd wished him an overdue demise more than once. "But I'm not ready for"—he gestured at the office—"this."

"That *is* going to be a problem." Shiro turned to face him, leaning against the window that was so clear Foster worried he might just fall through it.

The idea that saddling Foster with this burden was Calderon's sick, twisted version of revenge rampaged through him. Suns knew there was little he would've hated more than accepting his enemy's bloody empire built on lies and murder. "You think he did this just to shaft me?"

Shiro raised his brows, his expression still strangely guarded. "Do you?"

Foster took a deep breath, his hands strafing through his hair. Anyone else that got this deal would've thought they'd won Casolla's biggest lottery. Everyone except Foster. Even still, he mentally scrolled through every interaction he and Calderon had since he'd known the man. In *none* of them had he actually attempted to harm Foster, in word or deed. If anything, it seemed the man had been doing everything in his power to prepare Foster for this moment.

...With the scars you bear from my own hand...

Suns—killing Vieve, trying to kill his teammates—had it all been some psychotic test?

He studied the whorls of the obsidian desk. There was no understanding the man, especially now, but he had to consider the possibility that whatever the reason, Calderon hadn't done this as revenge. The man may have been psychotic, but he'd never wavered in his beliefs that he was working for the good of Casolla.

"Okay, maybe not," Foster finally said. "But this is crazy, Shiro."

Shiro crossed his arms, looking way too relaxed for this bombshell. "Is it crazier than anything else you've done?"

"Okay, look." Foster burst from his chair, the agitation suddenly all too much. "I get having a voice. And I used it. I get having a position. And I used that too. But this kind of power? The responsibility? I'm twenty years old, Shiro."

"Foster." Shiro held Foster's wild gaze with his cool one, a sigh seeping out of him. "I know you want to be young and care about things like romancing your girl and going to school just like everyone else." His lips tightened, his voice dropping with gravity. "But you're not everyone else, Foster Sterling."

Foster let out a humorless laugh, suddenly too hot as he ripped open the buttons on his ambassador's jacket. "Yeah, lucky me. People have been telling me that my whole life." He braced himself on the desk. "But I don't care who I am, I'm *not* ready to be the fodding owner of Calderon Industries, and everyone knows it."

Shiro snorted, his expression hardening. "Okay, Sterling, in what world are we ready for what the 'verse has in store for us?" He scoffed, bitterness tugging at his mouth as he stepped forward—his soldier's training evident in every line of his wiry body. "Preparation is a rare luxury, Foster. From the day we're born until the day we die, we're all just doing our best to survive what comes at us around the next corner."

Shiro was in the profession of life or death, and his truth quelled whatever furious obstinance Foster had been holding on to, his muscles uncoiling as he walked to the window. He leaned his forehead against the cool glass, his words barely above a whisper. "What if good enough is too high a bar?"

"Good enough rises and falls with the wind." Shiro turned toward him, and Foster met his dark stare. "But you have to understand too that you will underestimate yourself every single chaffing time. So don't call it your best before you're lying face down in the dirt with nothing left to give."

Foster let the words sink into his core, not sure if they were meant to be encouraging or just fact. Either way, he had a feeling this was going to end with him in the dirt. Yet somehow, the knowledge sent a wave of cold acceptance rolling through him. Because it wasn't just him taking on this burden.

Keep your doubles partner closer than a shadow.

It would be Ezren too.

And suns knew he would bleed out before he let someone scratch her.

He sighed, his shoulders finally settling under this new weight as he looked out to the city again. In the distance, he could just make out Petraskis University where he had planned to study nanite materials this year. The plans he'd made before Otho's fire had branded him. Before he'd accepted the lesser of two evils from an old enemy. Before, he now realized, he thought he could dodge what the 'verse had coming for him.

Hubris.

And now he was expected to step into the shoes he hated the most. The shoes of an enemy. Of a puppeteer. Of a deadly power.

He dragged in another cool breath, bracing one hand on the glass. "This isn't exactly the future I imagined." He swallowed, his jaw flexing. "The *life* I imagined."

"You and everybody else. Just hold your family close and give your best." Shiro clapped him on the shoulder and gave it a squeeze, his mouth quirking with a smile. "It's a good life. Even if it's not the one you planned."

"Right." Foster forced his spine straight, burning his uncertainty into a heated resolve as he buttoned up his jacket once more. "I need to tell Ezren."

Shiro nodded, turning with him toward the door. "That's a good first step."

But just as they reached the threshold, the room plunged into darkness.

In a blink, Shiro drew his gun, the beam of his goggs flashing around the empty room. "What the—"

The window turned opaque as a holo fluttered across it, and every cell in Foster's body froze.

A naked tree. A murder of crows. And a single, scraping caw.

This time, red words spilled across the dark canvas.

Foster Sterling, I do hope you'll be more amenable than your predecessor.

For a moment, only silence stretched across the darkness, and Foster's hands curled into fists at his sides.

"Well, okay then." Shiro lowered his weapon, his words heavy with resignation. "Now, there's no question who that one's for."

And with that, every doubt in Foster's mind evaporated.

Because whether Calderon had intended it or not, he was well and truly shafted.

CHAPTER 5

4.29.44B T-minus 5 days until the BRR

EZREN HAD to hand it to Micah and Sylvia for their efforts to distract her with chatter, dancing, and silly party games, but she still couldn't help but look to the doorway for Foster every five minutes. Though she enjoyed the company of the royalers as they buzzed with BRR anticipation, she wasn't sad when they drifted back to their dorms for the night. While it was still early, they would all need plenty of time to wind down and get the rest they needed this week.

Almost three hours after Foster left, Ezren still sat in the small study where Micah had dropped the news about Calderon's death. By now, everyone had heard, and her closest friends and family gathered in the room with her. Thankfully though, no one had tried to broach the topic. Ezren herself still didn't know how to feel—especially while Foster was with Calderon's *lawyer*.

The only people who knew that juicy tidbit were her and Sylvia, but from the nervous energy in the room, it was clear that everyone knew that Foster was obviously somewhere *else* when he should've been there. It wouldn't have taken a genius to link it to the Calderon news, and she had no doubt most of the people in the room had connected the dots.

As her anxiety spiked, Ezren took deep breaths to calm

herself again. Calderon was dead, but he'd been old. She was safe, Foster was safe with Shiro, and the rest of her family and friends were smiling and laughing around her. It would all work out.

Simon was in the middle of telling some ridiculous story of his illegal jet-racing days to Sam and Micah's delight, when Foster stepped through the door. Ezren's attention snapped toward him, but she couldn't read his expression as Shiro followed him in.

Sylvia looked from one to the other. "So how'd it go?"

"Yeah, where were you?" Micah added, bobbing in an armchair.

The rest of the group—Foster's parents, Ezren's family, and Grady/Guns—simply regarded him with their own tense expectation.

Foster shoved his hands into his pockets, his gaze sweeping over all of them. "Sorry, but I need to talk to Ezren first."

Ezren popped from the couch, alarm singing through her as she brushed past Foster through the doorway.

"Okay, but Shiro, you're going to tell us, right?" Simon asked.

Shiro grinned with a shrug as he leaned against the wall. "No way I'm cracking."

A chorus of groans erupted from the room just before the door closed.

As soon as they were alone, Ezren took Foster's hands in hers. "What's wrong?"

Foster stared out the huge wall of windows at the now calm night outside. "So, I saw we have a solid stretch of clear weather."

Ezren nodded. She'd set her algorithm to alert her for any clear spans over three hours, rejoicing as they'd become longer and more frequent with the intensive terraforming efforts.

Foster looked from her hands back to her face, the corner of his mouth lifting. "I brought our topsuits. You want to go for a run?"

Despite the uncertainty she sensed in his posture, his tone, even his hand in hers, Ezren smiled. "With you? Always."

In twenty minutes, the two of them bounded across Belethea's mauve surface with Casolla's lava-streaked face peeking at them between the racing cobalt clouds. Foster led her down their familiar path—one they'd taken many times since they'd started regularly escaping to his dad's for a weekend away from Petraskis. And though they ran in silence, there was a familiar comfort to it.

The weight of Calderon's death, the future of the council, and whatever Foster was holding sloughed off of Ezren's shoulders as her muscles stretched. Together they climbed a rock spire not three miles from the dome of his dad's compound. With a teasing smile, Ezren lurched ahead, climbing hand over foot until her chest heaved with the petrichor air and her arms burned.

Foster followed close behind, a smile in his crinkled eyes as they climbed over the plateau, the windswept valley opening beneath them, and the thick belweed rippling under the wild gusts. Together they took off their helmets and sat on the ledge, feet dangling in the low gravity. Ezren leaned her head on Foster's shoulder, savoring the glimpses of scarlet Otho and cerulean Crion through the whirling clouds as she waited for Foster to find his words.

She didn't know how much time passed before he finally sucked in a long breath, and in a calm, measured voice told her about the inheritance, the auction should he decline, the probable murder of Calderon, the message he'd left, and the second murder tree.

After the wind stole away the rumble of his deep voice,

Ezren sat silent for a moment, taking it all in. Trying to grasp this thing that seemed too huge to be possible. She thought of how Calderon's attacks had always been on the people around Foster rather than Foster himself. Thought of how he'd offered Foster the position in the council last year. And how he'd placed Foster on his right side at every opportunity in the months after.

"He knew this would happen." Ezren's stare drifted upward to where one of Casolla's twenty-two moons slipped from the clouds. "He's been prepping you for I don't know how long. Publicly endorsing you at every opportunity." She shook her head. "There have even been rumors on VSoc that you're secretly related."

Foster flinched. "The lawyer said we're not."

"The real question is why would the Crow kill him?"

Foster kicked his heel into the rocky shelf beneath them. "From the credible threats the lawyer described, I think it's not the first time the Crow has tried to kill him. If Shiro's right, they've been at odds for decades."

"Well, since he was leveraging your influence and backing all of these anti-corruption measures, he was probably a bigger threat to the syndicates than ever." Ezren wrinkled her nose. "But why would the Crow target you?"

"We have a voice in the luxie usage, terraforming, the Belethea Race Royale, and now..." Foster's jaw flexed. "Calderon Industries." He met her gaze. "We could do a lot of damage, Ezren."

"Or a lot of good." Ezren bumped one of her boots against his. "Unfortunately, the corrupt make doing good hard. And if we don't bend, I guess they'll try to replace you like they did Calderon." The very thought sent knives through her chest.

"Fod that." Foster reclined until he was on his back with Casolla's face shining down on him. "I'm tired of all this cloak-

and-dagger chaff. I want to be completely open about the messages we've seen and expose him to the public. Get Casolla on our side." Ezren lay down beside him, their shoulders touching. "Shiro's been compiling evidence against them for months. Let's enforce a crackdown and announce a transparent partnership between Calderon Industries and the people of Belethea."

Ezren couldn't help the grin that tickled her lips as she nudged him. "You're starting to sound like a CEO."

Foster scoffed. "Me, a CEO? That still seems impossible."

Ezren propped herself up on an elbow. "Foster, I don't pretend to understand all of Calderon's choices, but I do get this one. I'm not sure there's anyone better to replace him than you. It may not be what you set out to do, but it's who you are now. You're young, yes, but that only gives you more time to make an impact. And people listen to you. They trust you." She leaned down to push her forehead against his. "Don't underestimate yourself."

For a moment, Foster studied her, his stormy irises swirling in the moonlight. "Okay, Ezren Hart, but if I do this"—Foster's hands circled her waist, and he rolled them until he was looking down on her, the wild Belethean sky above him—"will you help me?" He captured a magenta strand of her hair and wound it around a finger. "I know this isn't what you signed up for either, but this goes beyond anything we've done before, and I don't think I can do this without you." He tucked the lock behind her ear, his finger skimming her jaw, and his voice barely audible against the melancholy song of the wind. "There's no going back from this."

"Foster." Ezren laid a hand across his, squeezing tight. "We've run side by side across the churn belt and the verge of interplanetary war; I certainly think we can weather this." She pressed her lips to his knuckles. "And even though we might not be totally ready for whatever comes next, I think we're as close as anyone." She smiled again, losing herself in the intensity of his gaze. "And through it all, good or bad or completely insane, I'm with you."

In a deep breath of relief, his forehead fell to her shoulder, resting there a moment as she dragged her fingers through his hair. When his head rose again, his eyes shone as they looked at her. "Ezren." He gripped her hands in both of his. "I don't think words can describe how I feel about you anymore. It's as if my heart beats in your chest instead of my own. And when we're together, somehow I feel stronger than I thought possible —like between us, we could take on anything." His fingers traced each one of hers, holding them like a prayer. "You're my yesterday and today and tomorrow. But before we do this and go under the 'verse's microscope, I want to do something just for us."

Ezren's chest filled with the endless warmth of the love that looped around them, of a bond too strong for words. Of an unbreakable tie forged in storms and fire and death.

"Anything," she breathed.

For a beat, his gaze held hers as if searching for something within them, and when he spoke, the hope in his voice nearly broke her. "Will you marry me?"

Ezren's voice caught in her chest. Perhaps it should've sounded ridiculous, but their promises had already been made, the cords of life already threaded between them, and all she could feel was the rightness of it soaking into her core. They were always meant for this, and if anything, she was struck by how natural the question felt. With Casolla's moons peering down on them from Belethea's wind-whipped expanse. Out here in the silence, the beauty of their home. She could think of nothing more perfect.

"Yes."

And yet the word didn't ease the tension in Foster's held breath. "Tonight."

"Tonight?" But even as Ezren's laughter bubbled up through the quiet, the appeal of it rang through her. Unlike Sylvia, she didn't want an extravagant ceremony or lots of people. She just wanted Foster and the Belethean sky, and they were both right here.

"Tonight," Foster repeated, his voice soft as Otho's garnet face peered down on them through the curling clouds. "Before our lives get more chaotic than they already are. I have pledged my life over and over to you, and I want everyone to know it. That you and I are one. Always."

The image of Ezren's father and mother running away for their own impromptu ceremony only widened her smile. She couldn't help but appreciate the precedent. Especially with Foster looking at her as though their lives hung on her next words—a sort of desperate need she longed to soothe.

She gripped his hand tighter. Because he was right, no matter what came next, they could have this joy. She wanted it with every fiber of her being. With both of their families already here, and the Belethean sky smiling down on them, there really was no better time. No reason not to acknowledge the vows that already lived in their bones.

"Okay," Ezren whispered. "Tonight."

And finally Foster's face lit up with a laugh of joy and relief as he swept her from the ground, swinging her under Casolla's smiling glow. "Thank the suns." Holding her tight against him, his lips found hers in a sweet, lingering kiss. Pulling away, he rested his forehead against hers. "I didn't think I could wait another day."

"It's the right time," Ezren agreed, her arms knotted around his neck. "But we're going to need witnesses." She arched an eyebrow. "And I know just where we can find a few volunteers."

CHAPTER 6

4.29.44B T-minus 5 days until the BRR

THE NEXT HOUR passed in a dreamlike blur, Foster's pulse thrumming through him as they raced back toward his dad's house. Just before they reached the airlock, he snatched Ezren around the waist, letting them tumble to the finish. Ezren laughed as he pulled off their helmets, and stole one last kiss, running his lips across her jaw.

By the time they made it inside, still sharing besotted grins, the rest of the party had migrated to the kitchen where they were having some kind of late supper around his father's massive kitchen island. Micah noticed them first, her teal irises lighting up as they stepped inside, still in their topsuits and Ezren's hand warm in his.

"Suns, took you long enough, are you finally going to spill or what?" She twirled around on her stool. "I'm *dying* over here."

"We'll get to that later, but first..." Ezren trailed off, peeking at Foster with an amused glint in her gaze, their secrets still swirling between them.

Squeezing her hand one last time, Foster walked up to Shiro. "First, we wanted to ask if, as a ship captain, you would marry us tonight." Shiro's eyes shot wide, and Foster pressed on. "In the garden."

The kitchen exploded with a simultaneous uproar of congratulations and questions, the room converging on them in a wave of excitement.

"What do you mean tonight?"

"Congrats, kin!"

"Well, we all knew this was coming."

"Okay, the other news must be insane. Someone tell me one of them isn't dying or something."

"How long have you been planning this?"

"You are *not* getting married in your topsuits!"

Finally, Shiro bobbed his head in a short bow. "It would be my honor." His gaze flicked to Ezren where Sam, Evangeline, and Micah were all talking to her simultaneously. "Are you ready now?"

"No!" Sylvia jumped on the table, banging two metal cups together. "Wait."

Grady cocked his head with a grin. "The objection part comes later, Syl."

She lifted a single, manicured finger tipped in gold. "Give me *one* hour!" Her expression was firm as she propped her fists on her full hips. "I'm overjoyed that you want to get married, but at least give me an hour to make it beautiful." Her face softened, eyes shining. "You both deserve that."

Foster looked to Ezren, and he wasn't sure if she could smile any bigger. She lifted a brow to him in question, and he gave a nod. A holo flicked out from Ezren's goggs. "Okay, Sylvia, since it's our wedding day, we'll give you sixty minutes."

The countdown began, and Sylvia once again turned to steel, barking out orders. "Foster and Ezren—I need you showered and changed. Micah, can you style Ezren's hair? Simon, you help Foster with his ink. Bex, I need you to get the wedding bander delivered. Shiro, when you have the ceremony script, you need to send it to Foster and Ezren. Dr. Evangeline, you're on cake. Gerard, you've got music..." Her list went on as everyone whirled suddenly in ten different directions.

Fifty-five minutes later found Foster in his long ambassador's coat with temporary black ink scrawled in a decorative goggs-design around his eyes. Passing Grady's scrutinizing muster, he stepped out into a garden wholly transformed. At what had to be Mach speed, someone had programmed the holo dome to turn his father's garden into what appeared to be a Belethea of someday. A rainbow of blooms covered its mauve dirt while the spires rose in the near-dawn sky in the distance. An arched trellis coated in ivy sat in the center of the circular dome with the floating hydroponic vines dipping in a verdant curtain around a dozen white chairs.

"Thank the suns your dad has had events here," Sylvia huffed, expertly applying a swirl of gold ink across her cheekbones.

"You did all of this?" Foster marveled at the projected fields of belweed that could one day be their future. "Ezren will love it."

"Sam did the holos," Sylvia said, ushering him toward the trellis where Shiro already waited in his crisp, gray CIF uniform. "Your mom arranged the garden."

Foster looked over to where his mom sat beside his dad, the two of them watching with proud smiles as they whispered to each other. His dad's guitar lay across his lap, and as his fingers moved absently over the strings, its sweet, light notes drifted across the gathering.

FOSTER: THANK YOU.

His mom smiled.

MOM: WE'RE GLAD TO BE A PART OF IT.

Grady clapped him on the shoulder from his other side, guiding him to the right of the pavilion. "Okay, we stand here. And you've got the script, right?"

"Yeah." Foster cued the ceremonial proceedings in his goggs as he turned to Shiro. "Are you ready?"

Shiro flashed him a huge grin. "If you've each got your two witnesses, I'm ready when the bride and groom are."

As his second witness, Bex stepped forward, handing him what looked like a thick metal band. "I programmed in the design you and Ezren chose. You'll just slide it on her finger, and it'll ink in the ring."

Foster nodded, pocketing the device. It was a tradition that had survived through the stars to thrive under Belethea's storms —a symbol of eternity in more ways than one—and the weight of it grounded him. "Thanks, Bex."

Sylvia stepped forward to straighten his jacket and style his hair away from his eyes with a twist of her fingers.

"Okay. You look great," she finally relented as she turned to Grady where he adjusted his own styled curls. "Do you have the cam?"

"Got it." Grady pulled the spherical hovercam from his pocket and tossed it in the air.

"Sylvia," Foster warned, his brow furrowing. "Tell me you're not going to broadcast this on VSoc." When he'd asked Ezren to marry him, he thought it would be easy, but now with a complicated vortex of activity spinning around them, he started to regret giving Sylvia her sixty minutes.

Sylvia lifted her chin indignantly. "Oh, c'mon, what do you take me for?" Expression softening, she leaned over to pick up one of the tiny fallen blooms littering the floor. "This may be a small, quick wedding, Foster, but this is one of the most important moments of your life, and one day, you'll want to remember it. This holo is just for you and Ezren, so the two of you can have it always." She tucked the small bloom into the pocket of his jacket. "For luck."

Foster softened, recognizing the monumental effort that

Sylvia had put in was for him and Ezren alone. Her gift to them. "Thank you, Sylvia."

"Holy chaff, you're appreciating your manager? It really is a big day." She threw her arms around him with a grin. "Seriously though, you're going to make me cry." Pulling away, she fanned herself as if she could ward off the swelling emotion. "But if your bride is going to be late to her own wedding, I'm going to have some words for her."

"I'm here!"

Foster and Sylvia both turned to see Ezren actually running to the altar, because of course she was. Her magenta-and-orange-streaked hair had been pulled up into an elaborate braid dotted with flowers, and someone had programmed her ambassador's jacket, skirt, and boots from black to a silvery white. She arrived at the arch with her pale cheeks flushed, her dark gaze practically sparkling beneath the silver ink decorating her pale skin in an ornate mask around her eyes.

And Foster couldn't breathe.

She was too beautiful. Nerves rippled through his chest with the impossibility of the dream before him. Could this really be happening? It was all too incredible to be reality.

Ezren flicked out her holo, checking the time with a laugh. "And look, I still have two minutes left." Her attention strayed to the garden around them, and her lips parted in shock. "Oh suns." Laughing again, she pulled Sylvia into her arms. "I can't believe you did all of this."

"Just wait until you see the cake!" Davis called from where he sat beside Foster's dad, chords now thrumming in earnest from his guitar.

Micah flounced behind Ezren and pulled her onto the left side. "C'mon, then, let's get it started!"

Trailing behind them with both Turnip and Waffle on his

heels, Sam turned to Foster, his expression strangely serious and his voice low. "You're going to look after her, right?"

Foster reached out and squeezed his shoulder. "Until my last breath."

Sam scanned Foster from his boots to his styled hair, his stiff regard unchanging as though he found something lacking. Finally Ezren called to him, and he stepped away to stand by her. Dr. Evangeline hugged Ezren, her eyes filled with tears as she took in both of her children at the archway.

Blowing out a tremoring breath, Foster turned to Grady and Bex. "You all must think this is crazy."

Grady snorted, brushing a bit of mauve dust from the shoulder of his teal jacket. "Give us some cred, kin. We all knew it was happening someday."

Foster shoved his hands in his pockets with a rueful grin. "I didn't realize we were so predictable."

"You wouldn't be a good royaler if you were predictable." Bex polished one of the silver buttons of his jacket with the cuff of her sleeve. "But we know you, Sterling. And we know Hart." She gave him the ghost of a smile. "This is right. We all feel it."

Bex and Grady gave way as Foster's parents stepped toward him.

His dad reached up with a hard hug. "I'd ask you if you're sure, but I already know." His dad released him so his mom could give him her own brief squeeze.

"Suns, Foster, I don't think I've ever seen you so happy," she said.

And he couldn't smother the grin that seemed to be taking over his face because in truth, she was right. "I don't think I knew I could ever be this happy."

Then Sylvia gave Shiro a pointed look, and he opened his arms, reading the script from the small holo glowing in front of his face. "If everyone could take their places, we'll begin."

Foster's parents smiled at him in tandem, his dad curling an arm around his mom as they walked back to their seats. With nerves scrabbling through his gut, and Grady and Bex on either side of him, Foster stepped up to Shiro's left side.

On Shiro's right, Ezren mirrored him with Sam and Micah a step behind her. Shiro nodded at all of them, a smile curving his lips. "The bride and groom have requested this to be short and sweet, so we'll get right to the good part."

Behind them, the romantic notes of a soft guitar lilted through the air, and Ezren's eyes lit up as she bounced on her toes. Foster chuckled softly, resolving to thank his dad later.

Shiro clasped his hands in front of him. "As a starship captain in this stretch of the 'verse, I've been asked to acknowledge the lifelong bond between two of our passengers. Do we have our witnesses?"

Four "ayes" resounded from Sam, Micah, Bex, and Grady.

"So it is witnessed." Shiro nodded. "Foster Sterling and Ezren Hart, are you of the same heart in wanting what is best for one another? Do you both believe this to be a right and true match with the devotion to hold your faith?"

Foster peeked at Ezren to find her with an impossibly big smile as they answered in unison. "We do."

"Then step forward and accept the ties."

Foster and Ezren stepped forward and extended their hands. Pulling a length of sleek white cloth from his jacket, Shiro tied their wrists together in a simple, tight loop. "This knot represents the ties that bind. Older than all you see around us, stretching back to our ancestors with earth beneath their feet. Though we may not always see them, they are always there."

Pulling the tie free of their hands, he retreated three paces until the arch was between himself and them, and draped the ribbon over it. "Stepping forward, you will now move as one, be as one." He paused, letting his words settle on the lilting notes of the love song. "If you accept these ties, then clasp hands."

Foster twined his fingers with Ezren's, his heart pounding in his chest.

Shiro smiled. "Now, do you swear to accept one another for the people you are, the strengths and the flaws?"

They answered as one. "We do."

"Then step forward with peace."

With Ezren's grip tight in his, together they stepped toward the arch.

"Do you swear to forever choose each other with every rise and fall of the sun?"

Again, they answered, voices unwavering. "We do."

"Then step forward with honor."

They complied, the lilting music at odds with the race of Foster's pulse.

"And do you swear to love and protect each other till death do you part?"

Ezren squeezed his hand, and Foster squeezed back. "We do," they said together.

"Then take your last step with strength and face each other," Shiro said, his voice level and calm. "To seal your vows, you will wear the mark that shows your heart is forever claimed by the other."

Their last step took them up to the arch, and Foster pulled the inking band from his pocket. Ezren proffered her slim fingers, and he slid it on the third. "With this mark, I am yours." The ink ring flashed as its mark sank into her. He slipped it off her finger to find the two silver lines it had inked on her skin—one bisected by the three dots of past, present, and future.

Ezren took the inking band, and he presented his hand for her to slip it on—the metal cool against his finger. She held his gaze as it flashed. "As I am yours." When she withdrew the ring, matching lines of silver ink adorned his own skin.

Shiro's grin widened as he addressed the observers, the music swelling. "Now in front of all who stand before us, let it be known and seen and felt that these two are bound as husband and wife." He turned to them once more. "Let the 'verse flow ever and between you as your lives weave into one. And though this may not be your first kiss, nor your last, let this be the one that brings you the final step together."

Foster turned to Ezren, cupping her face in his hands as he kissed her long and deep—to more than a few whoops from their attendants. When they parted, tears of joy pearled in her eyes, and he once again took her hand.

Together, they took the last step through the arch that represented the gateways of the 'verse that would lead them to new worlds—to a new life—the music rising in a joyous climax.

And Shiro burst into the full grin he'd been keeping unsuccessfully at bay. "May Belethea bless her newest union, Foster and Ezren, now husband and wife."

Scarcely had Foster turned toward Ezren than they were mobbed on all sides. Grins and congratulations and hugs passed by in a joyous blur as Sylvia carried in a huge white cake that smelled strongly of coffee.

"What's a wedding without cake?"

Ezren didn't hesitate to swipe a finger into the icing and smear it across his nose. Not to be outdone, he retaliated by rubbing his face against hers until the white sugar streaked both of their cheeks. Together, they cut the cake, and sent out delicious brown-and-gold-striped slices to the guests—all laughing and telling stories as they savored the sugar-sweet flavors on their tongues in the dawn-bathed garden. Turnip, of course, managed to turn over at least two glasses as she chased Waffle through the crowd until Micah captured them both with a delighted squeal.

Amidst the clamor, Ezren leaned in close, eyes dancing. "So, husband, do you feel different now that you're married?"

He grinned, leaning in to touch his forehead to hers. "Is it possible to be more in love with you?"

"This was a good idea," she whispered.

Foster nodded, reaching out to wipe the last bit of icing from her forehead with his thumb. "The best." He leaned and pressed a kiss to her lips. With his dad's music still weaving around them, surrounded by love and laughter, they'd found a truly perfect moment. A resounding connection vibrating through an air of joy he had no words for.

And Foster was sure his heart would never be this full again.

Finally, with all evidence of any sugary violence wiped from their faces, Ezren rose. "Thank you all so much for making this a moment to remember." She turned to Grady and Bex. "But it's getting late and you two are supposed to be resting up for the BRR this week."

Micah bounced to her feet, releasing her pink and brown captives. "So you're saying it's time for the sendoff?"

"What sendoff?" Ezren shot Foster a questioning glance, but he only shrugged. She turned to Sylvia. "I thought we were staying here."

Sylvia snorted from where Shiro's arms encircled her, his chin resting on her head and Turnip brushing against their ankles. "As if we wouldn't arrange something for the *newlyweds.*"

"It was short notice." Foster's mom looked up at his dad, his arm slung around her shoulders. "But we managed to find something for a few days."

"A few days?" Foster looked to Sylvia again. "What

happened to nineteen hours? With our schedule and the BRR in—"

"Foster." Sylvia shook her head, smile brightening. "You just got married. Enjoy some time off just being together."

Ezren launched herself at Sylvia. "Thank you so much!"

Grady frowned, crossing his arms. "Chaff, sounds like I need to find someone to marry."

"Oh, shut up, Grady," Bex said, a smile crooking her lips where she scratched Waffle behind the ears.

Sylvia waved them off. "All right, all right. Now you two get out of here. Have fun, relax, and we'll see you in three days for the pre-race press conference."

"But what about—" Ezren began.

"It's all taken care of—VSoc, cancellations, packed bags, everything. Shiro will drive you and set the security detail," Sylvia said, guiding them toward the front doors. "Now just get out of here before I change my mind."

Foster stopped, hardly able to believe the gift she'd given them as he met her tired gaze. "Seriously, Sylvia, thank you."

"Your lives are about to change in unfathomable ways." Sylvia's rainbow brows pinched, her words holding a gravity that said she'd managed to wheedle the afternoon's events out of Shiro. "Enjoy this peace together while you can."

After one last round of goodbyes and hugs, Foster and Ezren sank into the back of a storm truck with Shiro at the wheel. Though it wasn't quite midnight, the exhaustion of the day settled over Foster as Ezren leaned into him, and Shiro bumped along Belethea's rugged terrain. Had the day been real? Ever since he'd stepped into Calderon's office, he'd been existing in some kind of dream haze. First a nightmare, then a fantasy.

"It's not far," Shiro called back to them as they roared over the plain, the rising sun turning the clouds all hues of pink and purple. It was as if they were suspended in time, late and early all at once with Belethea's strange cadence of six-hour sols.

"There's another domed villa that's used as a vacation rental," Shiro continued. "As usual, Sylvia and your parents were able to pull a few strings to get you a vacancy on short notice. It's not much, but it's private, and fully stocked with everything you need for a couple days. I'll have security posted outside, and they'll check on you every evening."

"Thanks, Shiro," Foster said, his words weighty with gratitude. "And not just for the ride."

Shiro met his gaze in the rearview mirror, understanding clear in his dark eyes. "It was my honor." Then he smiled. "And maybe if I'm lucky, it'll inspire a certain someone to move up our own wedding celebration." He sobered. "Life is short. There's no use waiting for joy."

Knitting their hands together, Foster admired the matching silver ink circling their fingers, and Ezren grinned up at him. She snuggled deeper into his side, and he pressed a kiss to her hair. His wife. For the twenty-minute ride, they stayed like that, savoring the newness of it. The thought of falling asleep with Ezren every night from now on. Of waking up with her. The two of them linked in every way the 'verse had a name for.

The storm truck rolled to a stop in front of a small cluster of domes set in the shelter of a mountainside. Together they crawled out with the bags Sylvia had packed them. As they stepped out onto the mauve dirt, and the airlock door opened before them, Foster reveled in the quiet of it, the solitude. Even though he knew Shiro had security out here, he couldn't remember the last time they were this alone for a night—with this much emptiness around them.

Shiro only waved from the driver's seat.

Shiro: I've got security on the lookout from the

DOME NEXT TO YOU. LET ME KNOW IF YOU NEED ANYTHING.

EZREN: THANKS AGAIN, SHIRO.

SHIRO: ANYTHING FOR OUR ROYALERS.

And with that, the storm truck rolled away, leaving them as alone as it got.

For a moment, the two of them stood on the quiet Belethean plain, its roguish gusts unraveling their styled hair with the promise of incoming thunderstorms. The sweet fragrance of heavy rain steeped the air in a promise Foster could practically taste, the electricity quivering along his skin.

Ezren threw their bags in the airlock and smiled up at him. "Foster Sterling, my husband..." Her voice dropped, and her arms curled around his waist. "Is this real?"

"It is." Foster grinned down at her. "Ezren Hart. My *wife*." The word tasted sweet on his lips, as if she were always supposed to wear it.

"Thank you, Foster." Ezren's arms squeezed around him. "For making this the best day of my life."

"And it's not over yet." His grin took on a mischievous edge as he swept her up in his arms and carried her through the airlock to Ezren's delighted squeal. "I doubt it'll be as fancy as your dorm in Carmella, but I think it'll do for a couple days." The inner door opened to reveal a translucent dome, giving the impression that they were living under an open Belethea sky. In the dome itself, a kitchen and a plush living space opened up from the door with four vases of flowers adorning the long counter with a bright holopro:

For our favorite newlyweds, enjoy your happily ever after.

"Suns, I can't believe they did this for us," Ezren breathed as she slipped to the floor, her fingers tracing one of the bright petals. "I know we've already been through so much together, but somehow this feels like the start of everything."

Foster's chest heated as he took her in, still in her silvery ambassador jacket, her face relaxed with awe and wonder. So beautiful. He took three steps toward her and opened his arms. She gave him one glance before falling into them.

"Ezren," he whispered into her hair, his pulse racing all over again. "Every time I see you, it feels like the beginning and the best part and the ever after all at once." He breathed in her scent of lemon and sage, knowing he'd never get enough of her. Not now, not ever. But suns if he wasn't going to savor every second of his life trying. "And now that I get to wake up and feel that every morning for the rest of our lives..." He shook his head. "I'm almost scared to believe it."

"But you can, Foster." Ezren looked up at him with her warm, dark eyes—like the two steaming cups of coffee he would brew them in the morning. "We can believe in our forever."

Then his lips were on hers, and they were tumbling together—tasting, teasing, touching. They were breathy chuckles, and undone buttons, tongues and two heated bodies tangling into something new. With his jacket discarded next to hers on the floor and threatening to come undone, Foster swept Ezren into his arms again, her legs wrapping around his waist. Ezren's lips trailed down his neck as he just managed to find the bedroom, the door opening and hissing shut behind them. And for the hundredth time that night, he couldn't believe the dream they were living. That he was Ezren's, and she was his, and no matter what lay for them beyond these walls...

Tonight was theirs.

CHAPTER 7

5.01.44B T-minus 3 days until the BRR

IN THE END, they only got two blissful nights before the outside came knocking at their door. Literally. The ring of Ezren's goggs pulled her from her peaceful basin of sleep. Her eyelashes fluttered open where she lay with her cheek pressed against Foster's bare chest, his breaths rising and falling with easy slumber, and his arm curled around her.

With a smile tugging at her lips, she let her eyelids close again, tuning out her goggs on their charging dock with a mental chip command. Satisfied, she snuggled into Foster's heat, savoring the drum of the rain on the clear dome above them. She was just slipping back into a dream of sprawling fields when the ring of Foster's goggs picked up where hers had left off.

Foster's steady breaths stumbled as his eyes opened, his voice rough with sleep. "I thought I silenced them." The goggs fell quiet as he turned on his side, pressing an absent kiss to Ezren's hair and tucking her closer.

"Mine were silenced too," Ezren murmured. "Who would call this early anyway?"

Foster chuckled, a delicious rumble beneath her cheek. "It's not even early."

Ezren grinned. In truth, she had no idea what time it was,

and it was her new favorite thing. "Okay, well who's calling at all? Security checked in before we went to bed."

"Guess we'll never know."

Ezren let her fingers play over the muscled ridges of his shoulders. "You know, I could really get used to this days-off thing."

"Mm, once we move out of Carmella, maybe we could start every day like this." He pressed another warm kiss to her forehead.

Ezren closed her eyes as Foster kissed her bare shoulder, exposed by his oversized T-shirt. "This is definitely my favorite—"

A hollow banging made Ezren tense, and Foster's head jerked up. Another three bangs, and Ezren let herself relax with a relieved eye roll. "Ugh. Someone's at the door. It's got to be Sylvia."

Foster groaned, burying his face in her neck. "I thought she said we had three days."

"Something must've come up."

Foster stilled, and this time, when he looked up, they locked gazes, tension sparking from their shared understanding. Ezren reached for her goggs and connected them to the security cam by the entrance, projecting the holo above them. Sure enough, Shiro and Sylvia stood at the door, which Shiro kicked half-heartedly with a heavy boot.

Foster opened a voice channel. "Sylvia. Shiro."

"Oh thank the suns." Sylvia threw up her hands as she turned to face the cam. "I was starting to worry you were dead!"

Foster looked to Ezren with a sleepy grin. "To what do we owe the pleasure?"

"Look, I'm sorry," Sylvia continued. "This couldn't wait. We need to talk."

Now it was Ezren's turn to groan. Whatever Sylvia was about to say, she knew it would inevitably bring a swift end to their honeymoon. And she was nowhere near ready for it to be over. "Can we at least get a rain check on our third day off?"

"Not just that," Foster cut in. "I want a fourth day in interest."

"Oh, c'mon." Sylvia crossed her arms, her hip popping to one side. "I already feel terrible, and we brought apology cronuts."

Shiro lifted the box in his hands as proof.

Ezren raised her eyebrows at Foster, but he shook his head.

FOSTER: STAY STRONG.

"No deal," he said.

Sylvia bent down to pick up a heated jug. "Did I mention we also brought fresh coffee from Small Hour Café?"

Ezren's eyes flew wide, and Foster pressed a finger to her lips, suppressing a laugh. Ironing his expression, he spoke again. "Sylvia..."

"Oh, all right. *Fine!*" A holo flicked out from Sylvia's goggs. "I'll schedule it in. Just come open the chaffing door."

"We'll be right down!" Ezren called, shutting off the voice channel. She turned to Foster with a victorious giggle. "My, my, that was quite the bargain." She pressed a soft kiss to his pleased smirk. "I guess we'll consider this a pause on our honeymoon."

"Hmm, I don't think four days is enough." Foster met her lips with a deep languorous kiss. "Maybe I can bargain for a fifth."

"We're married, Foster." Ezren smiled as he stroked his thumb across her cheek. "Now we have forever."

His stormy eyes creased in soothed satisfaction, his head flopping on the pillow as she rose and stepped toward the bathroom. "Do you think that's what she wants to talk about?"

Ezren winced. "You think VSoc found out about the wedding somehow?" She slipped on her favorite black tights and her oversized sweater, hands knotting in the overlong sleeves.

Foster sighed and rolled out of bed in his shorts, his defined abs rippling as he stretched his arms above his head. "I guess, unfortunately, we need to go find out."

Ten minutes later found Ezren still rubbing sleep from her eyes as she sat across from Sylvia and Shiro at the circular breakfast table. A cronut and a steaming mug of vanilla-cream coffee sat in front of her while Foster slouched in the chair at her side.

"So," Sylvia started, glancing at Shiro as she tapped her rainbow nails on the table. "The news is out."

Ezren frowned, and Foster's head lolled backward. "But how?" she asked. "No one at the wedding would've leaked it."

Sylvia's lips pursed in a moment of confusion before understanding dawned on her. "Oh, no, not about the wedding."

Shiro's dark gaze met Foster's. "About the will."

Ezren's brows shot up. It wasn't that she'd forgotten about the will so much as she'd been deliberately ignoring it. "Oh, right." And strangely, the knot in Ezren's stomach eased. Under the table, Foster squeezed her hand, and she gave him a smile. At least this secret was still theirs for a little longer.

Foster leaned forward, his elbows on the table. "How'd it leak?"

"We don't know," Shiro said. "But they're asking you to address it at the pre-race press conference tomorrow."

A muscle in Foster's jaw ticked. "But we haven't even announced our decision."

"It sounds like someone's trying to force your hand." Ezren sipped her steaming coffee, savoring the sugar on her tongue—

still not worth getting shorted a day of her honeymoon, but chaffing close.

Shiro nodded, his angular face dark. "And I bet we could take a good guess as to who."

"But that doesn't mean we have to respond to this, Foster." Sylvia stabbed a finger into the table. "We can choose when and where to respond if you're not ready."

"No." Foster clasped his hands together and rested his chin on his knotted fingers, the furrow between his brows like a deep, brooding trench. "I'm tired of this, Sylvia. I've made my decision, and I want to make it clear that we're no one's pawns."

Ezren touched her knee to his in support, while Shiro and Sylvia shared a brief glance of surprise.

"You're sure about this?" Shiro twisted his mug on the metal table. "About taking the CEO position?"

"I am." Foster unlaced his hands, one of them finding Ezren's. "And I want to announce it at the conference tomorrow."

Sylvia let out a slow breath between her teeth, rubbing her temples with her fingers. "Okay then." Her holo flicked out of her goggs. "First we'll need to meet with the lawyer and maybe the Calderon advisors. Then talk about enhanced security measures. Write up a speech." She looked pointedly at their fingers, where the silver ink stood out against their skin. "And get some gloves. Unless you're planning on announcing that too?"

"Not yet." Ezren shifted in her seat as she considered everything that would undoubtedly spiral out of control after Foster announced his ownership of Calderon Industries. "I don't want to distract people from what's going on. And"—she smiled again at Foster—"we'd rather keep this between us for as long as we can."

"Makes sense." Shiro took a sip from his coffee and wiped

the cream from his upper lip with a hand. "Don't want to give Casolla a collective heart attack."

"That's not to say it won't happen anyway." Sylvia's fingers flicked through her holos three at a time. "But, Ezren, you're going to have to break that news to Micah. If someone leaks your nuptials before she does, we'll hear her scream from here."

Shiro chuckled. "And we won't be able to keep it secret forever. Technically speaking, your marriage license is public. The only reason it's not out yet is because people don't know to look for it. But with all of your other legal matters about to be dissected by VSoc's best wannabe holo detectives..." He gave an apologetic shrug. "I give it a week at most."

Ezren puffed out a resigned breath between her cheeks. "Sounds like in a week we'll be living different lives."

"Are you nervous?" Foster asked, tracing the silver ink around her finger.

"I'd be less nervous if you hadn't seen the Crow's murder tree," Ezren said.

"Don't worry about that." Shiro's gaze wandered out the clear dome wall to where the rain still poured down on the Belethean plain. "I'll need to gather up a few trusted faces, but I've got some ideas for some additional security at the press conference."

"And we've got a good team for everything else," Sylvia added, pushing her curls behind her shoulders. Shiro draped an arm over the back of her chair, and she gave him the slip of a smile. "We'll make sure you're safe."

"I know." Ezren swallowed, her skin prickling with a premonition she couldn't quite name. "It's a big step, but it's the right one."

For a moment, the words lingered under the steady thrum of Belethea's storm, the thunder rumbling as if in agreement. Ezren's regard swept from Foster to Shiro to Sylvia, the enormity of what lay before them twining around them all—holding them together.

The chime of Sylvia's goggs shattered the spell, and she gave an apologetic wince. "Well I hate to say this." Her lips tightened as she drew herself up straight, morphing from their friend to their manager in a blink. "But it's time to get back to work."

CHAPTER 8

5.02.44B T-minus 2 days until the BRR

AN HOUR before the press conference found Foster in a waiting room still whirling from the thirty-six-hour sprint of preparations. With his comms practically blowing up with urgent messages, he wistfully longed for the perfection of their unhurried honeymoon afternoons dozing under the Belethean storms.

Unlike their wedding, he and Ezren were dressed to the nines for the press conference. Today, Sylvia had forced him into a three-piece suit with long tails, his goggs strapped around a low top hat, and thin white gloves to obscure his inked ring. Beside him, Ezren's ruffled skirt fell to the floor with lace streaking up from her hips to the ends of her fingers. Matching geometric designs of black ink framed both of their eyes, and their holstered weapons were hidden beneath their clothes.

Together they stood in the small room clustered with Grady/Guns, Sylvia, Shiro, Micah, and strangely, Davis. Two newer guards, Emmett with a lime-green buzzcut, and Paula, a dark-haired woman with a tight bun, flanked Shiro, each of them looking like a wire ready to snap. With the record-breaking BRR crowds pouring in, people packed the streets around the press hall for a solid mile, and from *The Royaler*

Review's coverage in his goggs, Foster had no idea how they were going to escape the building once his speech was over.

He patted his pockets, sweat already prickling his brow at the thought of speaking in front of essentially all of Casolla. While Ezren had given more prepared speeches in the past year than he could count, he'd only ever been there with a supporting part. Now their roles would be reversed, and no one had any guess how the system's shock would manifest. If an angry mob stormed the stage, there was little Shiro and his two security guards could do about it.

Ezren wrapped herself around Foster's arm with a reassuring squeeze, and Paula grinned from beside them.

"Just wanted to say it's an honor to be a part of this," she whispered. "I have family on Exa, and the fall of the Kalashnik has completely changed their lives. You've already made such a huge difference, and we can't wait to see what's next for you."

Foster's lips parted, but he was at a loss. Though they received lots of messages and holos with the impact of their work, rarely did someone talk to them in person.

"We're so glad to be able to make a difference," Ezren whispered back, the glow of her cheeks matching Paula's.

Paula opened her mouth to say more when Shiro projected a large holo in the center of the makeshift waiting room. "Okay, listen closely." A short, three-dimensional model of the building and their exit routes rotated in the middle. "After your speech, I have three autocabs leaving in different directions from three different entrances." He glanced at Foster. "The highest risk will be on exit, so Davis and Simon here"—Shiro pointed to both of them standing by the door in suits identical to Foster's— "have ever so graciously agreed to be your doppelgangers."

Ezren groaned, rubbing a palm across her forehead. "I can't believe you managed to drag Davis into this again."

"What?" Grady grinned, knocking a forearm against Davis's. "He's in the group-comm."

Foster nodded to both of them. "Thanks for doing this." At this point, Davis was as much a part of their team as anyone.

"But they look nothing like Foster," Ezren said.

"Please." Shiro waved her away. "Their builds are close enough, and moving fast in a crowd with a holomask on, they'll work just fine." He pointed again to the holo, which had zoomed in on the conference hall. "When he's done with his speech, Davis and Simon will activate their holomasks and all three of them will move in different directions." Shiro pointed to her. "And since we're not taking any chances with you either, Ezren, Sylvia and Micah will be acting as your doppelgangers. You and Foster will be in different cars to maximize confusion. Then we'll deliver you back to your honeymoon suite for the rest of the night."

Foster frowned, but honestly they didn't have time to come up with an alternate plan, and the promise of getting another night with Ezren alone in the middle of nowhere was enough motivation to do just about anything. "Okay." He pulled up his exit path alongside his speech. "I've got it." Honestly, he'd barely looked at the route, but he had all the faith that between Sylvia and Shiro, they would get him to where he needed to go.

That is, if he got through this speech first.

"Are you ready?" Ezren asked, her attention darting to the huge holo clock in the middle of the room that said they had twenty-two seconds left.

Foster straightened, taking another long breath in and out. Just like before a race. Because at this point, it didn't really matter if he was ready or not. It was happening. "Let's do this."

Ezren nodded, squeezing him again. "In another hour, we'll be on our way back to the cottage."

He kissed her laced hand as Sylvia ushered them to the door. "If I don't get another word in, I'll see you there."

With that, Emmett opened the door to a veritable sea of shouting holologgers, screaming fans, and a few protesters waving signs he couldn't make out. Foster's hand tightened around Ezren's as they followed Shiro's quick steps through the lobby, into a back hallway, and then up the stairs to the stage wings where Senator Villegas stood giving her final remarks.

An event coordinator beckoned for Ezren, and she gave Foster one more smile before shuffling away. Foster's ears buzzed as Ezren strode onstage, confident and smiling. Her speech was a short, traditional BRR message that harked back to the history of how the BRR had unified and shaped Casolla. How it brought them together today as they developed exciting new technologies and planets in their shared system. With no polarizing messages about terraforming or the luxies, Ezren's words were meant to set the crowd at ease before Foster's rocked the system.

In another shower of applause and cheers, Ezren walked off the stage only to be shuffled away by Shiro.

EZREN: RELAX, YOU'LL DO GREAT. AND THEN WE GET TO GO HOME.

FOSTER: PROMISE?

EZREN: PROMISE.

Emmett positioned Micah more or less in Ezren's place, ready for the exit strategy, and out of the corner of his eye, Foster could see what looked like a member of the press whispering into Micah's ear. He had to hope Micah would be able to get rid of whoever it was before she turned on her holomask. The coordinator shuffled Foster forward for his cue, and from the other wing, Sylvia gave him a tight smile.

And then, there was no more time to stall as they guided him onto the stage to another raucous cheer from the crowd, one that seemed somehow three times louder than the last. He scanned the rows of cheering onlookers in the stadium seating of the dark auditorium, his gaze somehow immediately finding Ezren's in the corner of the first row, standing between Davis and Shiro. Her face glowed with pride as she cheered right along with the rest of the crowd, and the sight of her—of his *wife*—steadied his shaking hands. Foster strode up to the podium, adrenaline streaking through every inch of him as his goggs projected the small words of his speech in front of his eyes for him alone.

And for once, he was glad of all those speaking classes Sylvia had enrolled them in.

Taking one last deep breath, he let the words go. "To my fellow Casollans, I want to welcome you to another exciting BRR week." The cheers rose once again. "I know this year feels strange as we come together on the heels of Calderon's probable murder." The noise in the room ceased as if someone had turned off a switch. "Yes, as some of you may know, only four days before his sudden death, Calderon informed the authorities of a credible death threat. A death threat from the syndicate lord known as the Crow, which myself and others witnessed. After his murder, I received an identical threat." A few gasps were quickly smothered as the whole crowd leaned in to hear his words. "Perhaps it seems strange for us to speak of it, but as Ezren and I move forward, we no longer want to keep the shadows of our system a secret, but rather root them out." He swallowed, his mouth dry and the nerves turning his stomach. "This is all the more important since, as of yesterday, I have accepted Warner Calderon's bequest, and, effective today, officially accept the title as both owner and CEO of Calderon Industries."

For a single heartbeat, the auditorium was silent. Then all manner of shouts erupted from the crowd, though from his vantage, Foster couldn't discern if the shock was positive or negative. When they showed no signs of quieting down, he glanced at Sylvia, but she gestured him on.

"And while I'm young," he continued, raising his voice as the crowd fell quiet once more, "with a lot to learn, I'm in a good place to make a difference. I'm fortunate to have a seasoned team at my back that shares my commitment to Belethea's core values of honesty and industry as we partner with the CIF to crush out corruption. Together, we hope to not only mold a better Belethea but a better Casolla as well." He scanned the audience, but they were spellbound now, their feelings a mass pool of mystery. "Along with my doubles partner, Ezren Hart, we will remain on the BRR council in our ambassador capacity to continue our work in tandem with Calderon Industries. Despite the threats that have been levied on us from all quarters, Belethea will bow to no one. Especially not the syndicate shadows."

Foster's confidence grew with the nearing end of his speech, and he shifted his focus to bore into the crowd as if the Crow might be among them. "Although Warner Calderon and I had many differences, on that, I know we would agree."

He gripped the podium tighter, his tangled regard for Calderon constricting his chest. "Calderon may have left behind a checkered legacy, but we cannot deny that it has shaped the Belethea we know today, and it is through our continued, united efforts that we will honor all the Beletheans that came before us. The ones that first navigated its storms, who braved its surface, built this city, and who transformed its skies." He found Ezren's gaze once again to find her eyes shining, one hand on her chest, and he couldn't help the smile that lifted the corner of his mouth. "So on behalf of the Belethean council and Calderon Industries, Ezren and I thank you for your continued support as we move forward out of the shadows as one Casolla System."

For a beat, silence stretched through the crowd. Then the audience roared with such force, security surged forward to protect the stage. Though hovercams soared through the air and hologgers shouted questions, Foster couldn't discern a single one.

Then Sylvia was standing next to him. "Unfortunately since Foster Sterling is on a tight schedule, we have to limit questions—"

In the brief lull, a shout echoed through the room. "Does this mean Foster Sterling is the new Warner Calderon?"

It wasn't until then that Foster finally realized his years of race royales had, in fact, prepared him for this moment. Because if you didn't sound like a winner, act like a winner, and believe you were a winner, then you weren't going to win.

And he was so used to winning.

"That's a hard no." He stepped forward with a cocky grin on his face that would've made Simon Grady proud. "I'm Foster Sterling, and Calderon Industries is *mine*."

The feedback nearly deafened him.

"And that's all the time we have," Sylvia chirped, though there was no way anyone but a lip reader caught the words.

Sylvia: That's our cue to leave.

Out of the corner of his eye, Foster caught Villegas slowly applauding backstage with an amused smirk. Looping her arm through his, Sylvia pulled him into the opposite wing with Emmett right behind them.

Ezren: Well done, CEO. Now, was that so bad?

Foster threw her one last grin over his shoulder.

Foster: I couldn't do it without you.

Ezren: We'll celebrate at the cottage.

Foster: I'll race you there.

Safely behind a curtain in a veritable army of security, Sylvia grabbed Davis and Micah and dodged into an alcove. The three of them touched the sides of their neck to trigger the nanite layer molded to their skin, and their faces disappeared— to be replaced by two of Ezren's and one of Foster's.

"Holy chaff," Foster breathed.

Ezren's face smiled back at him, but it was Sylvia's voice that spoke. "Yes, yes, technology is wonderful, now we have to move. You two are going that way." She shoved him and Micah in the direction of Emmett, while she and Grady started down the opposite hall with Paula. "Enjoy your last peaceful evening for a while, and we'll see you at the BRR."

With that, Micah clamped down on Foster's arm as Emmett ushered them quickly down the brightly lit hallway, the thunderous noise of the crowd still echoing off the walls.

"This way," Emmett said, a smile creasing his broad features. "And I have to congratulate you on a stunning speech, Executive Sterling. That was something."

Executive Sterling. The title sent a chill down his spine.

Micah squealed with delight, Ezren's face uncanny on her much curvier body. "Mother suns, that was chaffing amazing. And I can't believe I got to see it in person! VSoc will be talking about this moment for *years* to come!"

"That could be good or bad." But even as he said it, he chuckled, the elation of relief coursing through him. It was *done.* Now, the world could take it how they would, and he could spend one more night in the closest thing that came to paradise. When they left tomorrow, then they would deal with whatever fallout awaited them—as a team.

"Oh please." Micah slapped his arm gently as they rounded another corner in the labyrinth of a building. "You're Foster Yunin-Sterling. Or well, you were. Not sure what last names you and Ezren will take now." She gave him a wink. "Ezren's fans might be more passionate, but you, by far, with your neutral equal-opportunity-grumpiness and your celebrity pedigree, have the widest reach. I mean you have fans that have followed you since you were a baby."

"Creepy, Micah," Foster said, catching her elbow as she tripped on her heeled boots.

Micah's Ezren face gave a snort-laugh. "Okay, yeah, maybe. But still." She poked him in the chest. *"Powerful."*

Foster sighed as Micah continued her unfiltered stream-of-consciousness commentary. "And I think you were totally right about not announcing the other thing. But maybe that would be the perfect statement after the BRR. I mean I could..."

Foster mentally tabulated the fifty-three minutes they'd be stuck in a car together. While he certainly considered Micah a friend, he found when she was in the midst of an obsessive VSoc high she was best taken in small doses. Maybe he could convince her to do some kind of live VSoc response in the car. At least then her attention wouldn't be on *him*. Maybe he could even put her up front with Emmett and have the backseat to himself?

She was rattling off *The Royaler Review*'s reaction to his speech when a door hissed open in front of them, and they stepped out into a backstreet magically devoid of rabid BRR fans. A humming autocab waited for them, the door slicing open as Emmett moved to the mouth of the alley, a hand on the gun at his hip.

Well done, Shiro.

The thought was barely out of his head before footsteps from behind them pricked his ears. He'd only made a quarter turn when something stabbed into his neck, an electric shock convulsing his body with an overwhelming tide of searing pain. Beside him, Micah screamed as a figure rushed her, covering her head as the crack of gunshots echoed off the buildings' metal walls, and a body fell to the ground. Micah's? Emmett's? The shooter's? With his vision blurred, he couldn't see.

Foster tried to push himself up from the street, his whole body trembling, but his muscles weren't cooperating. Someone crouched next to him, and his ears rang as another deafening volley of bullets pierced the air much too close.

Then a gray boot whistled through the air, impacting Foster's jaw with a sickening thud.

And a black curtain fell on Foster's world.

CHAPTER 9

5.02.44B T-minus 2 days until the BRR

(FIVE MINUTES EARLIER)

PRIDE WELLED in Ezren's chest as she watched Foster on the stage, his voice strong and steady as he became, without a doubt, one of the most powerful people in Casolla. And somehow, he'd managed to choose words that set him apart from the shoes Calderon had left for him—setting the stage with his own path of ideals.

The crowd roared around her as Sylvia stepped up to the podium to handle questions, and Shiro tugged Ezren back from the roiling mass of people. But still she couldn't turn away, her gaze lingering on Foster as Sylvia pulled him off the stage as well.

EZREN: WELL DONE, CEO. NOW, WAS THAT SO BAD?

He threw her one last glance over his shoulder with the cocky half-smile he usually reserved for besting Simon in a brawl.

FOSTER: I COULDN'T DO IT WITHOUT YOU.

EZREN: WE'LL CELEBRATE AT THE COTTAGE.

FOSTER: I'LL RACE YOU THERE.

"Time to go," Shiro said as he pulled her and Davis down

the stairs into the corridor with event workers bustling back and forth. "Davis, go ahead and hit the holo-mask."

Davis touched something on his neck, and in a blink, he looked like the mirror image of Foster. Ezren's jaw dropped, and Davis smiled brightly at her—a strange expression on Foster's face. "How do I look?"

"Bizarre," Ezren said as Shiro continued to press them through the hall, one hand on each of their backs.

"You don't think I pull it off?" Davis asked, striking an exaggerated scowl as he offered her his arm.

Ezren laughed outright, looping her hand through his elbow. Though technically the holomask was accurate, all the details screamed false. From the way he moved, to his slimmer, slightly shorter build, to the weird victory wiggle he was performing at that moment.

"Stop!" Ezren laughed. "I can't breathe."

"And you're supposed to be imitating Foster," Shiro said.

"Oh fine." Davis schooled his expression to neutral with a slight furrow of his brow.

Ezren cocked her head at him in appraisal. "Hey, that's not bad."

Davis gave her a half-smile that, while not Foster's, was closer than the huge beaming grin he usually had. "Why thank you. Casolla knows I see him enough on VSoc."

Shiro guided them through the basement of another building, putting as much space between them and the venue as possible before they rose to surface level.

"Thanks again for doing this, Davis." Ezren darted a glance over her shoulder at the stunned gazes of everyone they passed. Apparently, Shiro had been right, and the holomask was more than sufficient to fool casual observers.

"I'm proud to be a part of the team." Davis shrugged with a

sheepish smile as they walked into what looked like an underground garage. "Especially since I believe in every word that Foster said." He turned to her, his brows swept upward in the way that only Davis had. "I've always been proud of you, Ez, but it's so blime to see you and Foster rising to your potential. Having the courage to grow and change the world with you. First Belethea, then Casolla." He let out a dry laugh as they crossed the sloped metal floor of the garage. "Team Sterling/Hart has always been incredible. But I knew once you found your wings, you'd be unstoppable."

Ezren's lips quirked up, her eyes damp with the fullness of her chest. "Well, you're the one who told me to shout into the void."

He squeezed her hand. "And just look how it answered."

Scarcely were the words out of his mouth than the squeal of tires on metal tore through the garage. Ezren whipped toward the noise just as an autocab streaked up the ramp and straight into Shiro. Ezren screamed as he crashed into the windshield and rolled over the top—his limp body landing on the ground behind it.

Then a rough hand grabbed her arm, and with panic already surging through her, Ezren reacted. Wrenching the hand from her bicep, she just managed to dodge the needle-like device aimed for her neck. Stepping in, she grabbed the shirt of the dark-garbed figure and threw him to the ground. Shots rang out, and she dove to take cover behind a parked autocab, pulling her own gun from its holster at her ankle.

She popped over the cover, ready to fire, only to watch in horror as another figure in a dark holomask threw Davis's limp body in the back of the autocab. She squeezed off three shots in the man's direction but missed when he leapt into the car after Davis, the wheels already squealing.

Turning on her goggs' recording cam, Ezren continued to

fire at the driver's side as they peeled up the ramp, but her bolt-ammo did nothing against the hard hull of the vehicle.

"Fodding shaft it." She swept the garage once more before sprinting to where Shiro lay on the floor, her heart thrumming up her throat. "Shiro!" Blood streaked the floor, and a goggs scan warned of broken ribs, a gash to his head, and a concussion. Alive. Not life threatening. "C'mon, wake up!" She gently shook him as she sent out an emergency notification to Petraskis authorities.

Shiro, wincing as he returned to consciousness, lifted his head with a groan, blood dripping down his neck into his collar. "Ezren?" he whispered, eyes still unfocused. "Where's Davis?"

"They took him!" Her voice pitched into a near scream, chest still heaving.

"Took Davis?" Shiro rasped as he struggled to sit up and fell back with a wince. "But why?"

Ezren blinked, trying to align the pieces herself until they came together with a horrifying click. Her body began to shake as she forced the words out.

"Because they thought he was Foster."

"Ezren." Shiro's brows knitted.

"What?"

"You're bleeding."

But by the time Ezren registered the pool of dark crimson, the blackness was already taking over.

Ezren returned to consciousness with the holopro of trees swaying above her, and for a moment, could only stare at it, the where and when of her situation a fuzzy question mark. Slowly she took in the cot underneath her and the mellow chimes of the physical therapy machines—Carmella's recovery room.

Sitting up, she noted the nanite bandage around her thigh, and the grim murmurings of Micah, Shiro, and Sylvia huddled together amid the forest of holos lining the walls. Ezren rolled her aching shoulders. Why was her body so sore? Where was—

Then it all came rushing back to her.

The attackers.

"Davis!" Her voice was overloud in the silence of the recovery room. "Where is he? Is he okay?"

Shiro stepped away to the other corner of the room, hyper-focused on the other three figures pulled up in the sphere of holos surrounding him. But Micah and Sylvia turned toward her, their holos winking out as they moved to the side of the cot. Then Ezren's fuzzy vision started to take in more details. The bruises and cuts on their faces, the fear etched in their features, their torn clothes. Suns.

"What happened?" Ezren whispered, almost pleading.

Micah took Ezren's hand in hers, tears budding on her lashes. "I'm so sorry, Ezren."

Ezren's mouth went dry, fear spiking through her.

Sylvia took her other hand, her expression steely. "There's no easy way to say this." She blew a curl away from her mouth, her eyes glistening in the light beneath her rainbow brows. "Davis and Foster have both been taken."

Foster had been taken.

Her whole body went numb.

"Taken where?" She pressed her palms to her head as if she could gather her scattered thoughts. She needed to think. If she just had a second to pull herself together, surely she could figure this all out.

"No, Ezren." Sylvia leaned closer, the swirling ink around

her eyes smudged, and looking a decade older than her twenty-seven years. "We think it was a coordinated hit by the Crow."

"Hit?" Ezren's voice cracked, her heart rate spiking. "Like they're dead?"

Sylvia's full bottom lip wobbled as she looked to Shiro, but he was completely engrossed in what looked like an official CIF status report. "While we don't know," Sylvia began, something about the careful words sounding rehearsed, "it seems unlikely given that they weren't killed immediately."

Ezren squeezed their hands, trying to get a grip on this nightmare reality she'd found herself in. Surely Foster would wake her up any minute. *Just wake up.* "If they already took Foster, why would they take Davis too?" Maybe if she found a flaw, she could disprove this was all true.

"We think Davis's abduction was incidental." Sylvia's hands smoothed a stubborn wrinkle in the thin sheet. "Simon, Paula, and I were also attacked, but the crowd broke through the barrier, and we were able to lose the attackers in the chaos." A million questions stabbed through Ezren, but Sylvia continued on. "Right now, their abduction is being kept secret to quell panic. Not even Simon and Bex know. We sent them and the rest of your family to Gerard's for the extra security."

When Ezren spoke, her voice was small. "What do they want with Foster?"

"We don't know yet," Micah said. "They haven't sent a message or a ransom demand, but the CIF is trying their best to reach out and negotiate."

Ezren let herself fall back on the bed, a million worst-case scenarios warring to block out any semblance of rational thought. "Has the CIF ever negotiated with the Crow before?"

Sylvia's gaze fell to the floor with the smallest shake of her head.

"I'm so sorry, Ezren," Micah whispered. "It all happened so fast. I just... I didn't know what to do."

"They tried to take Micah too." Sylvia swallowed. "But Emmett was able to get her away before they..."

Ezren looked from one to the other, the grief plain on their faces. "He's dead, isn't he?" Though she hadn't known Emmett well, he had seemed like a solid, cheerful sort of man.

Sylvia nodded, wiping at the tears spilling onto her cheeks. "Paula too. The first bullet was to her head. If she hadn't been there, it would've hit me instead."

Ezren pressed her palms to her eyes, guilt and grief and fury all building within her as she thought of Paula's glowing smile. *It's an honor to be a part of this.*

Dead.

What did that mean for Foster and Davis?

"I couldn't save Davis either," Ezren said. "I didn't land a single shot, and Shiro almost..." Shaking her head, she bolted upright, the need to act whipping through her. She grappled for her anger to keep the grief at bay. "So what do we do now?"

"Well"—Sylvia dismissed a notification from her goggs with a flick of her fingers—"Shiro's coordinating a search with the CIF, and we've been combing through VSoc footage of the event looking for leads."

Ezren met Sylvia's gaze, the knowledge running between both of them like a death sentence. With no leads, there was really nothing they could do. And that thought sent another wave of fury through her.

"You might want to check your messages, Ezren," Micah murmured. "If there was a ransom message, they might send it to you as his... wife."

The whisper-soft word defused Ezren. If she wanted to find Foster, she had to stay focused.

"Right." She projected the holo from her goggs to find

34,223 unread messages. "Shaft." With a thought, she filtered it down to messages received since the time of Foster's speech two hours ago: 822. Ezren sighed. Her gaze swept down the list —most of them remarks on Foster's speech, offers for interviews and collaborations, terraforming updates, and a sprinkling of hate mail. She was about to open her mouth to rage at the futility of it when a message caught her eye:

IF YOU WANT TO SAVE FOSTER STERLING.

"I've got it!" Ezren hopped to her feet, and immediately regretted it when her thigh screamed in pain.

Shiro turned with a sparking glare. "Hey! Take it easy. We're trying to repair your chaffing artery."

"I got a message about Foster."

Shiro crossed the room in two huge strides as Ezren projected the message for them all to read.

Ezren Hart,
You don't know me, but you're the only hope I've held on to these last eighteen months, so I feel like I owe this to you. Foster's in lunar-hopper 9J8DF23 that departed from Petraskis spaceport bay at 2132 station time. Comms aren't safe, but I'll message as I can.
—A Fan

"Send it to me," Shiro barked as he swiveled to another CIF agent in his holo. "We've got a lead we need to trace. It's headed your way."

Frowning, Micah gestured at the glowing message. "If they want to help, why wouldn't they include more details?"

"Do you think it's a trap?" Sylvia whispered.

"We can't trace it." Shiro let out a frustrated growl, his jaw flexing. "It's been encrypted seven ways to the sun."

"At least that means it's not a trap," Micah said.

"I'm going to see if I can get a lock on that lunar hopper's location." Shiro's holos whirled in front of him. "If it's accurate, I should be able to get an idea of their potential trajectories."

Ezren's gaze sharpened, the beginnings of a plan striking a spark of hope in her chest. "And I'll arrange to have our ship readied." Ezren thought out the message to Gerard's staff. After their ambassador schedules had gone off the rails, Foster had insisted on buying their own lunar hopper—which he'd unimaginatively dubbed *The Wheels* and his dad graciously hosted in his private hangar.

"Okay, wait!" Micah waved her arms frantically. "You can't be thinking about going after him." Her round, beseeching eyes —violet today—peered down into Ezren's from her inch of a height advantage. "Think about what happened last time."

But Ezren was already planning four steps ahead, action smelting her fiery emotions into the cool hard steel of resolve. "I have no regrets about going to Otho, Micah. That was the right choice then. And this is the right choice now." She started to limp out the door, thinking of the items she'd need to collect from her room. "No matter how it ends, I will always put the people I love first." She looked at Shiro. "I just need to know how soon we can leave."

Shiro's attention skewed to Sylvia and he held her stare—a clear indication of a chip conversation Ezren wasn't privy to.

Finally, Sylvia's lips flattened into a thin line, and she gave a tense nod.

Dismissing his holos, Shiro moved with Ezren to the door. "I've already reported this to the CIF task team, but they'll take time to assemble a larger aggression strategy."

His dark gaze could've been cut from granite as he looked at her. This wasn't the laid-back security guard agent she'd gotten used to in the last nine months. This was the Shiro who'd gotten them in and out of Otho. The CIF agent responsible for their safety. And a professional Ezren trusted completely.

"If we want speed on our side, we have to go now," he said.

Micah looked from Shiro to Sylvia to Ezren with wild eyes. "You all can't be serious. The CIF can handle this." Her hands tugged on her pink pigtails as if they didn't know where else to go. "You're putting Ezren at risk for no reason, and her family has already lost so much."

"This *is* my family." Ezren limped to Micah's side and squeezed her shoulders. "There's absolutely no doubt. We'll be faster, and we care more." Ezren shook her head at Micah with a gentle smile. "There's nowhere I wouldn't go for Foster. Nothing I wouldn't do for him." And if they hurt him... Ezren's teeth ground together. The 'verse wouldn't be able to hold her fury.

Micah plucked at a tear in her formal jacket, pleading lines edging her mouth. "At one time, you would've picked Belethea. When this started, I had to basically shove you out of Tuzuno." She put a hand over Ezren's, a sad smile tilting her lips. "Is it selfish of me to want you to stay? To be safe?"

"The Crow didn't stop with Calderon, and he won't stop with Foster or me. This is about Belethea, maybe even Casolla, and to choose Foster is to choose all of it." Ezren gave Micah's shoulder another pat before turning and picking up her ankle holster from the pile of her bloodstained clothes. "Here, there are no safe choices, but this is the only one that I can live with."

"And this is why Belethea loves you so much." Micah folded her arms with a resigned sigh. "Well, don't forget to bring Davis home too." A worried line creased her forehead, and her teeth sank into her full lower lip. "Sammy..."

"I know," Ezren said, her voice thick as she thought of Davis and Sam laughing and inseparable at her wedding. How

Davis had gotten Sam through the last year when it seemed no one else could reach him.

She opened her mouth, the words, *"We'll bring them both home,"* ready on her tongue. But the last time she'd thought something like that, they'd been forced to leave her father's body on Otho. She told herself she didn't believe in jinxes, but she choked the words down anyway.

"We'll be back before you know it," she managed instead.

Conflict waged across Sylvia's expression as she turned to her. "With the BRR in two days, I have to stay for the team." She reached out a hand to Shiro and Ezren, connecting them. "Please take care of each other." Her voice was too soft, too desperate—more of a prayer than a command. "You're two of the people I love most. And Foster is..." She shook her head, tears caught in her long lashes as she wrapped Ezren in a hug. "Bring him back, Ezren."

SYLVIA: AND DON'T LET SHIRO MAKE ANY STUPID PLANS.

EZREN: I'LL DO MY BEST.

Releasing Ezren, Sylvia turned to her fiancé. "And you." Her brow furrowed as she pointed a finger at him, and Ezren braced for whatever rebuke was coming. But Sylvia only took one step before the tears burst from their dam, streaming down her cheeks in a wet sob.

Ezren's eyes widened at the sight. Not once during everything that'd happened to them had she seen Sylvia crack like that. She tossed a panicked glance at Micah, but Micah mirrored the alarm right back at her.

Shiro's face softened in the way it only did when he was talking to Sylvia. "Shh, Vi, shhhh." He cradled her to his chest and kissed her curls, his voice steady. "No crying. If you cry, I won't be able to go." He cupped her jaw in his hands, wiping the tears as he tilted her chin to meet his gaze. "And you know I have to go."

"I know. I'm just..." Sylvia sniffed, wiping at her cheeks. "I'm tired of this, Shiro. I'm tired of being scared." She gripped his blood-pocked shirt, lips trembling. "I need you to end this and come back to me after."

Shiro gently pushed a curl from her brow, but when he spoke, his tone left no room for doubt. "I will."

"Good." Sylvia nodded, the motion seeming to steady her somehow. "Because you promised to marry me." Her words steadied as she drew herself up—barely reaching Shiro's chin. "And if you die before our wedding, I'll be forced to bring you back and kill you all over again."

Shiro chuckled, his voice smooth and deep. "I promise, Sylvia Long, that I will make it back." He captured one of her hands and pressed a kiss to her fingers, her old-world ring glinting in the light. "And there will be one less shadow lurking in the dark."

"Go then. And hurry." Sylvia stepped back, her expression firm. She looked again to Ezren. "Be strong. Be swift."

Sylvia knocked her knuckles together three times in the symbol for entering the churn, and Ezren gave her a strained smile. As she limped out the door at a jog, the rest of the Belethean royalers' prayer rattled in her head.

Belethea, mother of mountains and skies...

Protect us.

CHAPTER 10

5.02.44B T-minus 2 days until the BRR

A SHOCK of pain brought Foster from empty blackness to a blinding white light. He gasped for air, his muscles jerking as if they might rip apart and tearing a muted scream from his clenched teeth before the agony finally eased.

"Ah, there he is," a smooth male voice said.

Forcing himself to lift his head, Foster took in the three people in front of him. A woman with chin-length navy hair stood to one side, a long, textured scar slicing her in half down the ridge of her nose. On the other side, a shorter, trim-haired man bared a smile of actual needles rather than teeth, and a bulkier man with a jagged oval of a scar circling his face from brow to chin stood directly in front of him—his eyes wild and hungry.

Sweat slid down Foster's spine as he struggled to stand, only to find his hands bound behind him and his ankles tied to the chair legs. His chest still heaved with the lingering pain of whatever abuse his body had endured in the transit from the street to here. A slight vibration in the floor and a hum in the air told him they were almost certainly on board a star ship with a rotating gravity liner, but he could tell no more than that. A quick scan of the metal room proved it to be empty, save the crumpled heap in the corner.

No, not a heap.

A body.

And not just any body.

Davis.

Suns shaft it. Was he dead? And where were Emmett and Micah? Foster stared at Davis, trying to make out the rise and fall of his chest. Another electric shock ripped through Foster's bones, and every muscle tensed against the pain. The jolt only lasted a moment before Foster sagged in the chair, sucking in ragged breaths. He lifted his gaze hatefully at the man in front of him.

"That's right. Eyes on me," the man crooned, his scarred visage glowing with pleasure.

The slight man with the needle smile stepped forward, his voice strangely musical. "Welcome, Foster Sterling. We're so glad you could join us. Allow me to introduce myself—"

"The Crow," Foster spat.

The man laughed in a crawling, high whinny. "Oh, no, no, no. You've not yet rated that introduction. I am merely Teeth, one of the Crow's Talons."

"Okay." Foster shifted in his seat, the exhaustion and pain edging out any fear he should've been feeling. "What do you want?"

"We want to give you another chance," Teeth said. "We understand that you, being young, may not appreciate the gravity of the situation you're in. Evidently Calderon didn't impart this to you, but his little company actually belongs to the Crow. He, and now you, are merely the pretty face we put out for the public."

"That's fodding shaft." There were many things Foster didn't like about Calderon, and although he had certainly suspected the Crow and Calderon of working together, he knew in his bones Calderon wouldn't have stooped to being anyone's figurehead. He was too proud for that.

"Now, now. Manners." Teeth gestured to the other man. "Face, if you would."

The second man winked, and another sharp electric shock rattled through Foster, jolting every inch of his body. Foster gasped in a hoarse breath. Suns. At least they didn't have Ezren, he reasoned with himself. As long as Ezren went free, he could endure this.

"You killed Calderon because he wouldn't work with you," Foster managed finally.

Teeth wiggled his hand as if it were up for debate. "He did become intractable there at the end. The alien-life situation unbalanced him. But make no mistake, the only reason he prevailed for seventy years was with the Crow's tolerance. Belethea has long lain beneath the Crow's notice, but with your little song and dance, it's about time you've been addressed."

"So you're saying now that Belethea is lucrative, you want it." Foster swallowed thickly, the iron tang of blood coating his mouth. Maybe if he kept these guys talking, he could find out something useful he could bargain with. "Of course you do. But the Crow is everything that's wrong with the stations, and I'll do whatever it takes to keep him out of Belethea."

"Such grand ideals." Teeth smiled, revealing the unsettling rows of his namesake. "But that's why we're here, after all. The Crow extended an olive branch on Crion, and you stomped all over it with your little council measures."

"But don't worry." Face nodded, his bulging eyes gleaming. "We're good at changing minds."

"Unfortunately his tolerance for pain is a touch high. A common flaw of royalers." Teeth tsked. "Thankfully, there are other ways to suffer."

He crooked his head, and the cables Foster hadn't noticed on the floor snapped taut. With two attached to Davis's ankles and two to his wrists, the cables yanked him upright, suspending him between the floor and ceiling with a crackle of electricity.

A scream juddered from his mouth, easing to a lower, sustained groan, his eyes still screwed shut.

"Leave him alone," Foster shouted. "He doesn't have anything to do with this."

"The first thing you'll learn about the Crow is that disobedience doesn't come without consequences." Teeth gave him a macabre smile with the grotesque charade of pity. "And I don't think you give this poor boy enough credit. He was doing a wonderful job of impersonating you, after all. And by the way you're sweating, I do believe you don't want him dead." His needles flashed in the low light. "Which is good enough for us."

Then Teeth leapt forward and bit Davis full on the neck. Davis and Foster screamed in horrified tandem, but Teeth only turned to grin at Foster, red coating his chin and gaze sparkling with delight.

It was then that Foster realized, the more he reacted to Davis's treatment, the worse it would be.

Suns save us

So, he welded his teeth shut as Face buried his fist into every inch of Davis, the spiked metal plate covering his knuckles glowing red with heat as it both stabbed and branded Davis simultaneously.

"Yes, horrifying, isn't it?" Teeth said, edging closer to Foster. "But if you swear your allegiance to the Crow, we could make it stop."

Foster dragged his attention away from Davis and met Teeth's crazed stare. "No matter what you do to Davis or me, I will not."

"Ah well." Teeth shrugged. "You can't fault us for trying.

And when this one dies, we'll grab another. Simon, Bex, Sylvia perhaps... so many potential weaknesses to exploit."

Foster forced himself not to react, but his mind raced. Why hadn't he mentioned Ezren? Was she already... no, she couldn't be.

Finally, after what seemed like eternity, Davis's screams stopped, his body went limp, and Foster's blood iced over. Had they really... Had they...

Face's fists stilled, his chest heaving. "Aw, he passed out." Leaning in, he pressed a finger into the wound on Davis's neck, and Foster bent over and retched on the floor.

"Alas," Teeth sighed. "He didn't last long at all."

No... he couldn't be... he wasn't... Hot tears gathered in Foster's gritty eyes.

Teeth turned his full-fledged grin on Foster, wiping a tear from Foster's cheek. Disgust crackled through Foster as he jerked away.

"Oh, don't weep, Foster Sterling. We won't let him die just yet. You see, to be in death is to reach the end of your suffering. The real torture is thinking the pain will never end. The real torture is having hope and seeing it shattered again and again until you learn not to hope at all. Only then will you meet the Crow." Teeth wrinkled his nose, glee glowing from his features. "Oh yes, don't worry, we're just beginning." He flicked a dismissive hand toward the girl. "Thread, get them ready to play again." With that, he spun on his heel and walked away, Face following after.

The girl waited for the door to slide closed before stepping from the shadows, and Foster could make out what resembled small *x*'s in the likeness of stitches carved around the scar that ran from her scalp down into the collar of her white spacer's jumpsuit. She moved quickly to Davis, pulling something from her pocket. Before Foster could object, she jabbed it into his neck, and he sucked in a rasping breath.

Foster's shoulders collapsed with relief. "Suns, he's alive."

The girl—Thread—gave him a tight glance, the holo words flicking out from her spacer's half visor.

Remember this moment, where you hoped he was still alive. The real trouble will come when you wish him to be dead. Or worse, when you envy his death.

Her words vibrated in Foster's bones as she began to strip Davis of his ragged and bloodied clothes—the ones that matched Foster's. The next question balanced on his tongue, his fear of the answer freezing the blood in his veins. He couldn't trust this girl, but neither could he suppress his need for answers. One answer in particular. "If they brought Davis to try to manipulate me, does that mean Ezren's already dead?"

The girl's gaze darted to the door before looking back at him, a surprising empathy softening her green eyes, and Foster realized she was young—probably no older than he was. Not only that, but something about her was familiar, like he'd seen her before.

Ezren Hart is alive. As the information is a comfort to you, Face and Teeth will not provide it. Instead, they'll exploit your fear of her death in the pain to come. However, your security guards, Paula Carney and Emmett Woodbridge, were killed in your acquisition.

Relief, confusion, and sorrow tangled in Foster's chest as Thread pulled a roll of nanite bandages from her pocket and wound the dark material around Davis's chest.

"You're... healing him?" Foster asked hoarsely. "But why? You work for the Crow, right? Or are you another prisoner?"

Thread snorted. *I believe it's most accurate to say both are true. If pain and despair become constant, one can become inured to it. Resist it even. Or they may find peace in madness or death—neither of which is useful to the Crow. But to know that hope is in the Talons of the Crow to give and take away will drive anyone to their knees in time. Believe me.*

She ran a finger along the thread-like scar from her brow to her lips, and Foster was suddenly certain she was projecting her words because she had no tongue to speak them.

I know.

"So your kindness is just part of the torture then?" Foster asked, the rage and helplessness bubbling under his skin.

Her sea-green eyes met his, but there was a sadness to them.

It is meant to be. She continued her work, her holo words still popping up in front of Foster. *I was created to be a weakness, and most beg me to let them die before the end.* Taking a strip of cloth from her pocket, she took Davis's head in her lap and began to clean the blood from Davis's chin, her strokes unbearably gentle. As he watched, Foster noticed her scars ran down each arm as well—to every finger. *But you are different. Despite what you will endure these next few days, you must remember that hope can come from beyond these four walls.*

Davis groaned, a wince contorting his mending face. Now wearing only his blood-stained T-shirt and torn pants, he blinked up at Thread, uncomprehending. "Who are you?"

She gave him a weak smile.

I have been no one for a very long time.

Her smile disappeared as quickly as it had come.

But unfortunately for you, I will be back.

With that, the last of the Crow's Talons walked out of the chamber. Foster watched the door close behind the strange girl before he whipped to Davis.

"Suns, Davis, I thought they'd killed you."

"I'm not sure they didn't." Davis let out a humorless laugh, not moving from his place on the floor.

Foster's brow furrowed, his own body aching. He couldn't even imagine what Davis was going through. "Are you okay?"

"I've definitely been better, but I think she gave me some kind of painkiller. I can't feel much of anything right now."

"Shaft." Foster hung his head. "Davis, I'm so sorry."

"Don't apologize." Davis's words held a strange sharpness. "This isn't your fault, and with what we're about to bear, you can't afford to carry the guilt on your conscience." Davis turned his head, his face contorting with the effort. "Just don't give in, no matter what happens. You can't."

"I don't understand why they don't just kill me," Foster said.

"They need a puppet, and you're young still. They probably see this as a golden opportunity. Maybe one they planned."

Foster tried to work through this, not at all liking the idea that they were already dancing on the Crow's strings. "And if they can't control me?"

Davis winced as he shifted his body, looking up at the ceiling once more. "If you die, then Calderon Industries goes to..."

"My wife." Foster swallowed. "Ezren."

The realization hit him and Davis at the same time with identical expressions of horrified shock.

Foster growled in frustration, his arms and legs struggling against his bonds. "So when they can't turn me..."

"They'll use you as the pressure point to control Ezren," Davis finished.

"And you..." Foster said, the larger puzzle coming together.

"Also have a history with Ezren." Davis's lips twisted into a humorless smile. "But I'm expendable."

Foster swallowed the urge to retch again as the enormity of what Davis was saying dawned on him. Of all their teammates, family members, friends... Davis had an almost nonexistent Virtual Society presence, and his relationship with them was almost unknown. He was an extra in their landscape.

If anyone else were to be killed—Ezren's family, Foster's, their teammates... their popularity would demand a riot from maybe all of Casolla. But Davis... Davis was nobody. In fact, there were probably even some who would paint him, Ezren's ex-boyfriend, as a villain in her life.

The certainty settled over Foster with a heavy thunk. While his future might still be uncertain, no matter what cards they played, Davis's death was almost assured.

"Davis..." he began, voice shaking.

But Davis turned to him with a smile, sweat and blood plastering his dark hair to his forehead. "So what'd you think about that girl?"

Foster stared at him a moment, but there was a plea hidden behind his crinkled gaze. A need for distraction.

Foster squeezed his eyes shut in resignation. Right now, he would've given Davis nearly anything.

"What about her?"

"At first I thought she was an Angel of Death bringing me back to the stars."

Foster snorted. "She might still be."

"Nah," Davis said, a smile curving his lips as his lashes fell. "She's going to help us."

"She's one of the Crow's Talons, Davis." Foster couldn't help shaking his head. "It's part of the manipulation to try to break us."

"Yeah, but she doesn't want to do it." He turned his head toward Foster with a wince. "I may not be a champion royaler, but I'm good with people. She's on our side."

Foster offered him a wry smile. "Are you saying I'm not good with people?"

An actual chuckle escaped Davis, and Foster marveled that he could laugh amidst the waking nightmare. "I'm saying we can't all be good at everything."

"You're grasping at straws, kin."

"We're alive, Foster," Davis said, a smile still lighting his blanched skin. "We have straws to work with."

But despite the hope that glowed from Davis's face, one word ricocheted through Foster's head over and over.

Expendable.

CHAPTER 11

EZREN AND SHIRO were in chaffing space. *Again.* Ezren's feet pounded into the treadmill—her steps automatic as she mentally scoured VSoc for word of the Crow. Of strange syndicate activity. Of potential sightings of Foster Sterling after his bombshell news the day before. But there was nothing. Nothing. Nothing.

When they'd left Belethea last year on the heels of a terroristic attack with a desperate hope to save her father from a death planet, Ezren couldn't have imagined worse circumstances.

But apparently her imagination couldn't match reality.

And this time, she only had Shiro at her back.

After she'd gotten used to the bustling team in Carmella over the past months, the speed-enhanced lunar hopper seemed empty with just the two of them. The two of them against a legendary ghost with unprecedented reach. While she trusted Shiro completely, she utterly missed her team.

Missed Bex.

Missed Sylvia.

And Foster... a visceral pain squeezed her chest, and she gasped in the recycled air.

She blew a strand of magenta hair out of her face, and

turned up the speed until the burn in her legs matched the rage kindling in her chest. He had to be alive.

Had to be.

With a concentrated effort, she forced her thoughts to shift from the downward spiral that threatened to destroy her in this tin can. Well, that was unfair. *The Wheels* was definitely not as claustrophobic as the *Tumble Bucket* had been. Here, both she and Shiro had plenty of space to get lost in their own tormented thoughts. She'd barely left the exercise room since they'd gotten there, and Shiro had stayed in the cockpit. Together they were hurtling through the blackness on a best-guess trajectory while they coordinated with the CIF to scrub Casollan space for any sign of their quarry.

Getting nowhere in the continuous gossip circles on VSoc, Ezren pivoted to searching the latest news on Calderon. She flicked through the hololog until a headline caught her eye.

WARNER CALDERON AND A HISTORY OF MURDER ON BELETHEA

THE SHOUT IN THE SOCIETY IS THE OLD MAN CALDERON MAY HAVE BEEN MURDERED. WHETHER YOU'RE CELE-BRATING OR MOURNING, THERE'S A SORT OF POETIC JUSTICE HERE. AND BEFORE YOU START CRYING INNO-CENT, I'M NOT JUST TALKING ABOUT HIS ALLEGED MURDER OF GENEVIEVE NAVARRO.

CALDERON'S BRUSH WITH DEATH GOES ALL THE WAY BACK TO THE ORIGINAL RACE FOR BELETHEA. THEN A BUDDING BELETHEAN SCIENTIST, HE AND HIS PARTNER, CARMELLA SAUNDERS, WERE THE FIRST TO POSTULATE ABOUT THE EXISTENCE—AND POWER—OF TERRANIUM. LITTLE DID

THEY KNOW THEY WOULD KICK OFF A PROVERBIAL INTER-SYSTEM GOLD RUSH INTO THE CENTER OF THE CHURN BELT.

FIVE GRUELING DAYS LATER FOUND CALDERON/SAUNDERS REACHING THE TERRANIUM DEPOSIT IN THE THICK OF THE CHURN… ONLY FOR DREITIS AND OBRONE TO SHOW UP AND TURN THE CANYON INTO A CHAFFING GUNFIGHT THAT THREATENED TO ESCALATE INTO WAR. ACCORDING TO LORE, IT WAS THEN THAT CALDERON, TIRED OF DEATH AND BLOODSHED, PROPOSED A TRUCE WITH THE IDEA OF ROTATING TERRANIUM RIGHTS BASED ON A RACE. NOW HERE'S WHERE IT GETS INTERESTING.

BECAUSE CARMELLA ARRIVED AT THE SITE ALIVE. AND NEVER LEFT. DID THE STORMS GET HER? WAS IT ANOTHER RACER? DID SHE DIE FROM INJURIES SUSTAINED UP TO THAT POINT? THE RACERS NEVER AGREED ON A STORY.

AND IF YOU'RE STILL WITH ME, IT GETS EVEN FRITZIER. BECAUSE OVER THE COURSE OF THE FOLLOWING TEN YEARS, OF ALL SIX OF THE RACERS WHO WERE PART OF THE DEAL, ONE LEFT THE SYSTEM, ONE COMMITTED SUICIDE, AND THE OTHER TWO SIMPLY DISAPPEARED. THE LAST… BECAME THE MOST POWERFUL MAN IN CASOLLA. SO IF YOU'VE GOTTEN THIS FAR, YOU HAVE TO ASK YOUR-SELF, DO YOU BELIEVE IN COINCIDENCES?

—THE ROYALER REVIEW

Ezren leapt from the treadmill, chest heaving. What did she just read? While admittedly, she'd never been the best student, she'd always been told Carmella's death in the churn belt had been a huge personal tragedy in what was a vicious and bloody event in Belethea's history. Was *The Royaler Review* saying Calderon killed her and the others too? Perhaps so he alone could profit? Or was it possible the others killed Carmella somehow, and Calderon took his revenge on them?

She frowned. Though she'd spent many an hour in meetings with Calderon over the past eight months, she didn't pretend to understand him. But still, as a self-proclaimed man of logic, she doubted he would kill without a reason. She searched for the names and faces of the other original royalers. They all had military or scientific backgrounds and one—she paused, still crouched on the floor of the lunar hopper's spherical gym—was Senator York's older brother.

Okay, that *was* a strange coincidence.

She was about to start a search on Carmella Saunders when a message chimed in her goggs. From an unknown sender.

Ezren,

We're in the outer orbit of X9-II. I don't know their plan, but they know you're following us. I want to tell you to be careful, but you need to hurry.

—A Fan

"Shiro!" Ezren yelled, running out the door and into the circular common area. "They sent another message." She vaulted over a couch and into the small cockpit where Shiro stood in a sphere of holos, running his hand repeatedly through his tangled hair.

"What'd they say?" He shot toward her as she projected the words, his eyes scraping over them. "Okay." He pulled up their course. "We weren't on that exact route, but we were close. If they have an actual destination, this should narrow it down. The CIF team is still a day behind us though."

Ezren nodded, trying to follow the trajectories in the holo

when something brushed against her leg. She looked down to see Shiro's six-tailed cat winding around her ankle with a mew.

Her brow furrowed. "Um... Shiro?"

"Yeah," Shiro said, enlarging a list of station orbits.

"I didn't know you brought Turnip on the ship."

"I didn't."

"Okay." Ezren picked up the small pink cat and stuck it in his face. "Then why is she here?"

"What?" Shiro blinked at the tiny animal before reaching out and taking her from Ezren. "I thought we left her at Gerard's with everyone else."

"So did I." Ezren shrugged, trying to remember if she'd seen the cat in the rush before takeoff. "Did she sneak aboard?"

"But we've been on this ship for sixteen hours already." Shiro draped the cat over his shoulder, his gaze narrowing. "There's no way she wouldn't have come crying for food."

Ezren thought of Waffle and Turnip playing at Gerard's party and at her wedding after, a furious suspicion building in her gut. "He'd better not be..."

She jogged off through the ship. Though it wasn't huge, they'd had no need to go into the spare bunk or the storage room. The first door to the spare bunk sliced open. Empty. In three steps she was at the next, the door retreating into the wall with a hiss.

And the rage burst out of her. "Mother shafting suns, what are you doing here?"

Micah, Sam, and Waffle looked up from their holos where they sat in the midst of the crates of supplies.

"I told you she'd be sparking pissed," Micah singsonged before turning to Ezren. "Honestly, I'm glad you finally found us. I wasn't sure how much longer I could keep sneaking around."

Shiro peeked in the room with Turnip rubbing her head

against his cheek. "You've gotta be shafting me." He ran a rueful hand over his five-o'clock shadow. "I guess that's what we get for not doing a security check on the ship before we left the ground."

"Make a stop at the nearest space station so we can drop them off," Ezren snapped, fury snarling through any kind of coherent thought.

Sam stood calmly, his hummingbot, Giles, whirring on his shoulder as he dusted off his dark pants. "You don't have time."

"The chaff we do," Ezren said, stepping to one side as he brushed past her. "What are you even doing here, Sam?" When he didn't answer, she turned back to where Micah scratched Waffle's nose. "Seriously, Micah, what the shaft?"

With a sigh, Micah met her gaze, her voice calm. "Well, he saw you and Shiro going to Gerard's hangar and confronted me. When I refused to tell him what was happening, he ran off. So naturally I had to chase after him, and then we were taking off and then we wanted to wait long enough so you wouldn't turn around... andddd here we are."

"Sam." Ezren spun on her heel to where her brother now lay stretched out on one of the couches. "Don't you realize how dangerous this is? Two people are already dead. You. Cannot. Come."

He shrugged, his unaffected expression stoking the fire within her. "Why not? You're going."

"You're *fourteen*." Ezren loomed over him, flailing her arms. "And I've done this before!"

"Not well." Her brother sat up, his blue eyes burning back at her. "And you only ever care about Foster. Someone has to save Davis."

Ezren gaped at him.

From beside her, Micah stage-whispered, "Okay, so I

might've filled him in during the sixteen hours we were in storage."

Ezren turned to Shiro, stabbing a finger toward Sam. "Tell them they have to take an escape pod."

"Don't look at me." Shiro held up his hands as if in surrender. "I'm not getting in the middle of this." Scratching Turnip's head from her perch on his shoulder, he started back toward the cockpit. "I'll be analyzing our routes if anyone needs me."

"Holy chaff." Ezren turned to Micah next. "C'mon, help me out here."

"You said there's no question about going for family." Micah's lips thinned, her expression thoughtful as she looked from Sam to Ezren and back, her voice soft. "I think Sam feels the same."

"And I can help." Sam's holo flicked out from his green goggs. "I already tracked where the messages are coming from and planned their route. I'm 99% certain they're going to the wormgate."

"Ninety-nine-point-seven-eight percent certain," Giles corrected from his shoulder.

"Wait, what?" Ezren frowned, and Shiro paused in his retreat. "How did you do that? Even Shiro's CIF friends couldn't track it."

Sam snorted. "Yeah, that's because they're probably looking at the message itself instead of the relays it came from. Knowing the timing, I was able to neck down the possibilities. Plus, if you know where to look on VSoc, there's tons of amateurs tracking space traffic as a hobby. With their added data, I was able to set executable parameters for Giles to parse." Waffle jumped on the couch next to Sam and put her huge rectangular head in his lap. "We were only at 78% confidence with the first message, but the second zeroed us in."

Shiro ran a hand through his nest of dark hair. "But why would they be going to the wormgate?"

"Well, it's right next to the largest space station in the Casolla system." Micah stretched her arms over her head, bending to one side. "It's also a great place to get rid of someone."

"Sam, send me your calculations," Shiro said as he strode toward the cockpit. "I'll adjust our course and update the CIF. They should have some agents on the ground there that might be able to help."

"Okay." Sam cracked his knuckles one at time. "But you don't have to go through the station to go through the wormgate."

"But why would they go through the wormgate at all?" Ezren asked, frustration still clouding her head. She couldn't believe she was arguing with her fourteen-year-old brother about this. He shouldn't even have been there to argue with. "That doesn't make any sense."

Sam looked at her as if she was missing something vital, his words slow. "Because when people disappear, it doesn't feel like they're dead."

Each word hit her like a punch to the gut. Because of course, she and her brother knew that better than anyone.

"VSoc would certainly have different opinions on someone cutting out through the wormgate versus getting assassinated," Micah said, draping herself over the top of the couch. "One might be a coward and the other a martyr."

"The legal implications would be different too," Shiro added from the cockpit.

"All right, Sam." With a bone-deep sigh, Ezren sank onto the couch next to her maddening brother. "Have you calculated if we'll be able to catch them before they get there?"

"Our calculations are a solid no," Giles chirped, and Ezren remembered just how annoying she found the little bot.

"Yes but..." Sam pulled up the numbers in his holo. "If we get close enough, I may be able to hack into their mainframe to slow them down."

Ezren propped her elbows on her knees and ground her palms into her eyes. While she had minor hacking chops she'd picked up from researchers during her internship, her brother, bedridden for much of his childhood, had made an art form of the practice. And from the genius-level scores coming back from his boarding school, his skills were certainly an asset they could use.

"Okay," Ezren said, a long exhale escaping her body.

Sam's head popped up. "Does this mean I can stay?"

Ezren didn't say anything, because she couldn't. There was no right answer to that question. Her options were to put her brother and Micah in an escape pod by themselves in the middle of space, forfeit Foster's rescue to deliver them safely to a space station, or let them come as they confronted murderous syndicate thugs.

Micah sandwiched her in from the other side, her voice uncharacteristically soft. "We know you've been depending on your royale friends for a lot recently, Ezren, but we can help too. We still want to be a part of your life." She bumped Ezren's shoulder with hers. "And not just for the parties."

Ezren's heart squeezed. She had tried to make time for Micah and Sam, but with all of her duties, she knew she hadn't been doing a great job. Especially with Sam. She looked at her little brother, the hope in his face practically glowing.

"Did you bring your regen meds?"

"Of course he did," Giles chirped from his shoulder. "As if I would let him go anywhere without them."

"Where does Mom think you are right now?"

Sam's gaze darted to one side. "I told her all the BRR stuff was too overwhelming, and I asked Davis to take me back to school."

"When she tries to murder me, I expect you to sacrifice your body to protect me."

"No way." A smile tilted his lips. "You're the family royaler —that's your job."

Ezren looked up at the blue sky projected on the ceiling but found no assistance there. "Okay, fine. But Sam, while I absolutely recognize that we need the help of your genius fritzing mind, you are to stay as far away from any violence as possible. Do you understand?"

Sam's head bobbed. "Absolutely."

"You too, Micah."

"Oh, come on, how long have we known each other?" Micah snorted. "I would never."

"I've seen plenty of your VSoc violence." Sam laughed.

"What can I say, I'm a virtual warrior of justice," Micah sniffed.

And as the two fell into their usual good-natured ribbing, a smile bowed Ezren's lips. Because even though they should never have been there, sitting on the couch sandwiched between her best friend and her genius little brother, a small part of Ezren couldn't help but be glad that they were.

CHAPTER 12

5.03.44B T-minus 1 day until the BRR

FOSTER'S SENSE of time had disappeared. Food, water, and light were scarce—his world instead ruled by pain and unconsciousness, or lack thereof. The cycle began when Teeth walked in with his usual ultimatum. After Foster declined, Face would beat him or Davis to unconsciousness while the other was forced to watch. When they were both suitably balanced on the edge of death, Thread would enter with just enough water and medical treatment to keep them alive. An indeterminate number of minutes later, Teeth would begin the process again.

They'd gone through it over a dozen times already, and now Foster understood the nature of Thread's cruelty. The notion that this could go on forever loomed like a suffocating shadow in his mind. A shadow that longed not to wake up if it meant more pain. A shadow that whispered he could give in. What did it matter?

But Ezren was still out there, Davis was in here, and these fodders didn't understand Foster at all.

Because every time they hit Davis, the fire in him they were trying to extinguish reignited with his rage. Every time they threatened his family or teammates. Every time they goaded him about the things Ezren would do for them, the rage grew, burning brighter than any shadow. With every blow, the grumble of defiance in his mind grew into a roar that said they'd either kill him or he'd kill them.

Those were the only two acceptable outcomes.

Beside him, Davis groaned on the floor, his eyelids fluttering as he returned to consciousness after their latest beating. Fury boiled under Foster's skin at the sight of him. Davis, who was fodding innocent. And good. Who'd always show up for them without a second thought. Who put his life on the line for them.

And this was what he got for it.

Oh yes. These motherfodders were going to die. And he was going to get Davis through if it killed him.

Which meant he had to keep him talking.

"Davis," Foster rasped, his throat impossibly dry. "You okay, kin?"

Davis let out a wet cough, blood speckling the metal floor. "Never been better."

"Always the optimist." The corner of Foster's mouth twitched up. "I've got to tell you I'm not feeling good about our chances."

The scrape of a chuckle grated between Davis's labored breaths. "Why am I not surprised?"

"And while I'm confessing," Foster continued. "I'm glad you're here with me. Is that a horrible thing to think?"

"Not at all, kin." A painful smile stretched across Davis's cracked lips, his eyes swollen shut. "Though I'd much prefer we were having a drink back at Gerard's."

"And what would we talk about?" Foster asked, trying to ignore the pain radiating from his broken fingers, currently encased in two medcasts, the nanites wriggling his bones back together.

"Hmm... well since I don't really care to dwell on our present, I'm going with past or future."

"Future," Foster said. They both needed something to look forward to after they got out of this. Needed to believe there would be an after. "What's the dream?"

"The dream?" Davis sucked in a rattling wheeze. "Well, one of these days when I finish my interstellar studies, the dream is to pilot a space ark to a new system."

"You're that desperate to escape Casolla?" Foster forced out a dry laugh. "Or is it this experience that's turned you?"

"Nah, I've always wanted to explore new galaxies. New planets. New stars. Since as far back as I could remember." Davis made a humming sound, his voice tinged with awe. "And what a world we can live in where that's possible."

Foster squinted in the dim light, trying to decide if he was happy Davis had something he was so obviously committed to. Or disappointed that he would one day leave them. "So when do you set sail then? Or whatever you 'verse crossers call it."

"Ark ship captains embark. Though when I finally get out of school in three years, I might have to start with something smaller like a wormgate maintenance craft or a comms rig." He swallowed, a strained motion that sounded like it hurt. "Sammy will be going to university then, so it'll be time."

"Suns, he'll miss you," Foster said, thinking of the fawning adoration Sam showered on Davis. Like the sun rose and fell with him. He couldn't even remember a time he'd seen Sam without Davis being there too. "Have you always been close?"

"Kinda, yeah. We were the Harts' welcoming family when they got to Tuzuno." He let out a sound somewhere between a cough and a laugh. "I'm an only child and there were six minors in Tuzuno when the Harts moved in, so I can't tell you how excited I was that we were getting a family with *two* kids. And Ezren being my exact age? That felt like winning some kind of lottery by itself, not to mention the bonus little brother I got along with it."

Last year, hearing how Davis and Ezren had met would've sent Foster into a whirlwind of jealousy. Now, when his existence was near complete suffering, he smiled along with Davis's joy. Because at a time when they thought they were losing their dad, when Sam was struggling with his regen complications—he couldn't imagine them having to bear it all alone. "I'm glad they had you."

"I was just as glad to have them. My parents live through their work, so in a lot of ways, the Harts became my family." He grinned at Foster. "And that makes you family now too."

The notion made Foster wince at the memory of Sam's distrust. In truth, since he and Ezren had been together, he could count the times he'd visited Tuzuno on one hand. "Yeah well, I wish I knew Ezren's family better."

"You will." Davis shifted on the metal floor. "Dr. Evangeline is a lot like Ezren, just a little quieter, more mellow. Sam, though, he's Ezren's opposite in a lot of ways. Not as trusting of people, a little suspicious of the world, always trying to hide how he feels—but while they're all brilliant, Sam's on a different level."

"Yeah well, I don't think he likes me very much."

"He just needs time to warm up." Davis's voice was soft in the hard room. "He's lost a lot, so he's cautious about making ties, and now he lives in Ezren's shadow. He liked the attention at first, but it makes things more complicated for him."

Foster grunted. He could understand that. When you were famous, it was harder to pick out actual friends from those looking to leach off the limelight.

"I try to help when I can," Davis continued, "But I can't be there all the time. Maybe when we get back, we could try to tag team it." A quiet filled their small cell, the hum of the engines barely perceptible in the vibration of the metal beneath their feet. "You know, so you could look out for him when I'm not there."

Foster's lips tightened as his brain involuntarily jumped to a future without Davis in it. A future in which he went home, and Davis didn't. *No.* He refused to entertain it. "Hey, you just said we get three more years of Davis bonding, so as far as I'm concerned, I expect you to be around all the time. Pilot, doppelganger... who knows what job Grady will pull you into next. At this point, I'm not sure he'll *let* you run off to another galaxy."

"Well, I'm glad for the time I have here," Davis said. "Wormgate hopping's not something you do on a whim. As soon as you cross, there's no going back, so you've got to be ready to leave everything behind and go forward."

"Better you than me," Foster scoffed. "Seems like an end to everything you've ever known."

"In many ways, it's the end of one life and the beginning of the other."

"Are you saying you don't like the torture we're offering you in this life over here?" Foster asked.

Another rough chuckle. "Maybe I want two lives just like this. Or maybe even more."

"Okay you cheerful fodding masochist." Foster's lips ached with a smile. "Do you think there's anything that would make you stay?"

Davis mirrored his grin. "More torture?"

If Foster could've thrown something at him, he would've. "You know what I mean."

For a moment Davis was quiet. "This past year, with you and Simon and the team, has probably been the best year of my life but—"

The hiss of the door cut him off.

Foster's pulse kicked with fear as his gaze lurched to the

doorway. But of course, if he'd been paying attention to the cycle, he would've known it was Thread. Her bare feet were nearly silent on the metal floor, the door shutting with a click behind her. While her presence wasn't unwelcome, her pale face held more tension than usual as she crouched in front of Foster, her words flashing out.

Do you think Ezren would follow simple commands to save your life?

Foster tensed as she took the casts from his hands—only thirty percent healed, but enough to break again. "What kinds of commands?" Suns, why did she look so familiar? He didn't know any girls with navy hair and green eyes... well, except Micah on some days. But anyone could change the colors, so maybe he had seen her somewhere before. But where?

She raised a tube of water to his lips, and he sucked greedily from it, a strangely sweet aftertaste tickling his tongue. *Commands that will give the Crow power over the Belethea council.*

"Fod no."

Thread moved to Davis next with another tube of water. *Think, and then answer. The truth is important. She loves you, no?*

And Foster forced himself to consider it. While he didn't trust Thread by any stretch, he had to agree with Davis that she ran on a separate circuit from the others.

"Yes, Ezren loves me. But she has strong ideals, and I don't think she would ever trust a promise from a murderer."

Thread nodded, injecting a healing stim into Davis's neck. *Take heart, then. Your pain will not be for much longer.*

Foster's brow furrowed, but it was Davis who answered. "Because they're going to kill us."

Thread pulled a scrap of cloth from her pocket and bathed

Davis's face with her gentle touch. *They will try, yes. But they will use you as bait first.*

Foster tensed at the thought of them doing anything to Ezren. "Oh yeah, that's just chaffing great."

"Why are you telling us this?" Davis asked.

Her sea-green eyes stared into his brown ones as if trying to tell him something, her fingers lingering on his.

Because I want you to be ready.

"To die?" Foster took back all the nice thoughts he'd had about the girl. She was just as twisted as the others. "Right, because that's going to fodding help."

But Davis held her gaze, his voice dropping. "What was in the tube?"

She looked at him, wiping the cloth down his cheek once more. *They have destroyed your bodies, and now they will try to destroy your mind. Though you will still have to experience the dream, the sedative should help you distinguish it from reality.*

"What does that even mean?" Foster snapped, his eyelids already drooping. "You drugged us?"

Thread looked at him, defiance hardening the line of her jaw. *I know you don't trust me, but no matter what—*

The slice of the door opened, and Thread's words disappeared as Teeth walked in. *Shaft.* He was earlier than usual. Thread rose to her feet, the emotion falling away from her features, and a hollow mask dropping in its place as she moved to the corner.

"Well, I must say the two of you have taken well to suffering of the body, as is expected for royalers, I suppose." Teeth bared his grotesque sneer. "Which means it's time to move on to test your mind, an entirely different creature."

"I'm not sure we're the ones that need the psychiatric evaluation," Foster said, his tongue feeling sluggish in his mouth.

"I see your cocky attitude isn't just a show for VSoc." Teeth paced to where Davis lay on the floor. "We'll see if you still have that same pluck after a little subconscious manipulation."

Face walked in with what looked like a neurochip-studded helmet, and his usual sick smile.

"Though we are running short on time, you still have a chance to play for the winning team here, Sterling," Teeth continued. "And let me assure you, no one here wants to see you fail."

Thread's wide eyes stared at him in silent apology, mouthing something he couldn't understand. Panic set in as Face forced the helmet onto his head, Teeth's voice still carrying on over his grunts of struggle. "Bones break, skin tears, but when the spirit dies... that can destroy a person."

His words faded away as a burning sensation gathered at Foster's right temple where his goggs chip was implanted, his vision going dark.

And then the real nightmare began.

CHAPTER 13

5.04.44B BRR Day 1

EZREN WRAPPED her hands in her overlong sleeves as she tried to decipher the virus code Sam had sent to the Crow ship. While she was supposed to be reviewing it for optimization potential, at this point she had to admit her brother's expertise far exceeded her own. But there was no way she was giving him the satisfaction of saying it aloud. After all, she had her reputation as an older sister to uphold.

"Hey, Ezren?" Micah called from where she lay curled in a ball on the couch, chewing on her knuckle as she studied something in her holo. "I think we're about to have a problem."

Ezren groaned. "Another one?"

Micah winced but couldn't quite mask the gleam of excitement in her eyes. "The news of Foster's abduction is about to break."

Ezren dropped onto the couch next to Micah, and Turnip blinked at her sleepily from her perch on the armrest. "What! How?"

"Apparently someone got a hold of the footage." Micah's brow furrowed as she concentrated on the message. "And they're looking to leak it for the right price."

"Give me their contact info," Shiro called across the ship.

"Since it's part of an active case, we can shut it down. We'll also need the holo for analysis."

"Okay, yeah, but even if he turns in the holo, I'd bet big creds he's still going to try to spill his eyewitness story. And when that story takes off, they'll probably dig up the wedding stuff too."

"Are you talking directly to this chaffer?" Ezren glanced at Micah's holo just as she swiped something away.

"No, someone else is sending me their comms." Micah swallowed, side-eyeing Ezren.

"Okay?" Ezren's eyes narrowed. "So why do you look weird? Who's the message from?"

Micah tugged on her mint-green pigtails. "It's... a trusted source."

Ezren frowned—why in the suns was Micah being so suspicious about this if she was trying to help? "Okay, which trusted source?"

"Sorry, it's, uh, confidential." And Micah Belanger actually *blushed.*

Okay, something was definitely going on. Ezren had known Micah for well over two years, and not once had she seen the girl blush. "Since when do you have a confidential source?"

"I don't know." Micah shifted deeper into the thick cushions, her gaze darting everywhere but at Ezren. "Since I'm the Belethea team's VSoc manager? Since some people have secrets."

"Suurreee." Ezren drew out the word low and slow, still not at all sure what to feel as she ran a hand along Turnip's soft fur. Of course she trusted Micah, but they were in an unprecedented situation. "So how do you know this confidential source isn't working with the syndicates?"

"He's not." Micah's blush deepened.

Holy shaft, there was a blush-worthy *he* involved. Ezren

INTO THE ABYSS   125

relaxed and came to attention all at the same time. "Okay, what is going on that I don't know about?" She looked to Sam where he sat on the other couch, Waffle snoring at his feet and Giles on his shoulder as he focused on his own holo.

"I don't know why you're looking at me." Sam didn't take his attention from the coordinates and code swirling around him. "Micah's always weird."

Micah gave him an overly innocent smile, and Ezren wrinkled her nose, resolving to dig deeper later. "Okay, whatever, I'll let it slide for now. So if this guy does rave about an abduction and a wedding, what does it mean for us?"

"Well, if he spills the wedding, it'll give more credence to the abduction story. And with the two of you not attending the BRR banquet last night, the general public may not take much convincing. Especially if others start to claim they witnessed it too. Then we've got the possibility of widespread panic. Maybe calls to postpone the BRR today. And if they dig really deep, they may even find in the Calderon Industries log that Foster Sterling-Hart is officially indisposed and his wife, Ezren, is technically currently recognized as the CEO of Calderon Industries."

"Okay, that's a lot." Ezren leaned back into the couch, the weight of it all crashing into her as Turnip jumped into her lap. "So what do you recommend?"

"We're pretty sure the best bet is to release the wedding news now before the BRR starts in a few hours. The honeymoon thing will explain why you're not there, and hype will be at its highest when we're at the most sensitive part of this operation. With any luck, the gossip of what your future children will look like combined with the usual BRR starting line conjecture will blot out some random guy ranting that he witnessed an abduction."

Ezren ran the story over in her mind, searching for holes as

Turnip purred in her lap. But with Micah being the VSoc savant that she was, it seemed she had all the bases covered. Which of course was why Sylvia hired her. But there was one burr she couldn't quite get over. "Who is *we* again?"

"Um... me and... Jabari and Sylvia."

Got her. "Really?" Ezren propped her chin on her hand with feigned interest. "Jabari's in on this? Because I thought we hadn't told anyone on the team so we wouldn't distract them from the BRR?"

Micah gave a nervous laugh as she swiped through holos rotating in a sphere around her. "Okay, you're right. Not Jabari, just Sylvia."

Ezren rolled her eyes, and Turnip leapt to the rug on the metal floor. "Seriously, Micah, who's giving you these leads? It could be important for the CIF's investigation." She didn't want to think about the possibility that an indiscretion on Micah's part—even with innocent intent—may have led to the abduction in the first place, but she couldn't help it popping into her mind.

Micah turned to Ezren, her face suddenly earnest as she cupped her hands between her own. "Ezren, I swear on the BRR itself that he doesn't have anything to do with the investigation. He knows what's going on, but not because I've said a word. Please, trust that if I thought it would help, I would tell you."

But why wasn't she telling? This still made no sense. Micah told Ezren everything, whether she wanted to know or not. That was basically her job as a VSoc manager to fan the flames of gossip. "Is... is the guy that's trying to cause trouble from *The Royaler Review*? I thought I saw him harassing you at the press conference."

"He wasn't harassing me," Micah said, her cheeks pinking all over.

And Ezren's eyes just about bulged out of her head.

"*The Royaler Review* is sometimes harsh, but that's because they don't play favorites," Micah continued. "They're actually one of the best news hololgs Belethea has."

A growing suspicion wriggled in the back of Ezren's mind, and she fought to keep her face impassive. "Don't let Sylvia hear you say that."

If Micah recognized the teasing lilt to Ezren's tone, she didn't give any sign as she played with the green strands of her pigtail. "I'm sure Sylvia knows. Even if they rub her the wrong way sometimes."

"Interesting." Ezren lay back on the couch, trying to act casual. "Because it's not like there's something going on with you and anyone from *The Royaler Review*."

Micah barked out a high, false laugh. "Definitely not."

EZREN STARED AT MICAH, CERTAINTY THRILLING THROUGH HER.

EZREN: THERE TOTALLY IS.

MICAH: THERE IS NOT!

EZREN: WHO IS IT? I KNOW THEY HAVE LIKE FIVE HOLOLOGGERS. IT MUST'VE BEEN THE ONE AT THE PRESS CONFERENCE! I'M LOOKING HIM UP.

"No, Ezren, don't!" Micah lurched across the couch, reaching for her goggs, and Ezren dodged, jumping up and running for the storage room. She pulled up the profile of a guy somewhere in his twenties with thick auburn curls falling across his forehead and a freckle-dotted nose.

EZREN: HOLY CHAFF. IS THIS HIM? LOWELL COPPEN?

"Ezren, no!" Micah jumped on her back, covering her eyes with her hands as the door shut behind them. "There's nothing to see here."

"Oh, c'mon, Micah." A smile tilted Ezren's lips—the first real one since they'd left Belethea. "Just tell me already. Is this

a work thing or a personal thing? I mean, what's the big deal?"
While she'd known Micah to have a crush on every royaler
under the sun, this was the first time she'd actually shown real
interest in someone.

Micah slipped from Ezren's back and threw her hands up.
"The big deal is Sylvia would *murder* me!"

"Because you're working with him?" Ezren leaned forward,
relishing this revenge after all the chaff Micah had given her
when she and Foster had first started dating. "Or because
you're in a relationship with him?"

Micah drew herself up, affecting an expression that strove
for placid and failed miserably. "You know, if you're on board
with me dropping the wedding news, I have to go live now."

"Are you going live with *Lowell*?" Ezren bounced her
eyebrows.

"If you have any objections, this is your last chance," Micah
said, shoving her toward the door.

"Well, I want to meet the guy first before I give you my
blessing." Ezren grinned as she slid into the hall.

"Ezren!"

"Okay, fine. Yes, it's a good plan. But—"

"Goodbye!" The door slid shut on their conversation.

"We're talking more about this later!" Ezren yelled through
the closed door.

Chaff. If Micah was this affected, and the guy was dishing
to her on sensitive news bombs, it had to have been going on for
a while. How could Ezren have possibly missed that? After all,
Micah had been living in the dorm with them for the past
month—ever since she'd resigned from her terraforming job to
take the full-time VSoc management position.

Still chuckling, Ezren walked back to the couches only to
find that Sam had retreated to the bunkroom. He stood in the
center of a jungle holopro, a lower bunk unfolded from the wall

so Waffle could stretch out on it. Equations and graphs glowed in the room around him while Giles rattled off calculations and probabilities. Waffle's nub of a tail wagged as Ezren sat down next to her and scratched her head, still smiling.

"Sam." She leaned forward in earnest. "Does Micah have a crush on someone from *The Royaler Review?*"

"I don't know." Sam didn't divert his attention from his holos, and Ezren didn't miss the tension in his voice. "She lives with you now, and I go to school."

"Okay, relax. I was just asking."

Sam's expression only clouded further. "Ask someone else, I'm actually busy, unlike some people."

"Well, I'm sorry I was taking a second to breathe and take my mind off this nightmare." Ezren rose to her feet, her voice shaking with frustration. "But if there's something you want me to do, I'll do it."

"Why don't you go make another VSoc holo or something."

The words hit Ezren like a slap in the face. Was that all he thought of her? "Okay, what is your problem right now?"

"Nothing."

"Sam, there's obviously something." Ezren drew in a deep breath, dragging the patience from deep within her as she grasped for understanding. "I just... I get what happened with Dad. I do. But—"

"Why'd you have to drag Davis into this too?" Sam burst out.

And Ezren's anger instantly cooled, her voice shrinking. "You're scared something will happen to him."

"Something already *has* happened to him, Ezren," Sam said, the full fury of his boiling blue irises on her. "And I get you're married and all now, but he's way more family than *Foster.*"

Ezren's lips tightened, trying to let the words blow past her.

While she knew Foster and Sam hadn't spent a lot of time together, she'd always thought they got along okay. Certainly better than the ire that was burning out of Sam right now. "Look, I know you and Davis are close, but he's going to be okay, Sam, we're going to get both—"

Another chime from Ezren's goggs cut Sam off, and Ezren's pulse raced at the unknown sender. "It's another message! Shiro!"

But this one wasn't words... it was a holo.

Ezren opened it up only to see Foster's bruised and blackened face. Sam gasped beside her as Shiro and Micah ran into the room, all eyes riveted on the scene before them.

The image of a man with what looked like a thousand needles protruding from his gums filled the room. "Well, hello there, Ezren Hart. Or is it Ezren Sterling-Hart? Ezren Sterling? I must say I have no idea what the Belethean custom is these days." Bile burned Ezren's throat. "As I'm sure you know, a couple of your loved ones have fallen into our esteemed company, courtesy of the Crow's invitation."

The image moved to Foster and Davis's bloody, swollen bodies, and Ezren stifled a cry.

"As Foster Sterling is currently indisposed, we understand that you, as his lovely wife, now have control of his assets." His voice was sickeningly pleasant, his mangled smile turning her stomach. "So we'll keep this simple. If you want them to survive the Crow's hospitality, you'll make a statement appointing Ambassadors Charles Wade and Susana Trevisani as members of the Belethean Council to replace Calderon. Because we understand you may be in shock, you have twenty-four hours to comply before we kill this one."

The cam flashed back to Davis in ragged pants—every inch of his skin flayed, bruised, or burned—retching onto the metal floor. The next scene showed a bloodied Foster with a helmet

on his head, tied to a chair as he screamed with such desperation, it made her want to cover her ears.

"It's a nightmare visor," Shiro whispered. "It evokes your
worst fears and makes them seem real." His lips tightened as
Foster screamed her name, his voice breaking with sobs. "In
long doses, the visions lead to madness."

Teeth's face filled the holo once more. "We want to assure
you we're looking after your loved ones' physical and mental
development during their stay with us, but we're also thinking
of their future too."

He grinned, and more images of Foster and Davis enduring
beating after beating filled the frame. Of them curled on the
floor. Of them coughing up blood. Sam finally looked away, and
Ezren pressed her hand to her mouth.

"In case you don't comply within the specified twenty-four
hours, we'll leave Davis Banda's body for you at the wormgate,
and Foster Sterling will be getting a one-way ticket without a
cryochamber." Teeth's revolting smile filled the cam, and
Micah gasped from her spot in the doorway. "As always, this
wonderful life is full of choices. So, which will you choose?
Your loving husband, or a forever losing battle to the Crow as
we pick off your family members one at a time?" His bony
shoulders shook with a shiver of excitement. "I can barely stand
the suspense."

The holo winked out, and Ezren's legs went weak beneath
her. She canted to one side just as Micah lurched in and threw
her arms around her. Ezren buried her face in Micah's shoulder, the sobs too much to hold in. After taking a few precious
moments to piece herself back together, Ezren straightened,
wiping at her cheeks.

"Can you send me the holo?" Though the blood had
drained from Shiro's features, his expression looked as if it had
been sharpened with a razor's murderous edge.

Ezren searched for the holo in her goggs, but just like the other messages, it was already gone. "No, it's disappeared." Beside Ezren, Micah looked like she was on the verge of throwing up. "What do we do now?"

"We do what we said we were going to." Shiro's jaw flexed, the anger clear in every precise move of his body. "We're going to find them and put a stop to this. I'll ask the CIF to run the ambassadors and see if they have a common thread that can point us in the direction of the Crow."

"What if this is a trap?" Micah asked.

"We have to assume that it is," Shiro replied. "But we don't have any other options. He gave us twenty-four hours, so let's first figure out if we can close the distance in that time and go from there." His gaze searched hers, and Ezren fisted her hands in her long sleeves to keep them from shaking, knowing that she would be seeing the images on the backs of her eyelids for the rest of her life.

"Okay, Ezren?" Shiro prompted, the question more command than solace.

Finally, Ezren nodded. "Okay." Ezren took a deep breath, forcing her voice steady. "Well, what do you..." Her question faded from her lips as she caught sight of Sam—pale and slack with shock. "Suns, Sam." He shouldn't have seen that. Why hadn't she pushed him from the room?

"They're going to kill Davis, Ezren." Tears spilled down his cheeks as he leaned his forehead onto her shoulder.

As much as she wanted to wrap her arms around him, they couldn't afford to waste time. Instead, she took him by the shoulders, and he lifted his gaze to hers. "Listen, Sam. They're trying to scare us, but at least now we know they're still alive." She wiped his tears with the sleeve of her sweater, just as she had countless times when he was younger. But now they had to put those feelings aside and focus on the problem. "You were right that they're going to the wormgate, but what did he mean about a cryochamber?"

Shiro leaned against the room's jungle holo and closed his eyes. "The wormgate jumps take anywhere from seventy to a hundred and twenty years. In cryosleep, it only feels like taking a long nap. You're the same age you were when you fell asleep, but the decades have passed. Without a cryochamber..." He shook his head. "Consider it like being in solitary confinement until you go mad or die. Either way, once you go through the wormgate, your course is set, so there's no turning around."

Suns. Not just any death. A slow, painful death. Afraid and alone.

Sam sniffed, stepping away from her as he turned his tear-stained face back to his holo, Waffle leaning against his leg as if to hold him up. "Giles and I have managed to degrade their engine performance with a few choice viruses, so we should get there about the same time."

"But how do we rescue them without them being killed?" Micah whispered.

"Them?" Sam scoffed, his voice dripping with resignation. "Davis is probably dead already."

"No." Shiro's eyes flashed open, hard and sure. "If he was, then they would've sent a holo of his corpse as proof of their ruthlessness."

Sam's shoulders relaxed, turning away as the tears brimmed again, but this time with relieved hope.

"It's a small ship that can only hold eight, and there are four of us," Ezren said, her own strength returning to smother her fear. "If we have surprise on our side, we could take them."

Shiro nodded. "Don't answer the message. We'll go dark when we get closer but we should go ahead and assume they know we're coming after them. They're bad odds, but..."

Ezren grinned, a feral, vicious thing—the rage and despair

finally flaming with the kindle of action. "Those are the kind we're used to."

Micah's wide, emerald-green gaze looked from Shiro to Ezren and back. "You're kidding me, right? You people are insane. We don't have four. Sam and I are the brains here. We don't do the run-run-shoot thing."

Sam straightened and turned to Ezren. "I'll do whatever I have to."

"Sam..." Ezren started, but the force of his glare stopped her. Nothing she said now would get past that.

"It's okay." Shiro put a hand on Micah's and Sam's shoulders, linking the three of them. "It's better that we play to our strengths. If we can divert their attention and control their cyber interfaces, that may be enough of a distraction for Ezren and me to get a jump and get our guys out."

"What kind of diversion did you have in mind?" Sam asked.

The light of an idea flickered on in Ezren's thoughts. "Micah, do you think your *Royaler Review* boyfriend might be able to break a story for us in about twelve hours?"

"Sounds doable," Micah said, narrowing her eyes slightly at the word boyfriend. "What kind of story are you thinking?"

A grim curve lifted Ezren's lips. "The kind that's going to drag the Crow's name all over VSoc." And as they cobbled together the beginnings of the plan, Ezren realized she wasn't scared anymore at all.

She was furious.

CHAPTER 14

5.05.44B BRR Day 2

WHATEVER GRIP FOSTER had on reality was slowly fading away. The physical beatings were now spliced between nightmarish visions of Ezren and everyone else he knew dying. Of floating through space without rescue. Of Ezren being tortured. Of being left in the dark alone with no way out. Of the churn belt sucking him up and smashing him against the rocks.

The only relief came when Thread delivered her doses of sweetly-flavored water that made his exhaustion too deep for the dreams. But that respite was all too temporary, and he couldn't tell if the reprieve was another calculated, tantalizing torture or if Thread was truly trying to help them beneath the notice of her fellow Talons.

He was in the middle of a million needles stabbing into his face, when a pressure was suddenly lifted from his head. The relief was instantaneous, the phantom pain and the fear dripping away from him as easily as an ordinary dream. He pried his bleary eyes open to find—a girl. Ezren? He blinked once, twice before she finally came into focus.

No, not Ezren, Thread.

Captor? Captive? He still didn't know.

He swung his head to Davis's spot by the wall, and his muscles relaxed another inch. He was still there, still alive—

even if he looked as bad as Foster felt. Fresh injuries and half-healed scars littered his body, and a long knife wound ran from his temple to his chin. Foster had seen that one—the sluggish blade inching across his skin at an unbearable crawl while Face drank in his pain with a greedy stare.

His stomach revolted at the thought, and he retched, but they'd had no food since they'd arrived, and he had nothing left to give.

"How much longer?" Davis asked, blood trickling from the corner of his mouth, and Foster had to rack his brain for the meaning of the words.

What did time matter in a place like this? Then it came back to him in a flash of clarity—Ezren's deadline. There would be an end for them. His heart nearly leapt with the thought until he remembered that their end would be a permanent one.

Thread injected the painkiller into his neck, and he winced at the sting.

We're only an hour from the wormgate, which means we need to prepare.

"Prepare how?" Foster let his body go limp against his bonds. "Do we get last words or something?"

Thread fixed him with her first firm look. *You still want to live, yes?*

Foster stretched his neck from side to side, his muscles stiff from the weight of the nightmare helmet. "Somehow, I was under the impression we weren't getting a choice."

Thread moved to Davis. *The choice is to trust me or not. I can't get you out of here otherwise.*

"I trust you." Davis's voice was barely above a whisper, but it held such confidence, Foster had to question if he was in his right mind. After all, while this girl may not have directly inflicted harm on them, her motives were a huge question mark.

And though Foster was desperate enough to hear her out, trust was entirely out of the question.

Thread placed a bandage on his arm, and he looked at her like she was the angel sent from the stars he'd originally thought her to be. Suns, he really had lost it.

"What's the plan?" Davis asked, struggling to sit up.

Thread helped Davis shift against the wall. *Only specially coded ships can travel through the wormgate, which means they're going to have to transfer you.* With gentle hands, she pressed a bandage to Davis's head, holding it there. *And since all wormgate ships have cryonic chambers, they'll need to take time to physically disable them.*

"Wait, why would they do that?" Foster asked.

Thread turned her green eyes on him. *So the system can see you leaving alive and well—avoiding martyrdom while also ensuring a long and lonely death of madness.*

For a moment, Foster stared, his mouth agape. Finally Davis let out a hoarse chuckle. "Suns, this guy hates us that much, huh?"

Thread winced, removing the nanite bandage to reveal a partially knitted wound. *I'm afraid it is a journey Foster is meant to take alone.*

A shadow passed briefly across Davis's face before his irrepressible grin returned. "Oh well, it seems like the Crow likes me better than you, Foster."

Thread sat back on her heels, her bandage moving to other wounds on Davis's body. *It's all part of the Crow's design to control the BRR, the terranium flowing out of it, and by extension, the Casolla system. Ezren Hart will either bend to the Crow's will, or she will go through the wormgate after you in a fit of crazed passion.*

"Also without a cryonic chamber," Davis whispered.

Precisely.

The gears of Foster's thoughts spun with fury. "Wait, but that means Ezren's on her way here."

Thread looked at him with surprise. *Of course she is.*

"But how does she know where we are?" he asked through gritted teeth.

I told her.

And despite his restraints, Foster tried to lunge for her anyway. "You're leading my wife into a trap!"

Lower your voice. Thread's expression remained placid. *While I have comm loops in place to shield us, the sound dampening in this room has limits.* She stood, moving to stand before Foster. *Yes, under the Crow's direction, I led her here under the pretense that she has an ally on board.* She reached out to grab his injured hand, but his fingers curled into an agonizing fist. *What the Crow doesn't know, is that she does.* Thread's brow creased with something dangerously close to grief. *Perhaps you will always hate me, but in the two years since I have been trapped on this ship, your and Ezren's journey has been my guiding star, giving me hope when I thought there was only darkness. When I had no one, I hung on your every word. Your every race. Your hopes and dreams and wins have kept me alive here.* She gave a shaky smile that didn't reach her mournful gaze. *You allowed me to believe in a better world with better people, and I swear that I will do everything in my power to help you create one.*

And then, with her face so close to his, he noticed the faded brown birthmark in the shape of a tear on her cheek, and it finally clicked exactly where he'd seen this girl. Foster reared back as if he'd seen a ghost. "You're Carmella Saunders, Calderon's doubles partner." He squinted, but there was no denying her high cheekbones and full lips. "How is that possible?"

Thread closed her eyes with a sigh. *I am not Carmella, but you are close. Genetically, I am the daughter of Carmella Saunders and Warner Calderon, crafted to resemble Calderon's greatest love and serve as the Crow's bargaining chip to manipulate him.* She reached out with a bandage for Foster's arm, and this time, he didn't flinch away. *The Crow made two attempts, both when I was a baby, and later as an adolescent, but Calderon never regarded me as anything but an abomination. So, the Crow saw fit to use me in other ways.*

Suns. Calderon's daughter? He studied her again but found nothing of the man in her features. Still, he couldn't see any reason for her to lie with such a strange story. Foster exchanged a glance with Davis. "So... who is the Crow?"

Thread shrugged as she stepped away from him. *There, I cannot help. The Crow takes many faces, and no one is sure which one is true. There are even rumors that the Crow isn't human.*

Foster's lips tightened, and he let his head drop. While he still didn't trust this girl, he couldn't deny that she had answered all of his questions without hesitation. He looked to Davis, but he returned his stare with a steady calm.

"She's our only chance Foster," Davis said. "We can trust her."

Thread's hands paused, her eyes wide as if waiting for his judgment.

"Okay, fine." Foster huffed out a resigned sigh. If this was some sick game, he imagined it couldn't have a worse outcome than the one that already awaited them. "I trust you." Thread lit up as if he had handed her the best gift in the 'verse. "What's the plan?"

For a moment, Thread bounced up and down on her toes in glee, and Foster thought he could see the girl she could've been if the Crow had never entered her life. Coming back to herself, she took a deep breath, schooling her features back into a tame smile.

Your best chance for escape is going to be during the transfer. When they take you across the dock, I'll incapacitate the other guards. Then we'll need to make a run for it and hide in the station till we can find help. You're too valuable to kill in public, and it's a big station to get lost in.

Foster had to stop himself from rolling his eyes. A five-year-old could have come up with that plan. But still, it wasn't as if he had a better one. "Do you have any weapons you can give us?"

Thread's bare feet shuffled on the metal floor. *Um, no, I'm not permitted, and the guards' weapons will be coded to them.*

"This is dangerous, Thread." Davis's voice was soft, Foster's doubt reflected in the lines of his frown. "You have to know our odds of surviving this are low. For us and you."

Thread nodded. *For me, staying would mean continuing this impossibly torturous existence.* Her chin trembled. *I've done... awful things, with no chance of escape, and though it is a slim chance, I can't miss this opportunity.* Her attention toggled between Davis and Foster, her fingers twisting together in front of her. *And you'll tell them I helped you, right? Perhaps I'll get a shorter sentence. I just want to start over.*

"We'll tell them," Davis said, his fervent words heavy in the quiet.

Thread gave him a grateful smile, her face shining with hope for the first time since they'd met. *Even when our odds are bad, our gains are worth the risk, yes? That's what royalers do?*

Foster nodded, a part of him knowing Ezren would love this girl. His chest ached with the thought. "Yeah, that's what royalers do."

Thread's cheeks practically glowed, her hands shaking as she patted her jumpsuit pockets filled with supplies. *I'm supposed to be knocking you out so they can transfer you. I'll need you to feign unconsciousness, but when I give the word, be ready to run.*

As she turned to go, Davis grabbed her hand—his brown gaze meeting her green one. "Thank you for helping us."

A hollow clang echoed in the corridor, and Thread's eyes blew wide with fear. *They're coming. Let's pray the elder suns are shining on us today.* Then, as quickly as it had come, her fear faded away, and Foster had to wonder which was the act. The fear? Or the plan? *Unconscious, now.* Foster let his body go limp as though drugged, forcing his breaths to steady and trying not to think about the thousands of ways this was about to go wrong.

Trying not to wonder if this was all just another heart-breaking ruse.

Instead he focused on the last time he'd seen Ezren, as he had so many times over the past three days. He thought of her smiling at him from the crowd as Sylvia tugged him offstage. If this went wrong, that might very well be the last time he ever saw her. And even amidst the constant agony racking his body, the thought sent a fresh wave of pain through him.

Still, they had to try.

Ezren would want them to try.

Foster didn't move as the door hissed open, or as his ankles and wrists were untied from the chair and rebound. With rough hands, they tossed his body into what felt like a coffin with Davis thrown on top of him, but he forced himself not to react. Inwardly, he thanked the low G of the ship for lessening the impact.

As their container, on a hover-dolly from the feel of it, began to move, he wondered how long they could afford to wait for Thread. What if she'd been found out? Or what if her little speech had been just another one of the Crow's traps to lure them into compliance? He thought of the gleam of desperate hope in Thread's gaze and had to dismiss it. Whether this worked or not, it wasn't because Thread had deceived them. But that didn't mean she hadn't deceived herself.

Still, without her help, they didn't stand a chance. And yet they certainly didn't stand a chance if they waited so long that they did nothing at all. The arguments warred back and forth in his head as time ticked away, the hover-dolly turning one way and then another while the voices of passersby swelled and faded. It was only when someone asked which ship it was that he could contain himself no longer. Thread wasn't getting them out, and they were at the point of no return.

He shifted, lifting his hand to test the lid when another hand caught his. *Davis*.

Davis's fingers tapped something out in his wrist that felt suspiciously like Morse code. Unfortunately, there was no way Foster could interpret without his goggs. Still, his message was obvious. Wait.

Foster's jaw tightened as he let his arm fall, his pulse spiking beneath his skin. They would kill Davis first—a death he'd already seen replayed a thousand times in the nightmare helmet. Even if they didn't open the box, he could still get the jump, he just had to—

The crack of a gunshot rang so loud, Foster thought he'd lost his hearing in his right ear. A second fell closely behind it, and before he could get his bearings, the lid of the container slid open.

Thread reached in, and with some kind of laser-knife, severed their restraints. *Come on.*

Not waiting, Foster leapt from the coffin, his legs weak beneath him as he staggered toward the navy-haired girl. One yawning wall seemed to be made entirely of glass, with an array of ships from small to gigantic docked directly into the other side. Beyond the ship, a complicated metal ring held the swirling rainbow miasma that was the wormgate.

GO!

Shouts rang from behind them as Thread pushed both him and Davis toward the far door in the corner of the loading dock. Fueled with pure adrenaline, they sprinted through the door and into a crowded hallway, people cringing away from them as they pushed past. Foster looked over his shoulder, and hope swelled in his chest. He could see no one chasing them, and now they were in the public eye. There was no way—

His thoughts were cut off as the alarm of an emergency airlock door blared from every direction. *Oh shaft.* Foster grabbed Davis, shoving him forward into a sprawling heap ahead of them.

"Fost—"

The airlock door slammed into place between them, cutting off the hall to the screams of the crowd. At least he'd gotten Davis through. That done, Foster turned on his heel, looking for another exit just as the second airlock door clanged down behind them, trapping them in.

Foster turned to Thread amidst the two dozen panicking spacers pounding their fists on the obviously locked side doors, her eyes huge with terror. Whatever was happening—it wasn't a setup. "Is there another way ou—"

One of the side doors opened, and automatic gunfire crackled through the hallway.

"Get down!" Gripping Thread's arm, Foster threw her slight form into the corner, protecting her with his body as the bullets cut through the crowd around him. Panic flared through him with each scream and crack, his body pleading to run even as he knew there was no place to go.

But it was only when the screams fell into silence that his hope truly died.

In the deathly quiet, Teeth and Face stepped over the litter of bodies toward them, with Face practically salivating over the innocent spacers lying motionless on the floor.

Teeth feigned a pout as he stepped delicately over a corpse still contorted in terror. "Now look at the mess you've made. All of these people dead, and for what? So you could stretch your legs?"

Foster looked at the bodies in horror, a sea of glassy eyes staring at him from the beyond in accusing silence. "But why?"

"Fear is good for business." Teeth flashed his unsightly grin. "And witnesses aren't."

But Foster had gotten Davis out. Davis might still make it. He tried to cling to the hope, but he couldn't ignore the unlikelihood of his survival. For all he knew, Davis was already dead on the other side of the wall.

"How did you..." Foster's voice faded away, the grief and revulsion overwhelming his senses.

"Know the girl was going to run?" Teeth raised his pistol and shot Thread in the knee. Thread convulsed as she let out a strangled cry in the clotted silence of fresh ghosts. "Because the Crow told us. How do we kill without people knowing?" He shot Thread in the other knee, her shriek echoing off the metal walls coated with a holopro of the open ocean. "Because the Crow has Talons in everything."

He bent down and looked Foster straight in the eye, his smile almost rueful, as if Foster were a disobedient child. With a shake of his head, he pressed the barrel of his gun into Foster's knee and fired. Foster's scream echoed through the silent chamber.

"And now that we've gotten all this running business out of the way, we can get to business," Teeth said, oozing good cheer. "You know, I'm not sure if your wife can't follow clear instructions, or if she doesn't love you after all, but either way, I'm so glad I'll be getting to meet her."

And as Face dragged the two of them back into the bay, the only thing Foster could think was: the Crow had been right all along.

Shattered hope was worse than no hope at all.

Don't come for me, Ezren.

Please, suns, don't let her come for me.

CHAPTER 15

5.05.44B BRR Day 2

STANDING IN THE COCKPIT, Ezren stared at the latest message, once again from an unknown sender.

Ezren, they know you're coming, and they're going to transfer them to a wormgate ship. I'm going to try to get them out, but we're going to need help. You have less than thirty minutes.

Ezren didn't know if this was an ally or an enemy, but she started the timer in her goggs anyway.

Ahead they could clearly see the massive station of Janusoth, ships of every shape and size ranging from one-man schooners to a massive space ark docked to the clear wall. Hovering only a few ship-lengths away from them, the soap bubble of a wormgate stood ready to ferry them to their next galaxy.

"We've got to get ahead of them." Ezren's mind spun as she grappled for options. "Sam, can you figure out which ship they're planning on using?"

"Uh, yeah." Sam zoomed in on the docked ships. "It takes a while for the engines to get ready. So if they're planning to leave soon, they should be giving off an energy signature."

"What are you thinking, Ezren?" Shiro asked, his bag of

supplies already strapped to his back and no less than four guns hanging from various holsters on his tactical topsuit.

"We're taking one of our escape pods and docking directly to the wormgate ship." Ezren checked to make sure she also had the four pistols Shiro had given her, one on each hip and one on each thigh. While over the last three days, she'd felt plenty of dread and trepidation, now she was left with only cool resolve.

"As good a plan as any." Shiro nodded to Micah. "Stay dark until you see us on our way back. Hopefully with *The Royaler Review* dropping the CIF's information bounty on the Crow, their attention will be on virtual damage control. But if you don't hear from us in an hour, let the CIF know it went wrong."

Sam crossed his arms, looking smaller than his fourteen years. "I don't know if I like this."

Ezren had no more time to coddle him. If he had chosen to be here, then he needed to understand. "There's no other way, Sam."

"But what if it goes wrong?" he asked, black shadows smudged beneath his blue eyes.

She held nothing for him but the truth as she followed Shiro to the escape pod. "It might."

"I don't want to lose you too," Sam said, the words barely audible.

Ezren's lips tightened. Though it killed her to think of leaving her brother and mother when they'd lost their father so recently, there was no question of her path forward. She wrapped him in a brief, tight hug. "Sometimes we have to do the right thing no matter the risk."

"I wouldn't let you do this if I didn't know that you could pull it off." Micah swooped in with her own embrace. "Just know, you're my hero. And my heroes always win in the end."

Shiro popped his head out of the escape pod. "What about me?"

"I'll let you know after you bring my people back." Micah wrinkled her nose at him. "But if you do bite it, I'm not going to be the one to tell Sylvia. Let someone else be the messenger she kills."

"It'll be okay, Micah." Ezren took a step back into the ship, meeting Sam's frantic gaze. "We'll be back in an hour with Foster *and* Davis."

Her brother nodded, and she closed the door before punching the eject button. The timer in her goggs read twenty-five minutes, and since they'd need seven minutes to dock, she certainly hoped their source was right.

Ezren breathed deep as she drew her gun from her thigh holster. She hadn't used it since Otho last year, but she was grateful Shiro had made them train with it almost every week since. "You've been on lots of missions, Shiro. What do you think about our chances?"

Shiro regarded her with shadowed eyes, his expression grim. "To be honest with you, I generally don't think about chances." He looked out the port window at the undeniable beauty of the wormgate. "I assess if the gain is worth the loss."

"And you think Davis and Foster's lives are worth yours?" Ezren cocked her head at him. While it was more than obvious what they meant to her, Shiro had only known them for a few months.

Shiro's mouth twitched. "Ezren, it was my job to protect them. And I failed. Just like you, I would do anything to get them back." His face darkened. "And the Crow killed two of my guards, so I have that score to settle as well."

A spark of fury kindled in Ezren's chest as she thought about the two lives already stolen from them—of what the Crow still aimed to take. Looking back out the window at the glass wall of the station, she connected with her brother in her goggs.

Ezren: Sam, can you jam their offboard cams so they don't see us coming in?

Sam: On it.

"We need to grab them, and then get out stat before they launch," Shiro continued. "Once the wormgate locks on, it will pull the ship in, and no one will be able to get off."

"Right." Ezren eyed the wormgate again, thinking of the gate her people had traveled through to get there. Of those that continued on to the farther systems. Involuntarily, she imagined Foster, suffering and alone, going through that gate without the blissful sleep to ease the decades, and her teeth ground together.

"Are you scared?" Shiro asked her.

Ezren shook her head, every muscle tight and hard. "I'm only scared of being too late." She shifted against her restraints as their ship neared the dock. "Is that foolish?"

"No. It's brave," Shiro said, his steely tone matching his expression. "Though sometimes brave and foolish can be the same thing."

Ezren gave him a grim smile as the ship docked into a mid-sized vessel, the seal latching on with a hiss. "Thanks for doing this, Shiro."

"I could say the same to you." Shiro moved to the door, his rifle already in hand. "And I want to let you know, in case anything happens, I would take this risk every time."

Ezren nodded. "Me too."

"Stay close behind me, and with any luck, we should be able to ambush them as they're boarding the ship." Shiro smiled at her once more. "You ready?"

Ezren forced her muscles to relax, just like she would before any race. In truth she'd never been a brawler, and even as an ambassador, many had criticized her for being the naïve, "tender heart" of Sterling/Hart. But here, in the darkest corner of Casolla, she would do whatever it took to get Foster back.

Whatever. It. Took.

"I'm ready."

"Then, let's end these fodders." With that, Shiro manually cracked open the door and strode onto the ship with nearly silent steps. Ezren followed behind him, rolling her feet from heel to toe as they moved down the hall's quiet forest holo, the branches swaying in the leaves and the birds chirping ahead. Shiro pulled a cam from his suit, about to toss it in the air when the muzzle of a barrel curved around the mouth of the corridor. A hulking man stepped into the hall, scars running down his face like tears.

Shiro jerked his gun up, but another voice cut through the air behind them. "Don't."

Ezren didn't have to turn around to feel the metal cylinder on her spine, and Shiro's resigned gaze confirmed their position. While she'd known it hadn't been a good plan, she'd expected to get farther than this.

The man with the tear scars stepped closer. "If you'll just put down your weapons, we'll take you to your friends."

Ezren: Now, Sam.

With a click, the spin of the ship's inner lining halted, cutting off the artificial gravity, and the four of them rose into the air, off-balance. It was only a moment's hesitation, but it was enough for Shiro. Two shots echoed through the cabin, and the men hung limp in the air. Ezren and Shiro bounded backwards as two more men took their places, the roar of gunfire filling the corridor. Pain ripped through Ezren's calf, and blood beaded in the air around her as she turned and kicked the weapon out of a man's hand. Another grabbed her in a headlock from behind, the two of them spinning through the zero-G.

Ezren bucked against him, choking for air as pain tore through her neck.

EZREN: SHIRO! HELP!

But wherever he was, he didn't respond. As the air was crushed from her lungs though, the anger in Ezren blazed. Anger at this man trying to end her life, anger at herself for not being strong enough to get past him, anger that she wouldn't get to see Foster one more time.

No. She refused.

Ezren extended her legs and her boots found purchase on the ceiling. She had one shot at this. Kicking off with all the strength in her legs, they rocketed toward the floor. The man's head hit the metal with a crack, and his arms loosened just enough.

Sucking in a burning breath, Ezren turned and shot the man directly in the chest—the jolt of a bullet electrifying his body until he lost consciousness.

"Shiro!" Ezren rasped.

"Here!" From around the corner, Shiro pushed a body away from him, a cloud of crimson surrounding them both. "But we gotta go."

Ezren poised to push off the wall when the hiss of a second pod's airlock caught her attention. "Shiro! There's another one."

She lifted her gun at the docking station, ready when the door sliced open, and revealed—

Her brother.

"Sam!" Ezren shrieked. "What are you—"

The rattle of gunfire cut her off, followed by Shiro's shout, "Ezren!"

With nothing left to do, Ezren threw her brother one of her pistols. "Stay here!"

Pushing off, she flew through the hall, hooking around the corner into the common room, just as another shot hit Shiro straight in the chest.

CHAPTER 16

5.05.44B BRR Day 2

LEAVING A THICK, crimson trail, Teeth's men dragged Foster and Thread onto the ship deck. The common room was surprisingly large with sleek couches, armchairs, tables, and entertainment centers bolted to the floor. Not that those things would do Foster any good on a seventy-year solo journey into the void.

Teeth gestured to two of his thugs with a flick of his fingers. "Ready the ship for its captain, if you will. Prep for launch and destroy the chambers."

With his leg screaming in pain, Foster turned to the bleeding, hyperventilating girl beside him. "Thank you for trying."

If she heard him, she gave no sign, her breaths becoming more irregular as her eyelids fluttered.

Teeth crouched beside her. "Really is a shame. She was such a unique creature. But without the other body on hand to paint the deck red, I suppose this one will have to do."

Foster winced as Face's thick fingers dug into his neck. "I thought you were waiting for Ezren," Foster said.

"We were." Teeth gave an apologetic grimace. "But your wife is running rather late, and I'm afraid we have a schedule to keep." With another flick of his fingers, Face hauled Foster to his one good leg, and somewhere an artificial voice said something about a countdown to launch.

"You know," Teeth continued. "They say it's seventy years to the next system, so maybe if you take care of yourself really well, you'll live to see—"

The gravity liner went silent, and they lifted off the floor as the echo of gunfire rippled through the ship. Teeth's head jerked toward the cacophony, his eyes narrowing as two more of his men went to investigate. "What is—"

"Hey!"

Foster turned at the familiar voice, his heart sinking. *No.* Because Davis Banda was wearing Foster's doppelganger mask and limping toward them up the gangplank with absolutely no weapons.

"You got the wrong Sterling," Davis said.

And in a heartbeat, as Face and Teeth turned to each other, Foster realized his odds would never be better than this. Wrenching out of Face's grasp, Foster tackled Teeth around the middle, grappling with him in the zero-G. Wrapping his hand around Teeth's fingers, he pointed the gun at Face and fired a shot. The bullet glanced off his shoulder as Face barreled toward Davis.

Teeth twisted in his grasp, and the gun spun from his fingers through the air.

Foster reached for the weapon, only for Teeth's spiked canines to sink into his back as more gunfire cracked through the ship. He screamed again, turning to bury his fist into Teeth's belly. But now four more men were running at Davis where he dodged Face on the gangplank, cutting them all off and leaving nowhere to go.

Teeth grabbed his gun, pointing it at Foster as his chest heaved. "You know, we really wanted a nice holo of you riding into the sunset for the fans. But now I'm thinking we could probably just—"

With another crack of a gun, Teeth convulsed, falling to the ground.

Foster turned to find Ezren with a gun raised and Shiro crumpled to the ground beside her. Hope and horror surged through him in a fresh wave of adrenaline. "Ezren!"

"Foster!" She tossed him a pistol, ducking as a muzzle swung in her direction, her guns flashing out in a strange dance. Foster lifted the pistol when another figure darted into the room, panicked and out of breath.

"*Sam?*" Foster ducked into a doorway as he returned fire.

Sam surveyed the chaos with his wide blue eyes, Giles hovering at his shoulder and a gun trembling in his hands. "Where's Davis?" Not waiting for an answer, he pushed off toward the front of the ship, swinging himself into the cryo room. "Davis!"

Ezren's panicked gaze followed him. "Sam, get back to the pod!"

Shiro had lifted himself onto one elbow, blood trickling from his mouth as he tried to pick off the men one by one.

Not pausing to think, Foster lurched into the room after Sam only to find a man with scars carved into his scalp already had Sam in a headlock, a gun to his head.

The man's face contorted into a sneer. "Don't—"

But Foster was *done* with hostage situations. His pulse pounding in his ears, he squeezed the trigger, and the man fell to the ground, electricity pumping through him. Sam screamed, but Foster didn't have time for hysterics.

He grabbed Sam by the arm and yanked him toward the door. "C'mon, we've got to go!"

"Where's Davis?" Sam rasped.

"He's here." Shielding Sam with his body, Foster peered into the ongoing gunfight, bodies now floating amidst the red mist now filling the lobby in the zero-G. Through the chaos though, he could see both Ezren and Shiro still laying down fire. But where was Davis?

Somewhere a sixty-second launch warning blared through the comms, and Foster's head whipped toward the holodash countdown. "Shaft. We've got to get off this ship before it goes into the wormgate."

"Get to the pods!" Ezren said from her and Shiro's position between a wall and a couch bolted to the floor.

Foster moved in that direction, only to find one of the men using the corridor as cover. "It's cut off!" The launch warning blared again, but Foster could barely hear it beneath the gunfire.

Shiro pulled something from his vest with a strangled cough. "Please note the exits." With that, he threw what looked like a grenade into the middle of the floor.

And everything dissolved into chaos.

CHAPTER 17

5.05.44B BRR Day 2

SMOKE FILLED Ezren's senses as she towed the semi-conscious Shiro toward the exit, shouting for Foster. Bodies shifted around her, but she couldn't tell if they were friend or foe—alive or dead. She could only hope Foster had gotten out with Sam, and she hadn't even seen Davis on the ship. Hopefully he'd already escaped.

With no alternative, she fumbled their way toward the gangplank, shoving Shiro ahead of her.

"Hart! If you leave, your Sterling dies."

Ezren turned in the gangway, the smoke clearing just enough to see the huge man with the scar circling his face holding a knife to Foster's throat with the other hand clamped around his mouth.

"No," Ezren whispered, cold terror freezing her in place.

"Come back aboard, and I'll consider letting him live."

Foster struggled, eyes wild, but the knife pressed into his throat broke his skin.

Oh, suns. Of course, there was only one choice. Ezren slid a shaky foot forward, and Foster's gaze hardened. Then, with an almost imperceptible shake of his head, the clear gangway doors slammed shut.

"No!" Panic vibrated through Ezren's every cell as she beat

her fists against the enforced glass, mentally trying to connect to the door. *Locked out.* This couldn't be happening. It *couldn't.* Chest heaving, she scrambled to start the override when another alarm jerked her head up.

An impartial, mechanical voice echoed through the chamber. "Vehicle embarking. Safe voyage."

"Wait!" Ezren screamed, her voice hoarse with smoke and tears stinging her eyes. *"You can't!"*

The bulky man holding Foster paused, his jaw going slack, and then a shot caught him in the head. A navy-haired girl Ezren had mistaken for dead had her hand wrapped around that of a dying man, using his fingers coded to the weapon to fire from her position near the ceiling. The gun slewed across the gloom, and one by one, she picked off the remaining men racing for the clear glass door locked from their side. The last gunman turned his weapon on her and caught her somewhere in the shoulder, her body jerking with the impact. In another breath, Foster snatched up the gun of the man floating behind him and brought an end to the firefight. He stilled, the last one standing as the ship accelerated steadily toward the wormgate.

He was alive... but he was leaving her.

And there was no getting him back.

She pressed her hand to the glass, a sob ripping through her chest, threatening to split her open.

Someone behind her screamed about Davis, but Ezren's mind couldn't parse the words. How could this be happening again? How could he—

Then someone shoved her aside as he launched himself against the door, kicking and screaming at it. *Sam.* Ezren turned toward him, the tears and snot streaming down his face. "Davis, stop!"

"Davis?"

Ezren turned toward the ship, her mind buzzing but blank.

Though growing smaller by the second, Foster walked toward the glass, something about his movements strange, his expression off. He touched his neck, and immediately Ezren sank to her knees in a flurry of emotions.

Because it wasn't Foster at all.

It was Davis.

"But where..." Ezren turned, and there was Foster—*her* Foster—scarlet dripping from a cut in his temple as he hobbled on one leg and pressed his red-stained fingers to the window.

"Davis, you chaffing motherfodder." His voice cracked, eyes glistening. "I'm so sorry."

Behind them, a gunshot scorched the wall a foot from Ezren's head. They flinched and Foster lurched to shield Ezren as she sealed the door to the hangar with a mental command, locking them in the clear gangway. Ezren's chest heaved as another knot of the Crow's thugs charged across the hangar.

Ezren: Micah, I need you to pick us up. We're on the gangway, and it won't be long before they break through the door.

Micah: On it.

"Davis, just hold on," Sam shouted into a comms channel. "We'll find a way to come get you!"

There was only a moment's pause before Davis's voice crackled into their goggs. "No, Sam. This is a one-way trip."

"It can't be," Sam sobbed, his body crumpling beneath him. "You have to come back. I'll get another ship." He looked wildly towards the other vessels docked beside them. "We'll bring you home. O-or I'll come with you."

"No, Sam." Davis gave him a sad smile, almost too small to make out as the ship gained speed, the massive wormgate spinning as it activated. "You belong on this side. You've got to go to school and grow up; your family needs you."

"But you're family," Sam choked out, his face soggy with tears. "We're supposed to stay together."

"It's okay, Sam," Davis said, his voice calm. "I was always headed toward the stars, just a little sooner than expected." He held up something in his hand now too small to see. "But I do have to thank you for bringing me Giles. He's a little beat up, but I'm sure he'll be a huge help, and someday, when you're ready, if you hear the stars calling, then you can make the journey too."

With Davis now only a silhouette in the multi-colored glow of the gate, Sam collapsed in on himself, the sobs racking his body.

"Someone tell Sylvia I'm sorry I won't be making it to the wedding," Davis said.

Ezren glanced to where Shiro lay on the floor, but he'd slipped into unconsciousness, pulse weak as his tactical topsuit compressed his injuries. Behind them, the thugs began to unload fire against the door.

EZREN: *HURRY,* MICAH.

MICAH: ALMOST THERE.

"I'm not going to forgive you for this," Foster said, tears soaking into his stubbled jaw.

"And just when we were starting to become friends." Davis chuckled over the line. "Well, just know that my one regret is not being able to see what you all do next. Sam, Foster, Ezren, I'm proud of you all, and I can't imagine what else you have in store for Casolla. It was truly my honor to witness you spreading your wings."

Tears spilled down Ezren's cheeks with renewed fervor as she thought about Davis greeting her at Tuzuno's storm truck station when she was fourteen years old. Thought of him playing with Sam and Waffle in Tuzuno's small park. Thought of him telling her to shout into the void.

No. It wasn't supposed to happen this way. Not like this.

"You saved me, Davis," Ezren whispered. "You didn't have to."

"Of course I did," Davis said, and she could hear the bittersweet smile in his voice. "Who else is going to take care of Foster while I'm gone?"

"You saved both of us." Foster shook his head, Ezren still caged in his arms as he leaned against the glass like it was holding him up. "I'll never be able to thank you enough."

"Be safe, Davis." Ezren sniffed, trying for a smile but not quite managing it. "I hope... I hope the stars welcome you with open arms."

Davis was now only a pinprick on the horizon, the ship standing at the giant maw of the spinning wheel of metal, colors across the spectrum whirling within. "At some point we all have to go into the abyss, Ezren. The void makes us look inward, finding ourselves in that blackness before we can escape it. But though the journey is dark, I like to believe the stars are worth the sail." His voice thickened. "Ezren, Foster, Shiro, Sam... it's been my pleasure."

And then the ship slipped through the gate, disappearing into the cosmic doorway, and Davis Banda was gone forever.

But there was no time to process. The door behind them buckled with the force of the gunfire on the other side, and Ezren knelt beside Shiro, his pulse much too weak.

Ezren: Micah, where are you?!

Micah: Fifteen seconds.

Ezren: I can't see you.

Micah: That's why they call it stealth.

Then Ezren saw it, the blue-black outline of the ship mirroring the stars in the expanse beyond. It loomed before the gangway for only a second before the hiss of the airtight seal reached her ears in a wave of relief. The door buckled again behind them, just as the ship chimed with a complete dock.

"Grab Sam." Ezren reached down for Shiro, his face growing sickeningly pale from blood loss. Foster pulled Sam into a bear hug, the boy still fighting him hysterically as the door to the ship opened. Favoring one leg, Foster tossed Sam in before hopping inside, and Ezren dragged Shiro through after. They were almost in the airlock when the hangar door cracked open, and a single shot sliced through the opening, scorching the ship's ocean wall holopro just before their door closed.

"Go, go, go!" Ezren yelled, the seal already whistling with release, and the ship pulling away as Ezren dragged Shiro down the corridor.

"Where's Shiro?" Micah called from the cockpit. "We're on autopilot, but if they come after us, I don't know what to do."

"Go stealth and hope for the best." Ezren's goggs scanned Shiro, and a half-dozen emergency notifications blared through her holo.

"Please tell me he has a pulse," Foster said as he turned on the paramedic chair in their closet-sized recovery room.

"I think he's had worse." Each taking one of his arms, Ezren and Foster moved Shiro to the medic chair, the nanites curling underneath them as they assessed. "But I think it's a low bar."

For a second, the medic chair's holo spooled in its loading protocol, and Ezren held her breath. While Shiro had taken shots that could've been fatal, she also knew his tactical topsuit provided a high degree of protection. Surely, if he could survive coding in the space above Otho, he could survive this. Still, as the holo stalled, the ball of dread in her stomach swelled. What if it wasn't working? What if he didn't make it back? What if—

A chime from the medic chair finally interrupted her downward spiral. *Healing Time: 30 hours.*

Beside her, Foster nearly collapsed, leaning back as his eyelids closed. "Thank the suns."

It was only then that Ezren let herself look at Foster—really look at him. He still wore his formal clothes from the press conference, but they hung from his body in stained rags. Bruises, blood, and burns covered every inch of his exposed skin, and Ezren flinched as her gaze caught on his mangled knee before shifting up to the haunted shadows in his gray-green eyes that hadn't been there before.

The pain was as visible as his other injuries, and something inside her blazed. Ezren didn't often take to rage, but she would find whoever had done this to him, and she would make sure they never hurt anyone ever again.

Foster shifted with a wince, and Ezren's furious protectiveness rushed to more pressing matters. As much as she wanted to collapse into his arms, she knew she couldn't, not this time. This time, she had to be the strong one. She reached for Shiro's bag of medical supplies, unbuckling them from his back and setting it onto the small table beside him.

"You and Shiro can trade off in the medic chair, but until then I have—"

She didn't get the words out before Foster's arms circled her from behind, his face buried in her neck. "Ezren..." Her name sounded almost desperate on his tongue. "Are you really here?"

"For better or for worse." Ezren turned, her bittersweet smile more of a wince as she cupped his abused jaw in her hands. "Suns, Foster, I'm so sorry we couldn't get here sooner."

"I can't believe you came for me." His voice cracked with emotion. "Just you and Shiro? What were you thinking?"

"Of course I came to get you." Ezren's smile wobbled on her lips, love and pain twisting through her in an inseparable weave of emotion. "That's what we do."

Sam peeked in through the door, his expression a dark mask. He glanced briefly at Shiro's status in the paramedic chair's holo before disappearing again with Waffle and Turnip on his heels. A moment later, the clank of a closing door echoed through the ship. Ezren's sigh felt like it weighed a thousand pounds. As much as she wanted to lose herself here in Foster's arms, the Crow was still out there, and she needed to check if Sam was hurt too. She unfolded the extra cot from the wall and guided Foster to it.

Her goggs scanned across his body, and though she had to scroll through his list of injuries, nothing mortal glared back at her. "Just relax here for a second while I check on Sam and Micah." She injected a painkiller in his thick bicep before throwing a blanket over him and propping his boots on Shiro's bag to ward off shock. Foster only nodded as he lay down, his eyes glazed, and Ezren's concern snowballed. She pressed a kiss to his forehead as his body started to tremble with the aftershocks of the adrenaline. "I'll be right back."

Ezren strode to the bunkroom and tapped on the door. "Sam, are you in there?"

"I do *not* want to talk to you."

"Are you injured?"

"No."

Ezren nodded. There would be time to dress the invisible wounds when he was ready... as long as he didn't run off in an escape pod again. She strode to the cockpit next to find Micah hopping from foot to foot as she scanned the holos.

"Micah."

Micah jumped with a yelp, pressing a hand to her chest. "Suns, Ezren, you scared the chaff out of me."

"Is anyone coming after us?"

Micah checked the holos again. "Not that I can tell, but Ezren, I'm no good at this. I have no idea what I'm doing."

"I know." Ezren wrapped her in a hug. "But thank you for doing it anyway."

Micah straightened, holding her by the shoulders as she took in Ezren's tear-stained face. "Wait, tell me what happened. You got them, right? Everyone's okay?"

"Everyone's alive. Shiro's in the medic chair, Foster's hurt bad, and Davis... well, Davis is gone."

Micah's eyes widened with understanding. "He went through the wormgate. By choice? With a cryochamber?"

"I... I don't know." Ezren shook her head, the tears welling all over again. "I've got to go help Foster, but then I'll come back. If something weird happens, just shout."

Micah nodded and pulled Ezren in for another squeeze, her voice quiet. "You did the best you could, Ezren. Even if you couldn't bring them both home, you all walked away, and that's a miracle."

"I thought miracles were supposed to feel better than this." Ezren sniffed.

Micah released her, a veil of tears shining in the muted light. "Not the ones you fight for."

Sucking in a deep breath to steady herself, Ezren gave her a grateful nod before staggering away on shaking legs. Grabbing food and drink rations from storage as well as fresh clothes for Foster, she stumbled back to the med bay, the ache in her body growing with each step. In the haze of adrenaline, she'd almost forgotten about her own injuries. Though they only added up to grazes and bruises, they still clawed at her with sharp fingers —the least on her long list of troubles.

When she returned to their glorified med bay closet, Foster was where she'd left him, lying down on the cot, his glazed stare pointed at the ceiling. Resting a gentle hand on his shoulder, she showed him her supplies, and his expression ignited with hunger. She helped him sit up, and he guzzled three water rations before she made him pause. He downed a nutrition tube next while she bent to retrieve bandages from Shiro's bag.

"I think I could eat about ten of these," he said, tossing the empty containers into the bag Ezren had brought them in.

Ezren frowned, wanting to ask if they'd fed him but knowing the answer was no. "Let's wait a little while before you take another one. If you eat too fast your stomach will reject it."

"What about a shower and fresh clothes?"

Foster swayed, and Ezren's hands shot out to catch him, maneuvering him back to a lying position. "We might have to hold off on the shower until you're a little stronger."

"Davis... he's gone," Foster whispered, his eyes half-lidded.

Ezren ran a hand across his forehead, his skin burning up beneath her palm. "Yeah, he is."

"But the cryonic chambers... they looked okay. He should be able to make it to the other side."

Ezren straightened. It was a fear she hadn't said aloud, but even one functioning chamber would change everything for Davis. "You're sure?"

"Sam and I ran into the guy trying to destroy them. He got two, but there were still three left. I guess they could've still disabled them somehow, but it seems unlikely with all the chaos."

Ezren nearly wilted with relief. *Thank the suns.* It was the answer to the question she'd been too afraid to ask—the one she knew would shatter her. Would shatter her whole family.

Foster caught her hand as she drew away. "Are you okay? Is Sam..."

Ezren shook her head, forcing herself to swallow the tears down. "We're fine. You're the one that needs fixing."

"He came back for me," Foster continued as Ezren loaded an injector with anti-fever medication. "He shouldn't have."

Ezren didn't fully understand what he meant, but knowing Davis, she could guess. "He saved my life too, Foster. If he hadn't closed the door, I would've been on that ship with him."

Foster's hand gripped hers tighter as she injected the meds into his thigh. "But if..."

He trailed off, and Ezren used a pair of small scissors to cut through most of his ragged, bloodstained outerwear. "It could've gone a hundred different ways." Ezren helped Foster into the clean spacer jumpsuit with gentle hands, each of his movements bringing a fresh hiss of pain, the vulnerability of the moment leaving Ezren raw. "Davis would be the first person to say we can't second-guess all the paths that could've been." Helping him back to the cot, she wrapped the gunshot wound in his knee, trying to keep the emotion from her voice. He didn't need that now. "It could've been better or worse. There was a moment there I thought we would all die, and then I thought we were all going out the wormgate instead."

"I know he's not dead." Foster's eyelids drifted closed like he was having a hard time keeping them open. "But I still feel like we lost him. And the navy-haired girl... did you see if she survived?"

Ezren thought of the girl picking off the thugs as the ship drifted toward the wormhole. She thought of her body convulsing as she took a bullet. "I... I don't know, Foster."

"She... I thought she was working for the Crow, but now I don't know. She tried to save us in the end." His eyes opened, and his hand found Ezren's, threading his fingers through hers. "She and Davis... they're the only reason I got through it. The way they got into our minds, destroying our bodies... at the end I was hoping for it to end. Ezren, I was so afraid it would happen to you; I was scared that you would come."

Ezren smoothed a dark lock of Foster's hair from his brow, her heart full of grief. "I'm sorry I wasn't there for you."

"I'm not." Foster pressed her hand to his cheek, his lashes falling as if savoring her touch. "I wouldn't wish that on anyone, much less my wife."

Ezren's breath caught in her chest, the word still new and tender. "What can I do?"

"Just..." Foster shifted on the cot. "Stay with me?"

The tremble of his voice nearly undid Ezren as she slid into the shelter of his arms, winding her body tightly around him as she drew the blanket over them both—as if she could shield him from the horrors of the past three days.

"I just... need to know you're here." He swallowed, and Ezren could feel his pulse still racing in his chest.

"For you, I'd stay forever." She burrowed in closer, savoring the heat of him—the life. And when his breaths finally deepened with slumber, Ezren let the tears stream unchecked down her cheeks. For him and all he had endured. For Davis and his lonely journey across the 'verse. And for a battle not yet won—the Crow still lurking out in the darkness, waiting for them.

Even though they might have been safe for the moment, their battle was far from over. But if they were to face the Crow head-on, first they would need rest. It was only with that thought that Ezren finally let herself relax into Foster.

They would rest, and then when she woke, she would hunt down the Crow herself.

CHAPTER 18

5.06.44B BRR Day 3

FOSTER HAD no idea how much time passed before he awoke to the sound of his name.

"Foster." The voice spoke a little louder. "Foster."

Foster's eyes flicked open, his pulse ratcheting up as he tried to remember where he was. Was Thread coming to tend to them? Or was it Face and Teeth arriving for the next round?

"It's okay, Foster, you're safe."

Foster's vision focused as he forced himself to take in his surroundings. Ezren's head was tucked underneath his chin, her body tucked into the curve of his, and her chest rising and falling with heavy breaths. That's right. He was on the ship. On his way home.

But Davis, where was—

Another jolt of panic followed quickly by the heavy realization. Davis was gone. Forever. The grief nearly threatened to drown him.

"Foster."

Foster lifted his gaze to finally take in Shiro standing above him. He jerked his head at the medic chair. "Get in. You need it more than I do now."

With a silent nod, Foster accepted Shiro's proffered hand to rise on his good leg from the cot. Leaning heavily on Shiro, he eased himself onto the medic chair, the nanites flooding through him like an instant balm to his burning body.

But Shiro was breathing heavily now too as he leaned against the wall.

"Are you sure this is okay?" Foster asked. "You were pretty bad."

"It's fine." Shiro squeezed the bridge of his nose. "You take this hour, and we'll swap again. I need to talk to Micah anyway to make sure she doesn't crash us into some passing asteroid."

Foster nodded. "Thanks, kin."

Shiro squeezed his shoulder, regret lining his face. "Foster, I just want to say I'm sorry. It's my job to protect you, and I failed." He took a deep breath. "I'll be handing in my resignation as soon—"

"Don't you dare." Foster's voice came out sharper than intended, and they both looked to Ezren, but of course, in her Ezren way, she slept on. "Shiro, with everything that I learned from the Talons, you're one of the few people in this 'verse I completely trust. If you couldn't have protected us, then no one could've." He lifted his arm. "Please don't leave us now."

Shiro looked at him for a beat before his expression eased into a grim smile. "While I'm afraid you may overestimate my skills, as long as you want my protection, you have it." He knocked his forearm against Foster's.

"Overestimate?" Foster scoffed. "You walked us into Otho, got Ezren off of York's ship alive, and escaped the Crow's thugs on Crion without losing a single life. And then somehow, with only Ezren at your back, you saved Davis and me from torture and death." He shook his head, a part of him still expecting to wake up in the Crow's torture chamber at any minute. "You underestimate yourself. But in any case, with the Crow still out there, we're going to need you now more than ever."

Shiro clapped him on the shoulder. "I swore to Sylvia

before I left that I would end this before I came home, and I still intend to." He winced, his hand moving to the hole in his tac-suit with a groan. "Just don't tell her I almost died again."

Foster snorted. "I won't tell her, but you know she's going to find out anyway."

"That I do." He gave his shoulder one more squeeze. "Rest easy for now, though, Foster. I'll be back."

Foster and Shiro swapped the medic chair three more times, and Foster gave him an abbreviated version of everything that had happened since he'd been taken. Eventually, Foster managed to limp his way into a shower and a fresh jumpsuit before Ezren finally awoke three hours later. Unlike him, she awoke slowly, rubbing at her eyes as if she could scrub away all that had transpired. She stared at the empty bed for three solid seconds before shooting up to sitting.

"Good morning," Foster said from his spot in the medic chair.

When she saw him, Ezren melted back onto the bed, her gaze soft and shining with relief. "Foster."

She crossed the distance between them before putting a hand to his head and checking his vitals in the medic holo. "Oh thank the suns, you're recovering well." Her forehead creased. "Is Shiro okay then?"

Foster nodded. "He's on his feet again and back in the cockpit, updating the CIF and all that." He shifted over to make room, and Ezren eased onto the chair beside him, her head pillowed on his chest.

"I guess it's time for us to think about our next steps then," Ezren whispered.

Foster curled one of her tangerine locks around a finger. "Yeah, I don't even know what's going on in the world right now. Has the BRR already started?"

"Yeah, I think it—"

"Mr. and Mrs. Sterling/Hart." Micah's now cyan-colored head popped into the room. "Sorry, but I couldn't help but overhear that you're both finally awake and well."

Ezren offered Micah an awkward grin from where she lay curled into Foster's side. "Oh, um. Hey."

Micah's smile widened. "So I was thinking maybe we could do a proof of life holo since you know... it was kind of touch and go there for a minute."

Foster frowned. After the biggest announcement of his life, he and Ezren had been very literally MIA during BRR week. Suns, VSoc must've been going insane. Honestly, he was surprised it had taken Micah this long to ask.

"You wouldn't have to move or anything," she continued, waving her hands for them to stay. "You could just stay here, and I'll do a holo edit so you don't look so..." She gestured to them before giving a pained grimace. "Almost dead?"

Exasperation carved Ezren's brow as she smoothed her tangled hair, dark shadows underscoring her eyes. "Okay... but what would we say? Hey, Belroy boys and babes, Foster was kidnapped, but now he's safe again?"

Micah's lips pursed as she shifted her weight from one leg to the other. "That may be a bit on the nose."

Foster ran a hand over his freshly shaven jaw as he considered it, the evidence of his healing wounds still littering his body.

Ezren peeked at him out of the corner of her eye, her pale face creasing with concern. "Micah, c'mon, surely this can wait."

"No, Micah's right," Foster said.

Ezren looked at Foster in surprise, and he squeezed her hand. "We need to send a message that we can't be intimidated. That we're survivors, and we're not going to bow down to the Crow's terrorism." His lips tightened, thinking of how hard

Teeth and Face had tried to break them. "With the BRR going on, we won't give details, but even the sight of us alive, smiling, and moving forward should be enough."

Micah raised a disbelieving brow. "*You*, Foster Sterling, are going to smile for a VSoc stunt?"

"Only under duress." Foster gave her a wry grimace, but he had to admire her chaotic buoyancy. "Don't get used to it."

"My, my, marriage has changed you." Micah fished a pair of hovercams from her pocket and tossed them into the air. "Okay, just remember, it doesn't have to be long, and you might want to at least mention the wedding since that kind of leaked out while you were away."

Foster blinked. "Wait, what?"

But Micah plowed on as if she hadn't heard him. "Ezren, are you in?"

Ezren met his gaze, concern radiating from her coffee-dark eyes. "Are you sure?"

The corner of Foster's mouth crooked up. He couldn't blame her for her uncertainty. In truth, he couldn't recall another time in their nearly two years together that he'd readily given a VSoc statement.

When he spoke, gravity weighed on his words as his thumb skated along the ring of silver ink on her finger. "I will use every tool at our disposal to destroy the Crow and make sure that other creatures like him don't rise up in his place. And I would be a fool not to use one of the greatest weapons at our disposal." Nausea turned his stomach as he thought of Davis bleeding on the floor. "That girl, Thread, I told you about who saved us. It was your messages that inspired her, Ezren." He swallowed, thinking of the spark in Thread's eyes as she'd rushed them through the station. Before Teeth had buried two laser-lead bullets in her knees. "VSoc and even the crowds around us always seem so nebulous, but I think that was the first time I realized the connection your message—our message—has made with real people across Casolla. That we could be saving lives."

He squeezed Ezren's hands, a glow returning to her pale cheeks. It was something he'd fought against for so long. His fame. Their responsibility. But now, he finally understood. He turned to Micah, all the torture and pain and grief welding into resolve in his chest. "So yeah, I'm all in."

A smile stretched across Ezren's face, and she planted a soft kiss on Foster's shoulder. "Me too."

Micah shrugged, beaming at both of them. "Well, all right then." The red dots flicked on the hovercams. "Short and sweet. Here we go."

He drew in a deep breath, thinking of his message as another bullet fired straight at the Crow. "I know we've been quiet since the Calderon Industries announcement, but as many of you know, Ezren and I took some time to celebrate after our wedding." He glanced at her, and she gave him a shy smile, hiding her blush in his shoulder. Leaning over, he pressed a light kiss to her hair, and behind the cams, Micah silently screamed in joy as she feigned a swoon. "These past few days, we've also had a few other..." His words failed him as he tried to sum up the atrocities he and Ezren had endured.

"Challenges," Ezren supplied.

Foster nodded, his grin bordering on feral. "*Challenges* we've also had to address that've kept us out of the public eye." *Challenges you can fod off with, Crow.* "But now that we're back, we just want to say good luck to all the BRR racers out there in the churn." He thought of Bex, Simon, and the Amarals fighting through the churn's storms at that very moment, and his muscles tensed. *Casolla keep them safe.* He wasn't sure he could lose someone else this week.

"May the storm winds blow you to the finish." Ezren gave the cam a warm smile. "We appreciate your patience during this time of great change, and we'll be sure to share more details as soon as we're able."

Micah gave a cutting motion with her hand, and the red dots of the cams turned off. "Aw, that was oh-so-completely adorable for a post-near-death statement." She performed a happy pirouette. "VSoc is going to love this! I can't wait to see all the honeymoon challenge rumors." She bounced on her toes with a cackle that had Foster rolling his eyes. Suns, he hoped he didn't have to see that pop up on *his* feed.

"Isn't everyone too wrapped up in the BRR right now to bother with us?" Ezren asked, stretching her arms over her head with a yawn.

"Hardly." Micah grinned as her fingers flew through her holos. "We may be in the middle of the ball, but you are still the queen and king." She pressed her hands to her chest, her expression going all gooey. "You're never far from our thoughts."

Foster raised an eyebrow. While he'd gotten—somewhat— used to Ezren's best friend over the course of the last few months, seeing the fangirl mentality up close was still weird as shaft. "Creepy."

Ezren wrinkled her nose as she rose to her feet. "I just hope it doesn't steal the racers' limelight. They deserve it right now."

"Oh please." Micah waved her off, her focus zeroing in on their faces in her holo as she edited out the still-healing wounds. "What they're going through has nothing on what you've survived." She scrunched her face at Foster. "Sorry about that, by the way. Shiro gave me the update." Her lips twisted to one side, thoughtful. "For the record, though. It all turned out way better than I expected."

Foster frowned, swinging his feet to the ground. "How's Sam doing with it?"

"Uh... less good?" Micah's attention darted to the hall. "I've been checking on him, but he hasn't come out of the bunkroom yet." She pulled on the ends of her cyan pigtails with a sigh. "I tried to explain that old potatoes—"

"Micah," Ezren snapped.

"Oh, c'mon, Ez, it's not like he's dead," Micah said. "And he ended up exactly where he wanted to be. He'll be *fine*."

"Micah." Ezren's voice was soft. "Davis is leaving behind everything he's known without any preparation. After everything he's been through, we can't ignore that it will be hard for him, and he made that choice without a second thought— for us."

"Okay, I'm sorry." Micah sank onto the cot. "I mean, I'll miss him too." Her lips pressed into a thin line as she stared at the ceiling. "It's just, when you left, and then Sam was gone too, I started to panic that none of you would be back." Her unshed tears glistened in the dull light, the holo of a peaceful river trickling through a meadow on the wall behind her. "So yeah, while I'm sad Davis left sooner than he wanted, for me, it felt like an unlikely gift from the 'verse. The best-case scenario I could've dared hope for."

"I know." Ezren moved to her side, squeezing her hand. "But Davis was a brother to Sam—maybe even like a father figure sometimes—and I broke my promise to bring him back." She swallowed, her eyes filling. "It'll take Sammy some time."

Foster stood, his own chest aching, and his voice rough. "I'll try to talk to him." Though he couldn't pretend to know what Sam was going through, he'd been the last person to see his dad alive... and he'd also been one of the last in Casolla to see Davis alive as well. While he hadn't known them as long, he couldn't deny that each one had taken part of Foster with them when they'd gone.

Foster glanced at Ezren, and an uncertain flicker of emotions ran across her features. "Okay." She nodded, her hands wringing as if she didn't know what to do with them. "I'll, uh, I'll take a shower."

With a nod, Foster limped down the corridor to the other bunkroom and tapped gently on the door.

"Go away, Ezren, I said I *don't* want to talk to you!" Sam shouted from the other side.

Foster glanced toward the med bay door to see Ezren's blushing cheeks disappear through it again.

"It's Foster."

For a moment, only the hum of the engine vibrated through the ship. The seconds stretched, and Foster was about to turn away when the door hissed open.

Foster stepped inside, and the door slid closed behind him. The lights were set on low with a foldable bunk hanging from each wall. Sam lay on the one farthest from the door, a holo glowing in front of him and Turnip tucked into the crook of his arm. At the foot of the bed, Waffle lifted her muzzle, her perked half-flopped ears betraying interest when her resting bored-face did not.

With the heaviness of the last few days weighing on him, Foster moved to the bunk on his left and lay down, his healing body still moving stiffly. A lake holo surrounded them as if they were on an island in the middle of the stars, and Foster let the silence flow between them. Waffle, however, snorted as she rolled around on the bed.

Finally, Sam spoke, his stare still fixed on his holopro. "So, did Ezren send you to talk to me?"

"No," Foster said.

Sam glanced at him, one arm pillowed behind his head. "Okay. So then, why are you here?"

"Because I'm hurting," Foster said. "And I know you are too."

Sam studied him, his blue eyes flicking from the scars on his face to the ones on his arms exposed by his rolled-up sleeves. "Yeah. It looks like you got pretty busted up."

"We were put through a lot." Foster met Sam's gaze. "But that's not what I meant."

"Davis looked pretty... pretty bad too." Sam swallowed, turning back to the holo. "I guess they tortured both of you?"

"They did."

Sam winced. "Davis didn't deserve that. He was just in the wrong place at the wrong time."

"Don't underestimate him like that," Foster said, his voice even but firm. "Davis knew exactly what he was getting into when he agreed to be a doppelganger. It was a knowing sacrifice, and to call it anything less is to discredit him."

Sam cocked his head, his attention sharpening on Foster like he hadn't really seen him before. "Yeah, I guess so. He was always doing stuff like that. Sticking up for people, forgiving people who didn't deserve it, helping out when he wasn't asked." His lips tightened. "And yet, he still got shafted."

"Bad things happen to even the best of us. As much as we would want to protect them from it, sometimes we can't fight what the 'verse has in store." Foster took in a slow, painful breath, and Turnip hopped down from her spot next to Sam to saunter over to him. She jumped onto the bunk beside him, her six tails flicking as she nuzzled his hand with her pink head. "Look, I know you would've rather traded Davis for me—"

"I didn't say that," Sam said, sitting up so sharply Waffle actually rolled off the bunk. She scuffled to right her plump body before giving him an indignant snort, but Sam's hard blue stare didn't stray from Foster. "I can be sad that Davis was taken and happy that you were saved. The problem is everyone's going to be happy that you were saved, and no one's going to care that Davis was thrown into the next galaxy unprepared and hurt and alone."

"I care, Sam!" Foster sat up, his voice trembling with his own grief.

"Since when?" Sam shot back.

"Suns." Foster let his head drop, the full weight of Davis's absence falling on him. "I don't even know. And trust me, I didn't want to. But Davis has showed up for me again and again, and I wouldn't have survived three days of torture from the Crow's Talons without him." He rubbed a shaking hand over his face. "Trust me when I tell you nothing brings you closer than that."

Sam swallowed, his shoulders relaxing and his fingers weaving into Waffle's thick fur. "What'd they do to you?" he whispered.

"Mental and physical torture." Foster shifted, and Turnip mewed beside him. He ran a hand along her back. "When they weren't hurting one of us, they were making us watch them hurt the other, and as much as I wish Davis had never been a part of it, I couldn't have asked for a stronger person to hold me together when I was threatening to break."

Sam's hand ran rhythmically along Waffle's head, and she scooted closer to him. "How'd you get through it?"

"Well, we talked... *a lot*. And Davis talked a lot about you." Foster's mouth tilted with a grief-laden smile. "Anyone listening would've thought you were brothers."

"We are," Sam said, his face grave. "In every way that counts."

"True enough." Foster scratched Turnip behind her ears, and she mewed with pleasure. "Well if it wasn't for you, we'd probably both be dead, so thanks for coming to get us."

"It didn't work." Sam kneaded his fingers into his right thigh in a massaging motion. "Davis is gone, and we'll never know if the cryonic chambers were working."

"They were." Foster dropped the words with a finality that

brooked no argument. He couldn't even entertain the alterna-tive. "You interrupted the guy there to destroy them, and there were three he hadn't touched." Foster leaned forward, intent. "He has Giles, and it's possible Thread might've survived too."

Sam blinked, brow wrinkled. "Who?"

"Thread was there with us—helped us get through it." Foster pressed his lips together, his voice dropping. "I really hope she made it too. After everything she's been through, she deserves it."

"I just... I wish he was here to tell me about it. You know I..." Sam's bottom lip trembled. "He was my best friend. I used to talk to him about everything, especially after my dad..." Sam shook his head, lying back down on the bed. "And now I've lost him too."

"But Davis isn't dead, Sam." Foster shifted on the bunk, shrinking the distance between them. "We'll miss him, but he lives on—chasing the stars like he always wanted. And one day, maybe if you want... maybe you'll meet him again."

Sam glanced up at the wisps of white clouds silently swirling across the ceiling. "I want to, you know." His gaze darted sideways at Foster. "Go through the wormgate. It's one of the things I liked to talk to Davis about." Concern pulled his mouth into a panicked grimace. "But you can't tell Ezren or my mom. I don't think they're ready for that yet."

Oh, suns, they certainly weren't. The very thought of Sam going through the wormgate would probably send Ezren into a panic attack. But they had at least eight years if he was following the same education path Davis had. Then, Sam would be an adult more than capable of chasing his own dreams, and so much could change between now and then, it would be impossible to predict where his path would take him.

Either way, definitely best not to start Ezren's panic storm now.

"I won't," Foster said. "Your dreams are your own to do as you please, but... I'm glad you have them."

A smile tugged at his lips as he thought back to the little brother Ezren had been fighting so hard to protect last year. A brother she feared couldn't walk to school by himself or make friends. Now he was jumping into syndicate gun fights and plotting a course across the galaxies.

Sam flopped back onto the bunk with a sigh, and Waffle gave her fur a shake. "This rescue didn't at all go like I wanted it to."

"Unfortunately, the dangerous ones rarely do."

"But I'm really glad we got you back, Foster." Sam offered him a half-smile—the first genuine one Foster had seen pointed in his direction since... well, maybe ever. "My sister needs you."

Foster returned his grin. "And I need her."

"And as brothers-in-law go"—Sam shrugged, a teasing lilt to the words—"I guess I could do worse."

"I could say the same." Foster chuckled. "But seriously though, if you ever need to talk about anything, I'm always here for you, Sam."

"Okay." Sam held his stare for a second before a smirk curved his mouth. "But first I need to know if you're better at homework than Ezren."

"I think I—"

A tap on the door cut Foster off.

"Sam?" Ezren's tentative question echoed in the small room. "Can I come in?"

Sam rolled his eyes before looking at Foster, but Foster's shrug was entirely noncommittal.

Pushing his mop of mousy brown hair from his brow, Sam got to his feet. "Yes, Ezren."

The door hissed open and Ezren took a small step inside,

her dark gaze uncertain as she looked from Foster to Sam and back.

But Sam didn't hesitate as he crossed the room and silently folded his arms around her shoulders. "I'm just going to miss him." All of the blame and anger had leached away from his words, leaving only sorrow behind.

"I know," Ezren said. "We all are."

Foster waited for the punch of jealousy, but there was none. Only the bone-aching certainty that Ezren was right. Davis would be so very missed.

"But I'm here for you, Sam," she said.

Foster rose to his feet. "And me too."

"And me!" Micah's cyan pigtails popped in the door along with a comically huge grin.

Sam rolled his eyes again with an overdramatic growl of frustration. "Were you eavesdropping?"

"Well yeah." Micah twirled the ends of one of her pigtails. "As your honorary older sister, it's basically my job."

"Whatever." Sam squeezed his temples. "Just get out of my room."

Micah pointed a silver fingernail at the bunks. "Um, your room? This is all of our—"

A chime from Ezren's goggs interrupted Micah, and as one, they all tensed.

Ezren's gaze swept the room, fear and something closer to fury flashing across her face. "It's the Crow."

"Shiro!" Micah yelled.

Foster's chest iced over and he stepped closer to Ezren as she flicked the holo into the dim room. A single crow flew across the walls to land in the skeletal tree, joined by another, and another.

As the murder burgeoned amidst the branches, a smooth, artificial voice reverberated through the room. "Ezren Hart and

Foster Sterling, I hope you're watching this together." Shiro leaned against the doorway, his features dark as he listened with the rest of them. "While I may admit, treating you with kid gloves was a mistake, the games are over. I could stomach Warner holding on to the Belethea Race Royale, but a naïve VSoc poster kid? Over my dead body. If I can't dispose of you artfully, I suppose it's time to wipe the board and start over. High time, I'm sure. I was always too soft on Warner. Now that he's returned to the stars, it feels right to go back to where it all started, don't you think? Of course, being the mindless infants that you are, you have no idea what I'm talking about, so let me just end by saying, with all the excitement, I hope you're still keeping up with the BRR this year. It's sure to have an explosive finish, and I can't wait to watch the fires burn."

A viscous, crimson liquid dripped through the holo until it blotted out the image, and the crows faded away completely. A chill ran down Foster's spine, goosebumps breaking out on every inch of his skin. "He means the finish line."

Ezren's horrified stare met his. "He's going to blow it up."

"But Sylvia's there right now," Shiro said, a muscle ticking in his jaw.

"And so is my mom," Foster said.

Micah ticked them off on her fingers. "And Bex and Simon and the Amarals and Lo—" Micah stopped short from whatever she was going to say. "Everyone else we know and love."

Sam sank onto the bunk, hugging Waffle around the neck. "The finish dome can hold up to two thousand people."

Ezren's holo illuminated the air in front of her, but this time it was the BRR feed. "Do we have time to get back?"

"It'll be close." Shiro pulled up his navigation holo as Turnip snaked around his ankles. "We're going to have to gun it, and we have to remember it's probably another trap."

"I don't care." Foster's hands curled into fists. "I'm not

letting this guy do this to us again. I'm done losing people. To the storms, the fire, the abyss—I'm *done*." Ezren nodded from beside him, the rage burning within him reflected in her eyes. In Sam's and in Shiro's too. "Whatever it takes, we're going to end this."

Because he'd had enough of waiting for the world to right itself. Of waiting for the darkness of the world to reach its claws out for them. This time, he was coming for them first.

CHAPTER 19

5.06.44B BRR Day 3

EZREN PROBABLY SHOULD'VE BEEN scared, but somewhere in the past twelve hours, she'd gone far beyond that. Now she only regarded the Crow's message as a loathsome problem to crush out. She squeezed her temples as she forced herself to rethink each word of the message, piecing together the threat and the consequences. "Okay, first, we need to warn everyone."

"We can't." Shiro ran his hands through his already wild hair, his eyes half crazed. "I just tried to send an update to the CIF, but someone's jamming our transmit comms. As it stands, I'm betting we won't be able to send a message until we're off this ship on Belethea."

Sam's face clouded as he tapped his lower lip. "Even then, I'd bet you that they'll be having comms issues at the finish line."

Foster nodded where he leaned against the lake holo on the wall. "It would be easy enough. Comms in the churn belt are already a dicey thing; it probably wouldn't even look suspicious for messages to be delayed or not get to them at all."

Ezren paced back and forth in the small bunkroom. "Okay, so Micah, you've been following the race. When are you expecting the winners to finish?"

Micah's holo glowed in front of her. "Based on their positions now, it looks like VSoc is guessing about forty-eight hours. It's a super close race this year and..." Her olive skin blanched. "Grady/Guns are in the top three."

Ezren's hands tightened behind her back, forcing herself to stay calm. "Okay, Shiro, when can you get us there?"

"Well, the closest dome with a spaceport is a four-hour underground train away." Shiro shook his head. "We'd be getting there with maybe a half hour to spare."

"*If* the trains are in your favor with all the crowds," Micah chimed in.

Foster crossed his arms, every muscle tight. "Is there a faster way?"

Ezren's mind raced. *Calderon, back to the beginning, churn belt.* "Do we have jetchutes?"

Foster slowly turned to her. "Why do I feel like I don't want to answer that question?"

Ezren held his gaze. "It's the fastest way in."

Foster's brows rose under the swath of dark hair falling across his forehead. "Yeah, and it's also the one that's most likely to kill us. This isn't just some storm, Ezren. This is the churn we're talking about."

"But we've collected so much more data on it." Ezren pulled up her weather files from the churn belt. "We could let the algorithm assess the conditions in real time and pick the best moment and location for the drop. It would only take me a couple tweaks, and with Micah here to help, we definitely have enough time to make the changes."

Foster turned away from her with a groan, scrubbing a hand over his face. "How much extra time would it buy us?"

Ezren and Micah shared a glance, but it was Micah who spoke. "Well that would totally depend on where the algorithm dropped you. Three hours from the epicenter is probably impossible due to the windspeeds, but outside of that radius could hypothetically be fair game."

"Even an hour is a lot of extra time to evacuate people," Sam said, his fingers raking through Waffle's brown fur.

Ezren nodded, reaching out to grab Foster's hand. She thought of them terrasailing through a storm. Of running through Walibista Channel injured while Talmadge tried to outright murder them. As the fear glinted in Foster's eyes, she knew he was reliving those memories too. But they'd survived them.

"We can do this," Ezren whispered.

"Suns, I'd thought we were done with the churn," Foster said, the deep line furrowing between his brows.

"Me too," Ezren said. "But I guess the churn isn't done with us."

He held her look for a long moment before his hand finally squeezed hers. "Fine, but if we're doing this, I need to spend more time in the medic chair." He pointed from Ezren to Micah and back. "And I want that algorithm to give us higher than a 90% survival rate before we go."

Ezren grinned, giving him a small push toward the med bay. "You got it. Heal up, and we'll take care of everything else."

Foster tugged her into the hall, the door hissing shut behind them. He shook his head as he pulled her close, his voice low. "Are we going to spend the rest of our lives with you trying to kill us?"

Ezren pretended to consider it. "Maybe just this one last time."

"That's the girl I married." He chuckled, the palms of his hands pressing into her back as his stormy irises swirled. "But I think after this, I'm demanding an extra honeymoon day."

Ezren grabbed a fistful of his spacer's suit and tugged him

toward her with a cocksure smirk. "After we find the Crow, I'm asking for a week."

"You think he'll be there?"

Ezren nodded. "Something about the message... it sounded like he was going there himself. Like he wanted to see it." Uncertainty fluttered in her chest, but she shoved it down. "And we've only got two days to figure out how to catch him."

Foster's gaze went distant. "That girl who helped us was biologically the daughter of Calderon and Carmella, engineered to look just like Carmella." His hand rubbed in circles along her back as he thought. "With this obsession with the BRR and Calderon and the Crow's decades-long record, do you think he could've been at the original BRR all those years ago?"

"With the luxie youth technology, it's certainly possible." Ezren chewed her bottom lip as she considered. "But I looked them up not too long ago, and allegedly, none of the other originals survived."

Foster cocked an eyebrow. "Allegedly isn't a word that's been kind to us. I'll do some more digging."

"No, you're supposed to be resting." Ezren pushed him another step toward the med bay.

He leaned down and pressed a soft kiss to her lips that lit her on fire. "And you're supposed to be working on the algorithm." Another kiss on her jaw, and Ezren melted into him. They hadn't had a spare second to—

The door hissed open, and they jumped apart as if they'd been electrocuted. Foster disappeared into the med bay with one last teasing glance. Smiling, Ezren turned to see Shiro— forehead wrinkled, hair wild, and Turnip draped around his neck—still fully focused on his holopro.

"It's not going to be easy to evacuate the finish line," he muttered. "There's one underground track in and out of there with three magtrains that each hold three hundred people. If there's eighteen hundred spectators there, it would take four hours to get the second half out." His jaw tightened, his hands fidgeting with the lapels of his long coat as if they didn't know where to go. "We don't have that kind of time... and you know Sylvia's going to make sure her royalers are safe before she takes a seat out."

But Ezren was feeling too light for fear, the adrenaline already racing through her as she thought of the course ahead. "Then we'll just have to disable the explosive somehow." Her fingers tapped along her legs as she thought. Then an idea hit her. With a grin, she poked her head into the bunkroom. "Sam."

Sam looked up from his current squabble with Micah. "Yeah?"

"Do you think you could devise some kind of code to neutralize a network-enabled explosive?"

Sam frowned, considering. "Yeah, I don't think it would be different from most other paralyzing viruses." His lips twitched one way and then the other. "But what if it's a physical trigger?"

"Then we'll have to physically remove it," Ezren said, "but I want to be prepared for all possibilities. Do you think you could put something usable together in the next thirty hours?"

"Yeah, it'll be harder without Giles." Sam rose to his feet, and Waffle looked up at him, obviously reluctant to leave her spot where she lay splayed on her back. "But I'll try to link into the ship's processor to see if I can go faster."

Shiro leaned against the narrow corridor as Sam passed by him. "And just how do you think you would physically take care of an explosive?" Shiro asked.

"Foster told you about the Carmella look-alike working for the Crow, right?" Ezren said.

"Yeah."

"I think the Crow might be one of the original racers, and from his message it sounds like he's going to be there to witness the carnage."

Shiro adjusted the goggs in his hair. "Okay, but with holo-mask tech, he could look like literally anyone."

"Surely the CIF has a way to see through it though."

"We have a way to detect a holomask," Shiro said. "But the more sophisticated ones would require you to disable it somehow."

"Physically or electronically?" Ezren asked.

"I'll talk to Sam and see if we can come up with something that could be used remotely." Shiro stretched his neck from side to side. "But with two thousand people there that we're trying to evacuate, you're going to need a better way to narrow down your suspects."

"Gotcha." Ezren's mind whirred as she sorted through the problem. They could do this; they just had to be prepared. "I think I have an idea for that too."

"Of course you do." Shiro snorted, but the tension eased from his face. He slipped Turnip from his shoulders and started toward the cockpit. "I would imagine Ezren Hart always has an idea."

Suns, let's hope so. Ezren continued to spin through the Crow's potential moves as she stepped into the bunkroom, letting Turnip in before closing the door behind her. So far, they'd tripped on nearly every trap, and they couldn't afford to be caught flat-footed this time.

Micah didn't look up from where she lay sprawled on her back in the middle of the floor, a dozen holos of BRR coverage glowing above her. "This jamming thing is totally chaffing with me," she groaned. "I can see everything that's happening, but I can't post anything about it. All my Belroy boys and babes are going to think I'm dead."

Ezren slid to the floor beside her, her back resting against one of the bunks. "How are the Beletheans doing?" Her stomach flipped at the question. Even with everything else happening, she couldn't help but want this for their racers. Ezren and Foster had trained beside Grady/Guns and the Amarals all year. They'd worked their asses off, and she was certain no one in the 'verse wanted it more than Simon and Bex.

"Grady/Guns are in good form on the wheels, but they're still in third. The top four are closer than I've ever seen them." Micah shuffled through her holos. "The Amarals were in the top ten early on, but they had a pretty bad scrap at the first checkpoint and have dropped to fifteenth now."

Ezren nodded as Turnip stepped into her lap, leaning into her chest. Though Ezren couldn't doubt the Amarals' talent, she always thought they needed another year of experience to be truly competitive. She scanned the feeds, the storms of the churn raging across each one. Her attention caught on the holo of *The Royaler Review*'s commentary taking up a central location amidst the swirl of Micah's feed.

Ezren tucked away the shadow of a smile as she absently stroked Turnip's soft fur. "What's *The Royaler Review* have to say about it?"

Micah narrowed her gaze at Ezren as the holo winked out. "I'm not telling you."

"Oh, c'mon." Ezren scooted closer, trying not to disturb Turnip from her lap. "What was his name again? Lowen? Lowry?"

"No, Ezren." Micah covered her face with her hands. "There's nothing to tell."

"Micah." Ezren pulled Micah's hands away, adopting a

pout that was almost solemn. Almost. "When I was nano-close to going through a wormgate, all I could think about was that I would never know this huge part of your life that I missed."

"Ha." Micah rolled her eyes. "As if I would fall for that."

Ezren smiled, sensing a crack in Micah's defenses. "Does anyone know?"

"Then it wouldn't be a *secret*."

"But I can keep a secret."

Micah snorted. "Like barely."

Ezren refrained from pointing out the irony of that comment coming from Micah, of all people. She tried to back-track instead. "Okay, but I know you've been working with him."

Micah rolled onto her belly, propping her chin up on a hand. "You're not going to leave me alone about this, are you?"

Ezren softened, her smile falling as she thought about how little she'd asked Micah about *her* life in the last year. "Look, I know I've been spending a lot of time with Foster and the royalers, especially after everything that happened on Otho. But Micah..." Ezren squeezed her hands. "You're still my best friend. I still want you in my life. And I want to be a part of yours... if you'll let me."

The waves of the lake holo lapped at the dock as Micah held her stare, slowly pointing a finger at her. "I see you manip-ulating me."

Ezren intensified the pout.

"Oh, all right." Micah hid her face in the crook of her arm, her voice muffled. "I have been working with Lowell Coppen from *The Royaler Review* for... some time now?"

Shifting Turnip onto the floor beside her, Ezren slid to her stomach, trying to contain her interest. With all the darkness closing in on them, she needed this spark of light. Just for a moment. "But how?"

"We run in the same circles of VSoc, Ezren." Resignation coated Micah's words. "Back when you started, there weren't that many holologgers covering the Belethea team, even in passing."

"Yeah, but *The Royaler Review* used to say the worst stuff about us," Ezren said. "I thought Sylvia was going to murder him."

"Well, actually there's four of them, but yeah, they used to be super critical of Belethea's team, and we butted heads too." Micah ran a finger across the holo of the wooden dock covering the floor. "But back when Calderon went on trial, Lowell actually wanted to know the real story instead of getting caught up in taking sides. So we started exchanging comms."

"And that's when they started to lay off on us," Ezren whispered.

Micah shrugged. "Maybe. Jabari came aboard not long after that too, and he's also pretty popular."

Ezren snorted, Turnip's tails tickling her nose from where she brushed against her. "Well, that's what you told Sylvia."

A shy smile curled Micah's lips. "Maybe."

"Okay, but that was still almost a year ago," Ezren said, scratching Turnip's ears. "And you're still"—she coughed with a bounce of her eyebrows—"*working* with him now. Have you ever met up?"

Micah's cheeks glowed pink. "Maybe."

"And you like him!" Ezren burst out just as the door slid open.

"Wait, your boyfriend works at *The Royaler Review*?"

Ezren and Micah's heads snapped up simultaneously to find Sam leaning against the doorjamb. Micah leapt to her feet. "Get out!"

"Hey, I'm allowed to eavesdrop too." He grinned.

"What's going on?" Shiro called from somewhere farther in the ship.

"Don't worry about it!" Ezren yelled back.

"If you make another peep about this, I will sing Gerard's *Star Jungle* at the top of my lungs for the rest of the trip." Micah shooed him out of the doorway, nudging Waffle aside with her foot.

"Suns, Sam," Foster yelled. "Just give her what she wants for all of our sakes."

"Excellent advice. Now go do your job, so I can do mine." With that, Micah shut the door in his face.

Ezren muffled a laugh as she tried to hide behind Turnip. "So, no one else knows about this?"

"No one." Micah dropped down on the floor cross-legged. "The powers that be at *The Royaler Review* have gained a following over the years that isn't exactly sympathetic to the"— she brandished her fingers in air quotes—"*Belethean upstarts.* Lowell's trying to change that gradually, but if people knew we had a connection, it would cast doubt on his impartiality."

"And then there's Sylvia." Ezren tapped her fingers on the metal floor, trying to think of how many times Sylvia and *The Royaler Review* had publicly lambasted each other over the last few years. *Uncountable.* Now, if she found out, she might even see Micah as a leak, fire her, and ask Jabari to take the lead VSoc position instead.

"Exactly."

"And you trust him?" Ezren asked, sitting up beside Micah.

"I do." Micah's expression sharpened as she faced Ezren. "But I swear I haven't given him any of your personal information, Ezren, or anything that's been going on in the last few days."

"I know, Micah." Ezren gave her an easy smile. "I trust you, and I trust the people you trust."

"Okay, Foster's right. We have to watch out for you." Micah raised a cyan eyebrow. "You should at least be a little suspicious. Because at least one of those chaffers at *The Royaler Review* is *not* quality."

Ezren laughed again, leaning her head against Micah's shoulder. "This Lowell guy though. He's going to be at the finish line, right?"

The shadow of worry that had been following all of them fell over Micah's normally carefree features, her voice like a whisper. "Yes, he'll be there."

Ezren took her hand, swallowing. Somehow, the Crow had truly managed to target all the people they cared for. "It's going to be okay. We've got a plan."

"I know." Micah let out a deep breath, meeting her gaze. "And I trust you too. It's just, I know I never really liked old potatoes, but that was a rough way to go for anyone. And if something happens to Lowell and Sylvia and Simon and Bex and... Suns, Ezren, I have so many friends who are at the finish line right now." She shook her head, her voice barely audible. "I'm scared."

The words sent a new wave of resolve coursing through Ezren's veins. This was only a small window into the pain and damage the Crow could bring. And if he blew up the finish line... with all of the interplanetary officials and visitors there, it could unbottle threats of war all over again.

And it was her duty as a Belethean ambassador to be sure that didn't happen.

"It's okay, Micah. I think we're all scared," Ezren finally said. "But that's what the plan is for. We need to make sure this syndicate asschaff doesn't get a chance to do this again. And for that, when we get there, we're going to need your boyfriend's help."

Micah gave her a flat look. "I didn't say he was my boyfriend."

Ezren offered an innocent shrug. "Lover? Husband? Coworker with feelings? Star-cross—"

"Okay, shut up already." Micah laughed, elbowing Ezren gently in the ribs. "What do you need him to do?"

Ezren looked up at the towering white thunderheads climbing in the simulated sky. "It's going to be hard to convince the organizers that this is a credible threat we need to evacuate for, but I think *The Royaler Review,* as an unbiased news source, could help us with that." Ezren frowned. "It'd be a huge leap of trust though, and he'd basically be risking his neck for us based on faith alone. Do you think he'll agree to help?"

"Yes." Micah said it with such finality, Ezren's brows rose. "He'll do it if I ask."

A bird song echoed through the holo, and Ezren stilled, suddenly realizing that this wasn't just some minor interest. "Wow, Micah. You two must be close."

"Lowell is... he's kind of my person." Micah gave her an expression somewhere between a blush and an apologetic pout as she tugged on her pigtails. "I can't wait for you to finally meet him."

Ezren leaned into Micah with a warm smile. Though Micah hadn't admitted it, Ezren could see the love shining from her eyes—could feel it in the confidence she had in Lowell. And the thought of her best friend finding love filled her chest with joy, even as anxiety edged Micah's face.

"He's probably so worried about you too," Ezren whispered.

A soft chuckle escaped Micah. "I know. He's already sent me about ten different messages since our transmit comms have been down. He's already a bit of a worrier... so, hopefully he doesn't have a panic attack over my radio silence in the next couple days." Micah shook herself, clapping her hands together. "But enough of that. Our time is ticking. Aren't we supposed to be working on your algorithm?"

"I'll start on the update, but I have something for you to do in the meantime. How much footage do you have of the press conference where Foster was abducted? And maybe even the expo bombing last year?"

"A ton." Micah swept the BRR holos to the other side of the room as she accessed her repository. "Why?"

"We need to go through the footage and see if we can pinpoint anyone acting strange. I have a feeling the Crow may have been wearing a holomask at both. But maybe we can find some other linking behaviors or patterns I can use as a baseline to look for him at the finish."

Micah let out a single bark of a laugh as she ran a hand over Turnip's insistent head. "Okay, so instead of watching the BRR —which is literally my favorite five days of the year—you want me to comb through hours of footage with no idea what we're looking for?"

"Exactly." Ezren grinned.

"Only for you, Queen of Casolla." Micah bumped her shoulder with a smile. "Let's hunt down this shafter."

CHAPTER 20

5.08.44B BRR Day 5

FOSTER WATCHED the navy swirl of the churn belt roil beneath them as *The Wheels* hovered in orbit above it. He stretched out his arms and legs, testing his freshly healed body as Ezren ran through the plan. Or as close to a plan as they were getting. They'd spent the last two days refining algorithms and running through potential scenarios the Crow might throw at them. And yet he could only hope it would be enough.

Ezren bounced from foot to foot next to the aft emergency hatch. "Okay, Shiro can get us about two and a half hours from the finish line, roughly in the opposite direction of the Walibista Channel. Which works out so we won't disrupt the race or attract attention."

"Ezren, there's a bomb threat at the finish line." He scanned her topsuit for tears for the third time. "There's no way we're not going to disrupt the race."

Ezren leaned down, hugging her thighs against her chest in a deep stretch. "You don't know that. The frontrunners are already in the arena, so if we could make it to the finish line and disable the bomb before they get there, we might still salvage the race."

Foster didn't say anything, but nor did he erase the doubt he knew was scrawled all over his face. He understood the interplanetary ramifications of disrupting the race as well as Ezren did, but as far as he was concerned, they would address that when the time came. Assuming they made it that far.

Ezren straightened, her features pinching when she saw his expression. "Well, we can at least try." Her holo flicked out from her goggs. "Micah and I found a handful of unidentified attendees at the press conference. After she gets on the ground, she and Lowell Coppen are going to see if they can find matches from the BRR coverage so far."

Foster massaged his spasming hand as he looked out at the storm that certainly looked ready to tear them to pieces. "Lowell Coppen, as in *Royaler Review* Lowell Coppen? And we trust him because..."

"Because Micah does."

"Right."

With a smile, Ezren nudged him with her shoulder. "I've sent you the files, so if your goggs find one of our candidates, it'll send you an alert." Ezren began bouncing again. "We still think he's one of Calderon's contemporaries, but with luxie treatments and holomasks and Thread's insider tip, he could look like anyone."

Foster caught her in his arms, wrapping his hands around her back. "And what're we going to do when this is another trap?"

"Then we'll fall back onto one of the contingency plans." Ezren met his gaze, her hands sliding up his shoulder blades over his topsuit. "Either way, we need to get there and spread the word as fast as we can in case it goes bad."

"*In case it goes bad*" had to be one of the biggest understatements in history. They were talking about the finish line blowing up along with them and a good number of people they cared about. But he wasn't going to say that aloud. Ezren knew the risks... even if she was trying to will them to success through a roughshod blend of grit, determination, and software. With anyone else, he would've abandoned the venture right there. But this was Ezren.

And he'd seen her come through with less.

Shiro crossed the common room toward them, his face like stone. "Are you ready?"

Foster shifted, his hand finding Ezren's. "As ready as we're going to be."

"I know you want to find the Crow and end this. But your first priority is getting everyone out safe. Including yourselves." Shiro's face darkened, and Foster couldn't even blame him. His fiancée's life depended on them, and if something happened to her, Foster knew it would kill Shiro too. Just like it would kill Foster if anything happened to Ezren—the two of them forever bound.

Foster glanced at Ezren out of the corner of his eye, chest tightening. "We will."

Micah, still surrounded by holos, rose from the couch, her teal eyes huge. "From *The Royaler Review*'s feed, it looks like Lowell is already down there." She twirled the ends of her hair around her fingers. "Predictably, the finish is reporting comms receipt issues, so I might not be able to fill him in before you arrive, but he'll help you once he knows what you need."

Foster opened his mouth to make another wry comment about *The Royaler Review* when he noticed Micah's hands were shaking. Though Ezren had told him she thought Micah had it bad for the guy, seeing it was a whole different thing. Both she and Shiro were depending on them to get their loved ones out. Not to mention the thousands of others who didn't yet know they were in danger—including Grady/Guns, the Amarals, and his mom.

He took a deep breath as he picked up the jetchute, sliding it across his shoulders. The image of an explosion tearing through their friends rippled through him, and his resolve hardened. As much as he wanted to keep Ezren safe, the atrocity before them was too huge to go unchecked. They had to find the Crow, and they had to end him.

Ezren stepped forward and hugged Micah. "We'll make sure Lowell's safe." She moved to Shiro next, giving him a quick squeeze. "And Sylvia too." Ezren paused as she came to Sam last, but the tension only lasted a breath before he threw his arms around her.

"I would be scared, but I know you can do this," he said.

"Thanks, Sam." Ezren stepped back to get her jetchute, and Sam turned to Foster, his expression grave. "You promised to take care of my sister."

"I did," Foster said, the gravity of the charge weighing on him with the danger that lay before them. He'd already failed Sam twice—first with his dad, and then with Davis. He wouldn't blame Sam in the least if he didn't trust him.

But then Sam barreled into him with a hug. "Just make sure you take care of yourself too. You're the only brother I've got left."

Foster gave him a brief squeeze before pulling away, his throat suddenly thick. "It's okay, we're coming back." He tried for a smile. "I did promise to help you with your homework after all."

"Wait, I'm not the homework person anymore?" Ezren asked with mock indignance.

Micah snorted. "Ez, I hate to break it to you, but you haven't been the homework person since Sam was ten."

A chuckle ran through their small circle, but an alert from Ezren's goggs cut it short.

"Four minutes." Ezren wrinkled her nose at Micah and Sam. "Hope we did our homework right this time."

"And I honestly hope we're relying on something a little

more substantial than hope." Shiro reached out and gave Foster his own rough hug. "Good luck, and don't be afraid to shoot first." He backed toward the cockpit. "Wait for the cue to jump. Micah and Sam, I need your help in the cockpit."

Micah gave them a wink. "Don't forget to record through your goggcams. After all, we wouldn't want some seriously epic footage going to waste."

"Always thinking about VSoc," Foster grumbled as he turned on his goggcam. Though honestly, they could very well need it as evidence once this all was over.

"That's my job," Micah chimed as she bounded away.

With their time counting down in Ezren's holo, Foster eyed the clear hatch beside her dubiously. "Looks like we're running the BRR after all."

"Just the final leg." Ezren grinned at him as if this really was just another race—one that they could win. "For the final time."

Even the sight of her adrenaline-fueled excitement kicked up his own pulse, but they couldn't underestimate how dangerous this would be. They were jumping through Belethea's atmosphere into the churn belt—something he wasn't sure anyone had ever done. From there, they had to traverse the deadly heart of Belethea's storms, and then they'd be entering into a terrorist situation searching for the most dangerous man in the 'verse.

At least this time, they both had pistols strapped to their thighs.

"Ezren." He pulled her into his arms, breathing her in. "Knowing how dangerous this is, I feel like I should be against it. I should be trying to find another way. Trying to protect you. But I want us to have a future that's safe, and this is the only way I see."

"I know." Ezren pulled back to look up at him, her smile

bittersweet now. "When I thought I was going to lose you to the wormgate, I just about shattered." She cupped his cheek with her hand, her skin warm and soft. "We want the same thing, and I think we both understand the risks here." She straightened, her brows furrowing over steely, dark eyes. "But if we survived the BRR, Otho, and the Crow's first assassination attempt, then we can certainly do this." Her hands found his, knotting them together. "He's targeting us because he knows that we can change Casolla. Because we can save them from his shadow. Doing the right thing is a risk, but that doesn't mean we don't do it anyway." She grinned as she attached the cable of her topsuit to his chest. "Besides, this isn't even our first time jumping out of a plane."

"But I'm really hoping it's our last." Dropping into the calm skies of Obrone was a far cry from what they were about to experience. "Somehow I think this one will hurt a little more."

"Maybe." Ezren gave a playful shrug. "But we live and breathe Belethea. We've won this race before, and no one knows the churn better than us."

"Right." Foster's expression creased into a tender smile. There was really no stopping Ezren. From the first time he'd seen her, he'd known she was a force of nature.

Her goggs chimed, and Ezren's eyes rounded. "Thirty seconds to jump."

Foster took her face between his hands in a fierce kiss—hard and brief—hoping to the suns it wouldn't be their last. He rested his forehead against hers, trying to memorize the moment as his thumbs traced her cheeks. "I'd cross a thousand storms for you."

Her gaze darkened with intensity. "And I would've crossed the 'verse for you."

Foster's stomach flipped, his hold on her tightening under the admission. Ezren loved her family—loved Belethea—above all. To follow him through the wormgate and sacrifice every-thing... he couldn't imagine what a price that would've been for her. And yet she held not a flicker of doubt, and he knew, deep in his core, that she would have. Unable to restrain himself, he kissed her again, pressing her against the wall—his emotions unchecked as he tried to drink her in, to absorb all of her, to make this moment last.

But then her goggs chirped again, and their time was up.

"Are you ready?" Shiro called from the cockpit.

Reluctantly, Foster stepped back, pulse pounding and voice rough. "Yeah."

Ezren held Foster's gaze for a stretched breath before grab-bing his helmet and handing it to him. "Just tell us when to jump." Together they slid their helmets on, adjusting their goggs over them. Foster checked Ezren's suit for any leaks as she did the same for him, tapping his chest in approval.

"I'll be doing a steep dive, and then pulling up hard so I can get you as close as I can without the churn sucking the ship in," Shiro said.

"I see the lull in the storm," Micah called. "But you're still going to get tossed around hard, so try to hold on to each other."

"I'm going to wait till the last minute to open the hatch," Sam added. "But it'll only be open for one point nine seconds before it snaps shut again."

Foster wound his arms around Ezren until they seemed almost of one body, the teal designs on their topsuits glowing in the dark. "Count us down."

"Diving now!" Shiro shouted.

The ship plummeted into Belethea's high atmosphere, and Foster's stomach rose into his throat. With one arm still holding Ezren to him, he held on to the bracing loop on the ceiling as they dropped, the ship already fishtailing with the force of the storm below.

"Three!" Sam yelled as the howling of the wind intensified. "Two!"

Foster's grip tightened on Ezren, lightning, wind, and water twisting into a horrifying vortex beneath them. And this was supposed to be a *lull*.

FOSTER: BELETHEA, MOTHER OF MOUNTAINS AND SKIES.

EZREN: PROTECT US.

"One!" The door slid open, and Foster didn't allow himself to hesitate before launching out of it, clutching Ezren to his chest as her limbs knotted around him. The wind whipped by them while the ship banked into a steep climb, and for a moment, whistling through the air, he thought they might survive after all.

And then they hit the clouds.

CHAPTER 21

5.08.44B BRR Day 5

THE FORCE of the wind nearly punched the breath out of Foster, whipping him head over heels through the blinding blast of rain.

The gale buffeted them in every direction through the navy thunderheads like a blade of belweed. It was all he could do to breathe through it, clutching Ezren as tight as he could as the storm tried to rip them apart. At one point in the dark swirl of mist and lightning, deafening wind and roaring thunder, he couldn't even tell if they were hurtling toward the ground anymore. Maybe they'd be falling forever.

EZREN: WE'LL NEED TO DEPLOY THE JETCHUTES IN TWENTY SECONDS... THEY SHOULD BE ABLE TO RIGHT US.

FOSTER: SHOULD IS NOT A GOOD WORD. ARE WE STILL ON COURSE?

EZREN: LET'S NOT WORRY ABOUT THAT UNTIL WE GET ON THE GROUND.

Which basically meant they were already fodded.

EZREN: DEPLOY NOW.

Their jetchutes fired to life in sporadic bursts as they tried to still their spinning trajectory. And yet still they flipped.

EZREN: WE HAVE TOO MUCH MOMENTUM! WE NEED TO SEPARATE!

Foster gripped her tighter.

FOSTER: NO, WE CAN'T. THE CABLE WILL SNAP.

Even as he thought it, the tall mauve spires of the Belethea landscape rushed toward them out of the blackness of the storm.

EZREN: WE HAVE TO!

With one last squeeze she pushed off of him, counter to the force of his spin. Ezren whipped out into the darkness, immediately lost to the driving rain. The cable yanked at his chest, but it was the second yank that threw his heart into a panicked gallop. The cable had snapped.

FOSTER: EZREN!

His jetchute capitalized on the cable's force to slow to a level his goggs assured him had a 78% survivable rate.

EZREN: I'M FINE. FOCUS, FOSTER!

Relief coursed through him in an icy rush, and he forced himself to consider landing. A yawning scar of a canyon cut into the ground before them, surrounded by a host of mossy spire sentries. Still falling much too fast, he angled toward a spire with a gradual slope. The jetchute roared in his ears as it tried to keep him upright at the same time as it pushed air toward the ground.

Praying he didn't break his legs, he let his heels drag against the side of the spire. Not dead yet, he leaned back against the rockface, his whole body from his heels to his shoulders grating against the mossy surface. He was about to congratulate himself on surviving yet another near-death experience when he saw Ezren sliding on her feet in a similar maneuver on an opposite spire.

He opened his mouth to call to her when she leapt over a rock jutting out of the slope. Her jetchute overcompensated for the leap, pitching her forward.

And straight into the canyon.

"Ezren!"

His attention off the ground in front of him, he tripped over an outcropping, sending him spinning into a roll down the slope. Pain radiated through his joints, the alarms in his suit whining as they tried to cushion the blow and maintain integrity. But it was nothing compared to the panic screaming through every cell of his body. What hubris to believe they could survive something like this. The wind howled as he rolled to his feet, and he lifted an arm to shield his goggs from the rain and debris showering down on him.

He sprinted to the edge of the canyon, sliding to his belly after the wind nearly toppled him into it. Turning on his thermal scan, courtesy of Shiro's tactical upgrades, he scoured the bottom of the canyon for Ezren's body—everything numb. How had he let this happen? He should've—

EZREN: FOSTER! LOOK RIGHT—YOUR TWO O'CLOCK.

Foster's gaze whipped to his right, where Ezren clung to the side of the canyon not twenty feet below the edge.

EZREN: CAN YOU DROP ME YOUR TOPSUIT CABLE? THE MOSS IS SO SLICK I CAN'T GET A GRIP.

Foster wasn't sure if he'd ever moved as fast as he did then. Pulling the retractable cord from his chest, he dropped it down to Ezren, shifting to compensate for the wind until the cable hung beside her. Hand over hand, he dragged up the cord until he could reach down and tug Ezren to relative safety.

FOSTER: SUNS, I THOUGHT I'D LOST YOU.

Ezren's chest shook with a chuckle.

EZREN: IN A LITTLE STRATOSPHERIC SKYDIVING? NO WAY.

FOSTER: ARE YOU OKAY?

EZREN: JUST BRUISED—NOTHING TOO BAD.

She pulled away, putting a hand affectionately on his helmet.

Ezren: But we need to move. The longer we stay, the worse the weather will get.

Her holo flicked out from her goggs, and Foster surveyed the storm raging around them. Lightning laced the sky, but so far, he hadn't seen any funnel clouds. Small favors.

Foster: How far off course are we?

Ezren: Aw, where's the faith?

Ezren looked up at him with crinkled eyes.

Foster: Ezren...

Ezren: Okay, so we're more like three hours away than two hours, but the course looks doable, and that still gives us an hour before the finishers are predicted to arrive.

Foster: Unless they're faster than expected.

A flicker of alarm vibrated through Ezren's shoulders, and she grabbed his hand.

Ezren: Right, so let's go.

He didn't miss the limp in her step as she started off, but a quick scan from his goggs told him it was only a sprain, and he knew from personal experience nothing short of amputation would keep Ezren from running. They picked up speed as their legs stretched in long strides in Belethea's 0.75 Earth gravity, debris and rainwater sluicing off their suits as the navy storm took on a furious green-gray tinge. Ezren's algorithm glowed in Foster's goggs, updating their track every three minutes.

While the terraforming research had allowed Ezren and Micah to further refine the algorithm, and it had saved their lives the last time they'd run the BRR, for whatever reason, it was currently only giving them a 64% accuracy estimate. To make it worse, each course update seemed to be significantly different than the last—creating a winding, circuitous route through the conditions.

They slid down into a steep gully, and Foster noted the worry sloping Ezren's brows.

FOSTER: WHAT'S UP WITH THE ALGORITHM?

EZREN: I DON'T KNOW. MY BEST GUESS IS THAT THE CURRENT CONDITIONS ARE OUTSIDE OF ITS RANGE OF EXPECTED PARAMETERS. THAT, OR THE WEATHER'S CHANGING TOO QUICKLY FOR AN ACCURATE PREDICTION.

FOSTER: CAN WE TRUST IT?

Ezren glanced at the sky where two funnel clouds circled each other like dueling serpents.

EZREN: IT MIGHT TAKE US SOME EXTRA TIME, BUT IT'S STILL BETTER THAN NOTHING.

Foster studied the ground around them again, chest pumping and legs burning as they picked up speed—adrenaline and urgency lending them wings. Belethea's spires and ridges fell behind them as they ran, and an open expanse of rocky ground lay open before them. Here, the winds and rains of time had worn the land down to a barren shell with little to no cover on the surface. The gusts were already starting to rise—at their backs for now, but here, the winds could change in a blink.

Though the BRR always followed the same channel to the finish, it seemed like their route currently had them hopping between a few on their way to the final dome still thirty miles away. But at least this, they knew. Together they skirted around a boulder and dipped into a shallow gully, avoiding the rapidly flowing river in the center. Though adrenaline flooded Foster's veins, they'd trained for this—and trained others. This was something they knew how to handle.

One of the twisters touched down a half mile off, and the wind intensified with a howling roar. Ezren stumbled to the side, and Foster grabbed her arm to keep her from going into the river—neither of them stopping their forward motion.

Here, they had to rely on their bodies and instincts.

Ezren: Down!

Foster didn't hesitate as Ezren tugged him into a dive, a rock the size of his helmet sailing overhead. Past them in a breath, Foster pulled Ezren to her feet to continue their relentless path forward. Though it was dangerous to continue, to stay or go backwards would've been suicide. Ezren's eyes crinkled at him, her gaze sparking as they climbed out of the gully, the second funnel cloud touching down with another clamorous roar up ahead.

Foster: What could you possibly be smiling about?

Despite himself, Foster found his own lips curving beneath his helmet. Here in death alley, where so many racers had lost their lives, even he couldn't believe Ezren had that effect on him.

They leapt into another gully, splashing into the narrow ravine as one tornado chased after them from behind, and another raced along beside them.

Ezren: Because we're good at this.

Foster's grin widened.

Foster: Not just good. The best.

Foster couldn't hear her laughter over the wind, but he saw it shake her shoulders as they ran, Belethea coursing over and beneath them. Satisfaction thrummed through Foster's veins—because whether it was true or not, it was something they certainly needed to believe if they were going to make it out of this.

Ezren: You know, we might be the first royalers to voluntarily run through the churn twice.

Foster: If that's true, I'm sure Micah will be posting about it first thing once we survive the bomb threat.

Ezren: Eh, with everything else right now, it

MIGHT TAKE A WHILE TO MAKE THE NEWS CYCLE. I'LL MAKE A NOTE TO REMIND HER IN A FEW WEEKS.

FOSTER: LOOK AT YOU COMING UP WITH CONTENT IDEAS. ARE YOU REALLY MY WIFE?

The glow of Ezren's face intensified.

EZREN: FOR THE REST OF OUR LIVES.

Foster's gaze traced the ring of debris lifting into a shard-studded stone tornado in the distance—a death sentence forming on the horizon.

FOSTER: WELL, LET'S HOPE THOSE LIVES STRETCH PAST TODAY.

The projectiles from the stone tornado thickened, and Foster focused on the terrain in their path. His attention flashed from his feet, to Ezren, to the spiraling vortexes around them. Nothing else existed beyond them and this moment. He couldn't afford it. Especially as somewhere high above the frantic clouds, the sun slipped away, plunging them into a near total darkness only punctuated by the constant flicker of lightning and the teal glow of their topsuits.

Stay in the moment. Focus on your breath.

How many times had he said that to Kit and Dean in the practice sessions? And now he was repeating it to himself.

Nothing had happened before this footstep in the mauve dirt, and he refused to let himself think ahead of it. Breathe in. Breathe out. Focusing on the immediate moment, he dropped into an almost meditative zone, taking in everything and nothing all at once. He wasn't sure how much time passed like that, so when a golden glow appeared on the horizon, it came as a surprise, and he entertained the idea that it might be a mirage, or a pervasive strike of lightning. Ezren, however, had no such qualms, and practically leapt in the air.

EZREN: THE FINISH! IT'S THERE, FOSTER! DO YOU SEE IT? LESS THAN A MILE LEFT!

Though it was a welcome sight, something in Foster's gut didn't quite trust it for some reason.

FOSTER: CAN WE GET IN FROM THIS SIDE?

EZREN: YES, MICAH AND I IDENTIFIED ALL THE ENTRANCES AND EXITS IN CASE WE NEED THEM.

Foster should've been filled with relief, and yet somehow, his dread only grew as they staggered through a channel toward the low-lying building. Then it hit him like a gut-punch—the memory of Ezren falling to the ground, screaming as her suit threatened to strangle her.

But Calderon was dead; there was no way that particular history could repeat itself.

He checked on Ezren, her glowing face and crinkled eyes a far cry from the state she'd been in the last time they'd arrived here, battered and exhausted after covering hundreds of miles. This time they were healthy and prepared for what came next.

But that still didn't stop his pulse from spiking as they rounded the last bend, didn't stop his feet from stumbling. He saw it all in slow motion as Ezren turned around, a questioning smile in her glance as she hugged the wall of the ravine. His gaze trailed to the building not a quarter mile ahead where a small side door opened. Instincts screaming, Foster grabbed Ezren, dragging her behind the channel's curve just as a spray of bullets ate into the rock where she'd been.

Diving to the ground, he covered her with his body, debris raining down on them until the onslaught ceased.

He lifted his head, checking her over with frantic hands.

FOSTER: ARE YOU OKAY?!

EZREN: IT'S OKAY. I'M OKAY.

Staying low, Foster peeked around the corner, only to be met by another volley of gunfire. Ezren yanked him backward, and the wind roared even louder—the algorithm updating in their goggs with a chime.

FOSTER: HE'S COMING TOWARD US.

EZREN: DO YOU THINK IT'S THE CROW?

FOSTER: HONESTLY, I DON'T THINK WE'RE THAT LUCKY.

Ezren drew her gun from her thigh holster and started to move toward the bend, when he caught her by the arm and dragged her backward.

FOSTER: NO, HE KNOWS EXACTLY WHERE WE ARE— HE'LL BE WAITING TO PICK YOU OFF. WE HAVE TO MOVE.

He pulled her to the side of the channel and began to climb.

Ezren followed him without hesitation.

EZREN: THERE'S NO WAY HE'S GOING TO LET US AROUND HIM. HE'S BASICALLY GUARDING OUR WAY IN.

FOSTER: IS THERE ANOTHER DOOR?

Ezren's gaze turned thoughtful as her holo flicked out, highlighting an entrance on each cardinal direction of the outpost.

EZREN: THINK WE CAN OUTRUN HIM?

Foster looked at her holo as she pointed to the mass of red coming up on their tail. Shaft.

FOSTER: I THINK WE'D BETTER BE FAST EITHER WAY.

He pressed a hand against Ezren's back, and together, they sprinted toward the door. The crack of a gun reverberated through the air, and Foster chanced a glance over his shoulder to see the man aiming at them over the lip of the gully. More concerning than that was the massive stone tornado still bearing down on them from behind, flinging man-sized boulders in their direction. While bullets scared him, they were nothing compared to that whipping monstrosity. Ezren stumbled with the force of the wind, and Foster grabbed her wrist to keep her upright even as the wind buffeted him into her.

FOSTER: WE HAVE TO GET LOW!

Ezren: The survival estimate of staying here is 8%.

Shaft. A rock slammed into Foster's spine as if to emphasize Ezren's words, and his mind went to that other storm two years ago. The one that had left Vieve's head cracked open and bleeding into the dirt. Another stone glanced off Ezren's shoulder, and she let out a sharp cry—fear spiking through Foster as another shower of bullets hit the ground beside them—the wind too strong for the auto-aim to compensate. They *had* to go faster. His hand traced the jetpack on Ezren's back, and his eyes widened with realization.

Foster: Hold on!

Linking into their jetchute interface, he turned them from auto to manual, a million warnings beeping through his goggs. Holding Ezren to his chest, he turned the jetchute to maximum propulsion, and they jetted across the dirt.

Ezren let out her manic laugh, and he squeezed her tighter as they cut through the storm headfirst, praying to Belethea's winds to sweep away the bullets and debris. Lightning struck the low dome in front of them, and Foster could've sworn the electricity sizzled on his skin.

He cut the jetchute power right before they could collide with the wall. Sliding to the ground, he turned to see their pursuer running for his own life... much too slow. Their attacker looked over his shoulder at the swirl of rock heading toward him, but it was his last mistake. A powerful gust knocked him to the ground, and in an instant, the tornado was upon him. The wind snatched him from the surface, and Foster thought he could just make out a faint scream. With no time to bear witness to the man's final moments, Foster tugged Ezren back into the channel.

Together they drew their guns as Ezren put in the door code. It hissed open, and Foster tensed—ready to face their next adversary. But no one waited for them in the airlock. With a shared smile of relief, they stepped in and closed the door behind them, shutting out the deadly tornadoes beyond.

Wasting no time, Foster pulled the helmet from his head as Ezren did the same beside him.

"How are we on time?" Foster's chest heaved as he holstered his gun and attached his helmet to his pack, Ezren doing the same beside him.

"Forty-five minutes."

Tugging her close, Foster kissed her hair before strapping his goggs on his head and opening the next door. "Let's go then." If they'd made it through the churn, surely they could handle whatever was next.

The door slid open, and Foster swallowed as they stepped into the huge chamber overflowing with noise and people. The girl next to the door glanced at them, only to do a double take with a strangled screech. In a span of seconds, her shock fanned out in a ripple through the packed audience, all eyes swiveling from the holos glowing across the dome. Foster grabbed Ezren's hand in his, but this time he didn't have to go down on one knee to have a voice.

Because everyone was already looking right at them.

CHAPTER 22

5.08.44B BRR Day 5

EZREN STOOD FROZEN, her breaths still ragged as the shouts echoed around the dome.

"Sterling/Hart is here!"

"But where did they come from?"

"Wait, they aren't racing, right?"

Foster squeezed her hand, and Ezren tried to collect her thoughts.

FOSTER: DO WE JUST ANNOUNCE THERE'S A BOMB?

EZREN: NO, THE PANIC COULD CAUSE A STAMPEDE. WE NEED TO FIND SYLVIA BEFORE WE GET MOBBED.

Which was... easier said than done. Already people were pressing closer with questions, and these were just the fans—once the holologgers found them, she wasn't sure they'd be able to move at all. While her long-range messages were no longer going through, her and Foster's shortwave comms still seemed to be working.

EZREN: SYLVIA, WHERE ARE YOU?

SYLVIA: I'M AT THE FINISH LINE. WHERE ARE YOU?!

EZREN: WE'RE ON THE WEST SIDE OF THE BUILDING, BUT THERE'S A BOMB SET TO GO OFF SOMEWHERE IN HERE,

AND THE CROW IS MESSING WITH COMMS. WE NEED TO
START AN EVACUATION WHILE WE TRY TO FIND IT.

SYLVIA: HOLY FODDING SHAFT. UM, OKAY. I'LL TALK TO
THE CIF ON SITE. WHERE'S SHIRO?

EZREN: HE'S ON HIS WAY. THIRTY MINUTES BEHIND US.

"We're here to deal with urgent ambassador affairs," Foster
said, holding up his arms to ward off the encroaching crowd.
"Let us through."

But Foster's request went unheeded as people pressed
closer to them, cams circling as people tried to squeeze in for a
holo shot or proffered pens for them to sign all manner of BRR
merch.

"Clear the way!" Ezren tried to push through the crowd,
only to realize they may have caused a stampede by their very
presence as the mob shoved back in a wave. Foster caught her
and tugged her to his side, shielding her from the brunt of the
pressure.

FOSTER: SUNS, SYLVIA, HOW'RE WE SUPPOSED TO GET
THROUGH THIS?

But before they got a response, a deafening voice rang
through the crowd.

"Let them pass!" A burly guard cut through the mob, and
Ezren didn't hesitate to duck into the gap he'd created, Foster
close on her heels. But when she nearly ran into Villegas's
furious face, she questioned her decision.

"In here." Villegas led them to a small side room for VIPs,
the door hissing shut behind them with her huge guard
standing like an impenetrable dam between the glass door and
the crowd. "Now." Villegas spread her gnarled hands on a table
in the middle of the room, BRR holos filling the walls as tension
thrummed from her. "Where the fod have you been? You've
been completely missing in action for a week. There were even
rumors you'd gone through the wormgate. And now..." She

gestured to their sweaty hair and scuffed suits. "Why are you coming in the side door looking like you ran the race yourselves?"

Ezren's impatience surged through her in a hot flame. "We don't have time for explanations, Ambassador."

Villegas gave a derisive snort. "Oh, I'm sorry, are you late for so—"

"The Crow planted a bomb, and it's set to go off when the winners arrive," Foster said, his voice flat. "We need to evacuate everyone immediately."

Villegas reared back as if she'd slapped him. "Do you have proof?"

"No," Ezren said, her hands fisting at her sides. "But you have to trust us. The Crow tried to get rid of Foster, and now he's striking back here."

Villegas dropped into one of the armchairs surrounding the table. "Okay. Yes, I see Sylvia has already alerted security." She took in a deep breath and sat up straight. "But we will physically have to pry people away from the finish line to get them out of here. Without proof, there's no way they'll believe this."

Ezren chewed her lip as she thought through their plans that now seemed so much more uncertain in the face of the chaos. "I think if we can get enough people they trust to back us, we can make an impact. Is there a good place I can address the crowd?"

"You'll have to turn off the race coverage first," Foster said, adjusting his goggs in his hair. "Or else there's no way they'll listen."

"I'll take you to the winner's podium." Villegas's lips thinned as she got to her feet. "Suns, what a mess."

With that, Villegas led them back into the suffocating crush of people. Her guard had managed to find backup, and the two of them jostled and barked their away across the dome. By the time they arrived at the winner's podium, Greta and Sylvia were both there with matching expressions of concern.

Sylvia bobbed her head to Villegas, not forgetting her courtesy even in the midst of crisis. "Security is moving into place to escort the first wave of spectators to the trains."

Villegas's lips twitched as she gestured to the open platform. "Well, here we go. Hart, you're walking the line between panic and survival. Tread lightly."

Not having any idea how to respond to something like that, Ezren only nodded as she turned to Foster. "You'll help me?"

He squeezed her hand. "Of course."

At once, the racing holos all winked out—the dome filling with gasps of confusion and outrage—and then together, Ezren and Foster stepped onto the stage.

A horde of hovercams descended upon them, and Ezren had to swallow her heart back down before she started to speak. "My name is Ezren Hart, and in the past year, I've asked for your attention as I've spoken on the race royale, on terraforming, and on extraterrestrial life. Today, I'm asking you to listen for your own safety. I know many of you have crossed the system to see the finish. That for many of you, this is a once-in-a-lifetime event. And please know that both as a royaler myself and a member of the BRR council, I do not make this announcement lightly. But security has received a credible threat, and we must ask all of you to evacuate while we attempt to neutralize the danger to both our royalers and the fans."

The crowd roared in dismay, but none of them moved toward the exits. Shouts spiked through the rising rabble, and Ezren had to fight to keep her expression neutral.

"Can they at least turn the race coverage back on?"

"What if we don't want to leave?"

"Get off the stage!"

Ezren looked to Foster, and he stepped forward, his face a

storm, and his voice nearly deafening as he artificially projected it through the sound system. *"She said."* He paused, and the dome fell into silence. "You need to leave. Now." Another, quieter murmur rippled through the crowd, and his gaze hardened. "Coverage of the BRR will only be continued in the trains themselves and in the waiting area. So if you want to watch the race, I suggest you move toward the exit. Security is in place to guide you."

"And if you see anything suspicious, please report it immediately to security," Ezren added. "This is not a situation to be taken lightly."

With another mass of grumbling, the crowd slowly turned toward the exit.

"Well, that was surprisingly well done," Villegas said, her arms crossed from where she stood off to one side.

Greta frowned. "I would've just told them there was a bomb and let them run each other over."

Sylvia let out a nervous laugh. "Yes, well, I'm not sure how effective that would be, but if you and Ambassador Villegas could make your own holos encouraging a calm evacuation, I'm sure that would go a long way."

Greta moved to Foster and Ezren, putting a hand on each of their arms as an anxious crease fissured her brow. "Are you okay? We've been so worried about you." Her frown deepened as she took in their grit-smudged cheeks and torn topsuits. "Apparently for good reason."

"We'll be fine once we get out of this," Ezren assured her, a familiar face in the crowd leaping out at her. "And I think I know someone else who can help."

Lowell Coppen's hazel eyes widened with alarm as Ezren zeroed in on him. He started to turn away just as she leapt down from the stage. "Hey!" She grabbed the rolled-up sleeve of his button-down before he could flee.

"Um... yes?" He adjusted the plain black goggs amidst his auburn curls, his cheeks pinking.

"You're Lowell Coppen from *The Royaler Review*."

"Yes, and I was just moving toward the evacuation—"

"Listen. Micah told me."

The blood drained from Lowell's face, and his gaze flicked to Sylvia—who was thankfully distracted by recording holo messages of Villegas and Greta onstage. "Micah? Belethea's holologger? She told you—"

"Oh, stop." Ezren pulled him into the corner between the stage and the dome wall, Foster watching them protectively from above. "The Crow's planted a bomb in this building, and I need your help." She flicked the file she and Micah had compiled to his goggs.

Lowell's already huge eyes shot wide. "But what can I—"

"Shh, pay attention." Ezren pointed to her holopro flickering between them. "I need you to cross-reference these people with the footage you have from today to see if any of them are present. Can you do that?"

His expression grew thoughtful as he regarded the holo. "Yeah, I should be able to pull from both my cache and the latest VSoc coverage. We got quite a few leads when we put out the information bounty for the Crow." He scratched at his fluffy auburn hair, apology and anxiety mixing in the lines of his frown. "But... if it's a large bomb, you know that not everyone here will be able to get out on the first train."

"I know; we're working on it."

He nodded a little too quickly, his Adam's apple bobbing. "Did, uh, Micah come with you?"

"No, she's safe."

He blew out a relieved breath, his shoulders sagging. "Thank the suns."

And in that moment, Ezren realized that no matter who he

worked for, Ezren was going to like this guy. "We're going to be friends, you and I." She clapped him on the shoulder with a smile. "Stay safe, Lowell, and if you get a match let me know."

"I will." He offered her a grim smile. "Good luck, Ezren."

"Ezren," Sylvia called, her voice strung taut.

Ezren leapt onto the stage and jogged to her side. "What's wrong?"

"Was *The Royaler Review* bothering you? At a time like this?" Sylvia glared over Ezren's shoulder at Lowell. "I'll kill him myself."

"No, no, no." Ezren waved her arms frantically. "He's helping." But before she could defend Lowell further, Foster's stony face caught her eye. "What's wrong?

Foster turned away from the crowd, his voice low. "The trains are down, and the storms outside are getting worse."

"We're turning the race coverage back on to distract them." Sylvia glanced to where both Villegas and Greta troubleshot with the race organizers. "And we've got maintenance trying to diagnose the train problem, but we think it's a cyberattack."

"It's only a matter of time before people start to panic," Foster added.

"The storms?" Ezren pulled up her weather holo to find that, indeed, since their arrival, storm intensity had tripled. The windspeed now would soon be too strong to run through—maybe even enough to compromise the dome. "But that's so strange. What could've caused such a sudden escalation?"

Foster's gaze held hers. "What if the bomb is made of terranium?"

Ezren's heart sank as she grappled with the possibility. The energy-dense terranium was hypothesized to be the cause of Belethea's vicious storms and unpredictable weather. And it was also used to power arks, domes, and the wormgate itself. Though it was much too valuable to be used as a common explosive it was... Suns, they weren't talking about a small bomb.

"If it's strong enough to affect the weather, it'll level this whole place," Ezren whispered.

Ezren's algorithm updated with another alert, the winds continuing to intensify, and the survival odds dropping to 60%.

Foster turned to Sylvia. "You have to get them to hold the racers at the brawl arena until we sort this out."

Sylvia ran her hands through her mane of curls. "We already have, but unfortunately there were five teams that had already left."

Ezren covered her mouth with a hand. "And Grady/Guns is one of them." It wasn't a question. "Can someone go and get them?"

"They can't," Foster said. "We'd just be sending out more people to die. If anyone can survive out there, it's them." His stormy eyes softened as they met hers, his words gentle. "We have to trust them and do what we can here. If it slows them down though, it might buy us some time to find the bomb."

"Right." Ezren checked the time in her goggs. With fifteen minutes passed, she was tracking they had forty-five left to find the bomb. But at least now she knew what they were looking for. She brought the schematic up in her goggs. The outpost had a half-dozen floors reaching deep in the ground, and with the density of terranium, it didn't have to be that big to do a lot of damage. "If it was on this floor, someone would've seen it already. We'll start at the bottom and work our way to the top."

"Be careful," Sylvia said, tugging at her curls. "I'll send Shiro to help you once he gets here."

"The first priority is to get the trains working," Foster said as he followed Ezren toward the stairwell. "Then we go from there."

Ezren sent a mental command to open the dome's interior

door only for an error to pop up in her goggs. Frowning, she reached out to manually slide it open, but it didn't give. Her breath caught in her throat, the icy fear coating her lungs. "*Foster.*"

Foster reached out and tried to force the door open. Nothing. "Shaft." He pulled again as Ezren jogged down to an exterior door a few strides away. Heart racing, she sent the mental command. *Error.* No, no, no, no, no. She yanked on it, but the heavy metal door remained shut as if welded there.

"Foster!" Her wide eyes met his, and she took in the crowded room once more.

Ezren: We're locked in.

Which meant... even if the racers did get here, there was no way to let them in. Ezren leaned against the door as the realization hit her. They had walked into the trap, and it had snapped closed. Now that they were here, there was no way in or out. Her heart raced, the swirl of sharpening panic punctuated by the blare of a mayday call.

And then the sharp cut of silence as it turned off.

A horrified gasp ran through the crowd when another mayday rang through the dome—and then once again fell silent.

Silence dropped over the crowd in a suffocating blanket, two large holos in the middle of the dome now shining a bright red.

And then the soft, trembling notes of the storm dirge began to play over the comms.

The death knell of a royaler.

CHAPTER 23

5.08.44B BRR Day 5

FOSTER WHIRLED TOWARD THE HOLOS, and then to Sylvia. "Who was it?" His voice cracked with desperation. "Tell me they weren't ours."

A bead of sweat streaked down Sylvia's temple, her eyes glistening as she shook her head, her voice quiet. "It wasn't, Foster." She enlarged two of her holos. "Kit and Dean are still on the wheels and Grady/Guns are crawling in the corner of the channel. They're fine."

"For now." Ezren staggered over to them, her countenance a sheet of white. "Survival rates in the channel are dropping by the second."

Distress bubbled through the crowd, the scent of panic not far off, but there was nothing they could do about it that they weren't already doing. The place was built like a fortress, and now it was on lockdown.

"Foster," Ezren whispered.

Foster turned to see a holopro glowing from her goggs. A raven cawed in a skeletal tree with bloody letters written across the bark.

The change of plans was worth it to watch you squirm. The poetry of watching it all come crashing down right where it began. Even separated by generations, the blood smells the same.

Foster's ears began to ring—the clamor in the crowds, the horror on Ezren's face, despair shaking Sylvia's shoulders, Grady and Bex desperately clinging to life in an impossible storm. Enough.

He turned to Ezren, squeezing her elbows as his voice pitched. "Ezren, you told me we could do anything, right?"

Ezren nodded, but he could see the tremble of her chin, her teeth chattering with adrenaline. "I did."

"Well, now's the time," Foster said, his mind racing. "There's got to be room for pedestrians in the train tunnel."

"Right," his mom said, already running toward the trains. "I'll direct them."

"And I'll get you some help," Sylvia said as she moved toward the race organizers. On their other side, the guy with reddish hair and the hololgger badge of *The Royaler Review* on his sports jacket jumped onto the stage. Foster's hand clenched into a fist, his voice a growl. "If you're here for an interview, I'm going to throw you off the stage."

"It's okay." Ezren put a calming hand on Foster's chest. "Lowell, what do you have for us?"

Foster frowned in confusion. *Lowell?* How was Ezren already on a first-name basis with this guy?

With a nervous glance at Foster, Lowell edged closer to Ezren, projecting a holo. "Well, I figured looking for suspicious faces would take too long. After I saw we were locked in, I did a check of the last people to use the doors out of the atrium, and I found one that was also present during the press conference." He pulled up the image of a man with a medium build, tan skin, and close-cropped brown hair. "Recognize him? He has on a security event badge."

Foster shook his head. The man was so nondescript, he could've passed him a dozen times in the crowd without noticing. "No. Not familiar."

Ezren's lips twisted. "I just sent it to Sylvia and Villegas, but they don't recognize him either."

"And if it's a holomask, he may have changed his appearance already. Or it could even be one of his Talons." Foster scraped a hand over his jaw. From the messages, he was almost certain that the Crow was a contemporary of Calderon's that had been present for the original race. But that guy was too young, and he didn't match any of the original holos they'd seen. "But if his security badge is legit, no one would question him."

"Well, he was the last one to go out, and that's also the last time he's caught on any of the building cams." Lowell brushed away the holo to bring up a schematic of the building. "The door he went out of leads to the south elevator bank, and he left about ten minutes ago."

"Lowell, put out a BOLO for this guy." Foster was already moving in the direction of the exit. "We're going to try to break through the doors."

"Comms are back up!" Sylvia shouted to them across the crowd.

Foster paused and turned to Ezren. "Why does that just make me feel worse?"

Somehow, Ezren's already pale skin managed to go a shade whiter. "Because at this point there's no time for help to get here, and no warning would help either. Plus..." Ezren rolled one shoulder and then the other, a strange, almost angry tension to her—like she was about to jump into a brawl. "He probably wants the 'verse to watch what he's about to do."

They passed by Sylvia, and Foster squeezed her arm. "We're going to try to find the Crow. If something happens to Grady and Bex..."

"It won't. I'm going to get them out." Sylvia put a hand over his and lifted her chin, her firm gaze shifting to Ezren. "Just make sure you're back for Simon's stupid umbrella drinks."

Ezren gave her a slim smile. "We wouldn't miss it."

Then Foster was pulling Ezren through the crowd toward the door. While people still noticed them, with the evacuation in progress, security barking all manner of commands, and the increasing danger to the royalers in the channel, they were now old news.

Foster shouldered through the final knot of people to the secluded side doors their suspect had left through. "Please tell me you can use your hacking magic to open the doors."

"I've already tried, but these have an added cyber lock on them to keep people out." The dome shuddered above them as a boulder smashed into it, and Ezren snapped up with a sudden realization. "But luckily, I know someone we can call."

Her holopro glowed in front of them until Sam's angular features appeared. "Ezren! I saw comms are back up; does that mean you fixed everything?"

Foster added "a false sense of security" to their current list of problems.

"No, Sam," Ezren said. "But I need to get through this door. Can you remote hack into it for us?"

"Let me see." Sam's nose scrunched as he connected to the door with a chime. "Um, yeah. Actually, it looks like this is the same security that was on the Crow ship."

A smile that could've rivaled a sunny day lit Ezren's face. "I thought so."

"Just give me thirty seconds," Sam said. "I'm sending you the virus code in case you run into any other Crow tech barricades."

Foster's mouth quirked up. "I thought you said the magic wouldn't work?"

"You said *my* hacking magic," Ezren said. "This is Sam's."

"So, it runs in the family." Foster hugged her to him with a surge of affection. "That's good to know."

"Stop being gross. I'm right here," Sam said. "And your door's unlocked."

Foster released Ezren with a grin. "Thanks, Sam, do you think you can work on the other doors too?"

"And the trains," Ezren added.

"On it," Sam said. "Good luck."

Sam's holo winked out, and Foster drew his gun as the doors opened, ready for whatever was waiting on the other side. But only an open elevator beckoned them forward. Foster took a step toward it when the rattling of the dome reached its peak. The algorithm in Foster's goggs blared in a long low tone he'd never heard before.

"What is that?" But when he turned to Ezren, her gaze was on the ceiling, her face a sheet white.

"Oh no," she whispered.

Barely were the words out of her mouth before the shriek of tearing metal echoed through the building. Screams ripped through the crowd as the dome peeled from the surface like the lid of a tin can. And above them, no less than a dozen stone-strewn twisters of a whip squall streaked the sky.

"Sylvia!" Ezren yelled, but Foster grabbed her around the middle, adrenaline sharpening every point of him as rain, hail, and rock began to pelt the mob—announcements about evacuating cycling through his goggs. "Let me go, Foster, we have to help them!"

Foster shook his head. "We have to trust that they can handle it." He hauled her into the elevator and jammed the code for the freight train floor on the fourth basement level. "If the storms are this bad, Ezren, the terranium has to be insane. We need to get it out before it causes more damage."

Breathing deep, Ezren forced her shaking hands into fists.

"Yes. Terranium has a natural energy emanation, but for this magnitude, I think it would have to be destabilized terranium. While a small amount of terranium becomes destabilized naturally in nature—especially in the churn belt—to cause this magnitude of a change, it would have to be on the order of several tons." Her expression clouded as she shook her head. "I don't even know how we could move that, Foster, and we don't have the equipment or time to try to stabilize it again."

The elevator chimed as it dropped them on the third to lowest level of the outpost. Foster raised his gun as the doors slid open, an eerie silence greeting them from the dark bowels of the basement. His heart pounded in his throat as he took a slow step into the inky blackness, the beam of light from his goggs sweeping across the bare metal corridor. "Ezren, do they store terranium here?"

Ezren shook her head as she drew her own gun. "No, after last year's drama, Calderon moved all of their research activities to other outposts."

"Then that means they had to transport the terranium in." He swallowed, swiveling as a shadow flickered across the gray wall. "Which means we can get it out." Turning a corner, Foster stepped on something soft and retreated a quick step, putting a protective arm out to shield Ezren.

"What?" She peered around him, and then stifled a gasp. "Oh suns."

A body lay in the hall, a blank stare like two hollow pinpricks in the darkness. From his uniform, it looked like a member of event security. Well, that explained why no one had called in any suspicious activity. The iron tang of blood filled the air, and Foster's stomach rolled, images of the Crow's torture chamber flooding his mind.

No, stay in the moment.

With a hand, he shifted Ezren until she was squarely

behind him. If someone shot him from the darkness, he wanted to be sure she had a chance to run. "The train tunnel isn't far."

Stepping over the body, they continued down the hall, the roar of the storm just barely audible through the floors above. Foster could only hope Sam had managed to open the doors in time for them to evacuate, but he couldn't afford the distraction of checking.

EZREN: WHAT IF THE CROW BROUGHT A WHOLE CREW?

FOSTER: THEN WE'RE GOING TO HAVE TO BE READY TO RUN. BUT THE FINISH LINE IS NOTORIOUSLY HARD TO GET INTO. I'M ALREADY IMPRESSED THE CROW HAD TWO PEOPLE IN HERE.

EZREN: FOSTER, IF SOMETHING HAPPENS...

She didn't finish the thought, and Foster sucked in a breath as he rounded the next corner. For a moment, he let the words sit between them. Because the fact of the matter was, if something happened, the odds that they were both leaving the world together were incredibly high.

FOSTER: EZREN, IF SOMETHING HAPPENS, JUST KNOW THAT I'LL LOVE YOU IN THIS LIFE AND INTO THE NEXT. IN STORMS, FIRE, AND THE BEYOND. I'LL BE WITH YOU.

Her fingers slid down the length of his back.

FOSTER: BUT KNOW THAT I WILL DO EVERYTHING IN MY POWER TO MAKE SURE THAT DOESN'T HAPPEN.

EZREN: I KNOW. EVEN HERE IN THE CENTER OF THE STORM, IN THE BELLY OF DARKNESS, I FEEL SAFE WALKING WITH YOU. THE ODDS MAY BE STACKED AGAINST US, BUT I STILL BELIEVE WE CAN DO ANYTHING.

It was at that moment that Foster almost tripped over the second body. His mag-boots splashed in the puddle of dark liquid, and he looked down to find that this one had lost a head.

Fodding shaft.

Ezren peeked around him before bending over, stifling a

gag as she covered her nose with her arm. Foster's head spun, the rusted stench assaulting all of his senses at once before Ezren pushed him on and past.

EZREN: WE HAVE TO KEEP MOVING. YOU OKAY?

FOSTER: No. BUT YOU'RE RIGHT. WE HAVE TO KEEP MOVING.

Even separated by generations, the blood smells the same.

At least there was no doubt that it was the Crow down here. A small consolation, but at this point, he'd cling to each and every sliver of information they could get.

Finally they rounded the last corner, emerging into a dark, metal tunnel with mag-tracks running down the center of it but no train. Foster swore inwardly, continuing his sweep across the platform until he finally encountered what they were looking for. There, in the farthest corner, sat a terranium cube as tall as him glowing a deep green, and written in blood along the wall was yet another message for them.

Welcome Sterling/Hart, to your grand finale.

Nausea coiled in Foster's belly as his gaze dropped to the side of the bomb where a timer glowed with a countdown. A bead of sweat trickled along Foster's temple.

Because they had only nineteen minutes left.

And time was ticking.

CHAPTER 24

5.08.44B BRR Day 5

AS SOON AS Ezren laid eyes on the three-ton block of terranium, her heart sank. Her attention flicked to the small holos in her goggs where Simon and Bex had taken shelter in a crevice. Another holo showed the live feed of the destroyed atrium with its ceiling open to the elements and survivors huddled amidst the wreckage. Most of the spectators had evacuated to the train tubes, but from the messages in her goggs, Sam still hadn't managed to get the trains working.

She shook her head, trying to toss off the despair threatening to suffocate her. If the Crow could get this monstrosity down here, there had to be some way to get it out. She crossed to the terranium, careful not to touch it as she bent to examine the base.

"It's still on a hover-dolly, so we should be able to move it between the two of us." Her lips pressed into a thin line. "But there's no way we could fit it in the elevator or the stairs. We have to get a train, but the two here are still on lockdown. In eighteen minutes..." She shook her head. "I'll call Micah and see if she can help Sam."

Foster nodded as he moved beside her, his gaze still strafing the darkness. "We could program the hover-dolly to go down the tracks too, right?"

Ezren's frown deepened. "The hover-dolly moves at walking speed, and by the size of it, it wouldn't do us much good."

EZREN: MICAH, ARE YOU HELPING SAM WITH THE TRAIN ISSUE?

MICAH: YES, BUT WE SUSPECT THERE'S A MANUAL SWITCH. I'M ACTUALLY ON MY WAY TO CHECK IT OUT RIGHT NOW.

Ezren shared a confused glance with Foster.

EZREN: WHAT? WHERE ARE YOU?

MICAH: I'M AT THE FINISH LINE WITH SHIRO. WE JUST GOT HERE.

Ezren's heart leapt. She'd forgotten Shiro was coming, but Micah tagging along on the train was not in the plan. Suns, she'd better not have come for better finish line coverage. In any event, Ezren didn't have time to grill her for putting her life at risk unnecessarily. At least Sam wasn't there—that she knew of. The thought was enough to send a fresh wave of anxiety erupting into gooseflesh across her arms.

EZREN: WAIT, YOU CAME ON A TRAIN, RIGHT?

MICAH: WELL, YEAH. HAVE YOU SEEN THIS WEATHER?

FOSTER: MICAH. WE NEED THE TRAIN THAT YOU CAME IN. SEND IT DOWN TO LEVEL 4B RIGHT NOW.

MICAH: YOU DON'T WANT TO USE IT FOR THE EVACUATION?

EZREN: MICAH, PLEASE JUST DO IT. WE'LL EXPLAIN LATER.

MICAH: YOU GOT IT.

Ezren added Shiro to their comm channel.

EZREN: ALSO YOU AND SHIRO NEED TO EVACUATE IMMEDIATELY. IT'S NOT SAFE FOR ANYONE.

SHIRO: WE KNOW. THAT'S WHY WE'RE HERE. THERE'S

STILL A LOT OF PEOPLE UPSTAIRS WE NEED TO GET TO SAFETY.

FOSTER: STAY AS FAR AWAY FROM 4B AS POSSIBLE AND USE THE EASTERN TUNNELS. ALSO, CAN YOU MAKE SURE MY MOM GETS OUT? I'M WORRIED SHE WON'T LEAVE WITHOUT HER ROYALERS.

SHIRO: SHE AND SYLVIA BOTH.

MICAH: ...LOWELL TOO.

EZREN: IN SEVENTEEN MINUTES, YOU'RE ALL GOING TO BE BETTER OFF OUT IN THE STORM THAN INSIDE.

MICAH: UM, EZREN, SERIOUSLY, ARE YOU SEEING THIS STORM RIGHT NOW? WE'RE TALKING RECORD-BREAKING.

EZREN: TRUST ME, MICAH. IF THERE ARE EXTRA TOPSUITS SOMEWHERE, I RECOMMEND YOU ALL PUT THEM ON.

FOSTER: AND PLEASE TELL ME THAT SAM DIDN'T COME WITH YOU THIS TIME.

MICAH: HE DIDN'T. HE'S STILL SAFE ON THE SHIP.

EZREN: AND YOU SHOULD BE WITH HIM.

MICAH: I CAN HELP JUST LIKE EVERYONE ELSE. AND... I ALSO HAVE TO GET LOWELL OUT.

SHIRO: SPEAKING OF, HE TOLD US ABOUT THE IMPOSTOR. DON'T FORGET TO USE THE GOGGS MOD I SENT YOU IF YOU RUN INTO ANYONE DOWN THERE.

FOSTER: THANKS, SHIRO. BUT I IMAGINE WHOEVER SET THIS BOMB PROBABLY WENT THEIR WAY ON THE TRAIN.

SHIRO: SO WHAT ARE YOU GOING TO DO WITH IT?

The sound of smoothly oiled tracks echoed through the tunnel, and Ezren's heart soared as the magtrain rolled into the freight station.

EZREN: WE'RE GOING TO MOVE IT. I'M SENDING YOU THE TIMER, BUT WE ONLY HAVE FIFTEEN MINUTES.

The train doors slid open, and Ezren smiled at Foster. "Let's do this."

Foster activated the hover-dolly, and it came to life with a cheery hum, lifting the huge mass of terranium an eighth of an inch from the ground. Bracing their shoulders carefully against the cube, the two of them began to move it onto the train when Ezren's goggs chimed again.

LOWELL: HEY, I JUST WANTED TO LET YOU KNOW, I WAS LOOKING AT THE FOOTAGE, AND I THINK WHOEVER IS UNDER THE HOLOMASK IS ACTUALLY A WOMAN.

Ezren's brow furrowed.

EZREN: WHY DO YOU THINK THAT?

LOWELL: THE WAY THE GUY WALKS, THE WAY HIS CLOTHES FIT... THEN I DID A REVERSE SEARCH AND DUG UP A VIDEO OF THAT GUY WITH THE SAME FACE FROM A COUPLE YEARS AGO ON VSOC. THAT GUY WAS 6′ 4″ AND 250 LBS., AND WALKED COMPLETELY DIFFERENTLY THAN THE 5′ 11″ 150 LB. PERSON WEARING THE MASK.

EZREN: OKAY, THANKS, LOWELL. ALSO, MICAH'S COMING TO YOU. MAKE SURE YOU KEEP HER SAFE.

LOWELL: WHAT?!!? I TOLD HER SPECIFICALLY NOT TO COME. I'VE BEEN FRITZING OUT FOR DAYS THINKING SHE WAS DEAD AND NOW... JUST WHY?

LOWELL: NO, IT'S FINE. IT'LL BE FINE. I'LL FIND HER. THANKS FOR LETTING ME KNOW.

Ezren turned to Foster as they eased the dolly onto the train. "So, Lowell says he thinks the person behind the mask is a woman."

"A woman?" Foster's brow creased. "Interesting. Thread did say she had no idea who the actual Crow was. I guess I just assumed a man. Does it make a difference?"

"Well." With a series of quick mental commands, Ezren deactivated the hover-dolly so the terranium sank to the floor of the train and activated the empty freight train's mag-restraints. They belted to the metal dolly with a sharp snap. "It's just weird because if we think that the Crow is actually one of the original racers, the only possibilities are Carmella, who died in the churn, and another spacer, who died a couple months later." Ezren started to link to the train as they turned to exit, but something was blocking her.

"So either we're wrong or—"

"Foster," Ezren interrupted him as she whirled toward the driver's compartment. "Someone's trying to take control of the train."

"What?" Foster's body jolted to attention as he followed her. "Remotely?"

"I don't know." Ezren sprinted into the manual control station. "But I think I can override it."

Ezren opened the cab door and raced in, booting up the manual controls and following the instructions for the override before shoving up the lever to lock the accelerator into place. "Okay, it's fine. I got it. Now we just need to get off. Hurry!"

The train was slowly edging forward as they reached the exterior doors. Ezren linked to them with her chip but got no response.

Shaft.

"Foster, someone's locked the doors!" she shouted, the tunnel walls already starting to blur around them.

"But how did they—"

Foster didn't finish his sentence before Ezren saw a silhouette stalking down the train toward them.

"In here!" She yanked Foster into the driver's cab, jamming the door closed just as a shower of laser-lead scorched the door.

"Who the fod is that?" Foster shouted.

Ezren's eyes widened as a message came in through the goggs.

Oh come now, Sterling/Hart, you already know.

CHAPTER 25

5.08.44B BRR Day 5

FOSTER TRIED to focus on the figure stalking toward them in the rapidly accelerating train, a storm of rage and fear bolting through him.

"They're hacking the door!" Ezren strained to hold the door closed. "It's trying to open."

Foster braced against the door with her, jamming his shoulder and back against it. "How long do we have to stall before the blast is out of range?"

Ezren consulted the holo in her goggs. "Not long. We're already moving at over two hundred miles an hour, so we'll be out of range in a minute or two."

Foster consulted his goggs, understanding the problem immediately. There were still eleven minutes to the blast. If the Crow could turn the train around, they had to get it far enough so that it didn't have time to return if they lost control. "Okay, so we need to ride it for six minutes and then get off."

Ezren groaned as she strained against the door. "Yeah, and between our jetchutes and topsuits, I think we might be able to exit without slowing... if we can get the doors to open."

"Forget the doors." A bullet smashed into the reinforced glass window above them, shattering it, and Foster pulled

Ezren low. "We can break the doors down. We just need to take care of our visitor first."

Ezren nodded, her face dark. "It's the only way to ensure he won't mess with the bomb timing. Somehow I doubt he would blow us up with himself on board."

"Don't be so sure. I don't think we can assume sanity at this point. I'm getting the feeling that whoever this is would rather die than lose here."

"Okay, but they'll try to kill us first and turn the train around for maximum impact."

Foster peeked over the now broken window, and his breath caught in his chest. Because the spitting image of Thread stalked down the ramp—her hair now a honey-gold, her eyes a bright green, and a tear-like birthmark on her cheek. Even though they shared the exact same features, he could tell in an instant this was not the tortured, kindhearted Thread that had healed Davis and him time and time again. This woman's face was twisted with a murderous hate, her stare wild, and a cruel, unhinged smile stretched across her cheeks.

"It's Carmella," he breathed.

Ezren yanked him down just as another volley of shots cascaded above their heads. "But I thought she died in the original royale."

A silky-smooth voice cut through the train, much too close for comfort. "Now, now, let's not go around spreading false rumors."

Foster popped up and squeezed off three shots before ducking back down.

EZREN: Maybe we can stall her.

"But I don't understand," Ezren called. "I thought you were Calderon's love—that the BRR was your dream."

Foster let the door crack open, wedging the muzzle of his

gun in the space and firing again, but Carmella was now too close to the bomb to risk a direct shot.

"Take care, Sterling," Carmella crooned. "I don't think a fiery, self-sacrificing end was the legacy dear Warner had in mind for you."

"But why are you doing this?" Ezren called again.

"Warner and I were partners when we discovered the terranium. Of course the other planets tried to steal it, so we came up with the BRR to save our skins. While I did come a hair's breadth from dying, Warner was able to resuscitate me unbeknownst to the others, but we decided my death was just part of the sob story legacy we would build to sell the deal. Through it all, we'd always planned to build Belethea into a power able to take it all back." Her smile grew, her canines the same kind of sharp that Calderon's had been in the old-world style. "I started taking out our enemies from the darkness, priming for our rise to power... but then Warner had to get a fodding conscience."

She ran a finger along the edge of the bomb. "At first we just kept to our own separate worlds, and it seemed like we could divide the system between the two of us." She rolled her eyes. "But then, he started to interfere and the cracks between us grew." She stalked toward them, the bomb directly behind her. "I suppose he fell in love with the BRR, and Belethea herself. He wanted to preserve us all in amber, even as he rejected the fountain of youth when we found it." She shook her head, anger etched into her unnaturally young face. "He was a fool, and though I loved him once, eventually his sanctimony grew too much to bear."

Foster took a deep breath as he tried to measure Carmella's steps. Though they couldn't risk taking a shot at her, soon she would be close enough to angle her gun through the door window, and they couldn't wait that long. Foster squeezed Ezren's shoulder.

Foster: I'm going to try to disarm her and go hand-to-hand. If you can swing around back, I think we can easily overpower her.

Ezren: Don't underestimate her—I'm fairly certain she's been cybernetically enhanced. Her footsteps are too heavy, and the way she's moving is too smooth.

Fodding shaft. While cybernetic enhancements were intensely regulated, of course that wouldn't at all affect a syndicate king—no, queen—with access to literally anything and everything. While he'd never had any firsthand experience with an augmented adversary, he'd heard from Shiro that they could be up to twenty-percent stronger and faster than even the best topsuit boost.

But there was nothing for it. She was too close now, and his window was small. Attack was the last defense they had.

"Still, I was shocked when he chose you, Sterling," Carmella continued. "And a little jealous. Especially after I'd made us the perfect heir. Perfectly malleable, perfectly us—and he rejected it." Venom coated her words. "And for what? Some faddish, nepotistic upstart?"

Foster: Just be sure she doesn't get to the train controls. Let the door go.

With that, they let the door slam open, and Foster leapt forward, barreling into Carmella's knees. It should have knocked her to the ground, but instead Foster felt like he hit a steel wall. *Shaft.*

Carmella chuckled as she pointed her gun down at him. "Mistake."

A shot caught her straight in the chest, the bolt crackling through her as Ezren stood in the cab. *"Don't touch him."*

Foster seized the moment to wrench the gun from Carmella's grasp while Ezren fired again. But the electric arcs rippling over Carmella only gave her the slightest pause. Foster fired a shot, tearing a hole into her space suit, but no blood flowed. Foster's chest iced over with horror as he shifted back toward the controls.

"Suns, are you human at all?" he whispered, Thread's warning echoing back to him all too late.

"An excellent question. Philosophical really." Carmella smiled as she shook away the electricity like one might flick off the rain. "In fairness, after the storms got me the first time, regeneration technology wasn't as advanced as it is now... and it took them eight hours of resuscitation measures to get a heartbeat. My brain functionality was mildly compromised, so naturally the augmentation started there. And then my heart, which wasn't working so well. With my legs and arms gone to frostbite, those came next. It took years before the regen technology advanced enough to heal my scars. By then, all the new things felt so good, I had to wonder, why stop there?" Carmella wrinkled her nose, but there was an emptiness to her expression that sent a chill through Foster. "But it's so hard to just tell you things—it works so much better if I show you."

Carmella lunged for the control room, and Foster tossed the laser-lead gun to Ezren as he rose to intercept the cybernetic monstrosity, knocking her off her feet. Maybe an inch shorter than him, she had to be at least 100 lbs. heavier than Lowell's estimated 150. Ezren fired into her from the control room, but the laser lead barely broke the surface of whatever mechanical shell lay beneath Carmella's skin.

She turned to Foster and, moving impossibly fast, drove her fist into the side of his face. Black edged Foster's vision, his topsuit rushing to compensate as he went sliding across the train. Still, he staggered to his feet, putting his body between Carmella and the control room.

He spat blood onto the floor, the tang of it bitter on his

tongue. "I didn't know that they allowed senior citizens in the BRR." He feinted high and buried a fist low in her belly, but even though his hand sank into what felt like flesh and muscle, Carmella's smile only widened.

Ezren: I don't think she feels pain, Foster. Her receptors must be turned off. Just hold her for thirty seconds, I have an idea.

Though Foster trusted Ezren with every fiber of his being, thirty seconds was a high ask against this thing.

Carmella swiveled to return the blow, and Foster blocked, the impact ringing through his forearm as he dodged a second swing.

"Please." Carmella snorted. "You think you can beat me? I've been doing this for eighty years. Just because I walk in the shadows doesn't mean I lack brute strength."

Her third strike glanced off his shoulder and pain ricocheted through him as he darted away. With that kind of strength, a direct blow to the head could very well kill him. "I think you need a new hobby."

Ezren: See if you can get her closer to the bomb.

Foster: Closer?!

Ezren: Please, Foster!

Carmella charged forward, and Foster's muscles burned as he tried to dodge. Despite his topsuit-enhanced speed, for every blow he blocked, another hit home, knocking the breath out of him and sending him spinning.

"I gave you the chance to choose the winning side, Sterling." Carmella landed a blow to his stomach with an audible crack of his ribs. Her other fist connected with his face, and he dropped to the ground. Even as Ezren's gunshots hit home, there was no stopping Carmella as she stalked toward his battered form.

"With the luxies, regen, and cybernetics, my body is

immortal. I am forever. No matter what politicians, royalers, or planets pass through, I am consistent. But you know, I'm almost happy you didn't bow to me. I never tire of crushing out a life with my own hands." Blood coated her sharp fangs, and a glimmer of satisfaction flashed through Foster at the sight as he tried to suck in oxygen.

"The spacers that left me for dead. The Obronians and Dreitians that held me hostage—that tortured me until Warner compromised. I got them all eventually." Foster raised his arms to defend himself as Carmella tried to kick at him, skittering back as he staggered to his feet, scarlet now dripping from his nose and mouth. "But I had to laugh when I saw Warner repeating history with your doubles partner. Almost felt sorry for you really."

Foster tried to swing, but Carmella sidestepped with another blow to the head, and his world spun before his back hit the floor.

Carmella stomped on his hand with a crunch, dragging a scream from his throat. "You see, we cannot help but repeat history, unless we become history ourselves." Carmella walked around to his other hand. "Warner always saw himself as so self-righteous, but I waited until the unrest was just right, until he was just enough out of favor, and then I savored that moment when the light faded from his eyes too."

Carmella crushed her boot down on Foster's other hand, the bones cracking with his scream. "Now with you, we will be at an end. I'll turn this train around and find a scapegoat. I'll whisper in the ear of VSoc the salacious story of how you two tried to run and save yourselves, only to be taken by the storm. My puppets will be back on the stage again." She crouched, her bloody smile an inch from his. "But know when I kill you, that I gave you a choice."

We never had a choice. The words were on Foster's lips

before he realized how wrong they were. Of course they'd had a choice, they'd just always taken the hard road. The right road. And even now, he found he could regret nothing. He'd given it his all to try to stop this monster, and he could think of no better sacrifice. His only regret was not getting to spend a lifetime with Ezren. Of no giggling, dark-eyed children running under Belethea's teal skies.

Foster lifted an arm to defend himself as Carmella reached for his neck, but she swatted his broken hand away. Her murderous stare gleamed as her fingers grazed his skin...and then stopped. Carmella's brows knitted as her hand flexed, her eyelids jittering as if glitching.

His gaze flicked to where Ezren stood, her holo glowing in front of her. In three long strides, Ezren kicked Carmella away from Foster and onto the unused mag-restraints next to the bomb. With another mental command from her chip, the restraints latched into place—tethering her securely to the floor.

"You... you hacked her?" Foster choked out.

"No, it's Sam's viru—"

Carmella's hand found Ezren's ankle, and with a yank, she fell to the floor. In another blink, Carmella's hand was on her throat, crushing her windpipe.

Forgetting the pain and his broken hands, Foster launched from the ground with a roar. He desperately kicked at the cyborg's arms as Ezren's face turned a horrifying shade of gray-blue, her eyes bloodshot as they bulged from her sockets, and her hands scrabbling at Carmella's wrist. Finally, he forced his head to clear, turned the attraction on his mag-boots to their maximum strength, and let his foot slam down onto Carmella's arm.

With the groan of bent metal, the fingers twitched, and Ezren tore away from them with four bloody gouges in her neck. Suns, he would kill the motherfodder.

"Ezren!" He rested his broken hands on her shoulders as he tried to assess the damage, her breath coming in choked gasps that reminded him all too much of their last BRR near-death experience. "Are you okay?"

She nodded, still wheezing as she pointed to the timer on the bomb: four minutes and thirty-two seconds remaining.

Ezren: We have to jump. I don't know how long the virus and restraints will hold her.

"Th-th-this is my s-system," Carmella said, her voice jittering with the virus. "I—I won this p-p-planet."

"The planet belongs to all of us." Foster smashed a boot through one of the windows, the tunnel screaming by, and the wall seeming all too close. He turned to Ezren, one hand still clutching her throat. "We are going to have to be incredibly precise if we don't want to hit the wall." Otherwise they'd be ricocheting off of it at two hundred miles per hour, and he wasn't sure their topsuits could handle that.

Ezren nodded, placing his topsuit helmet on his head and adjusting his goggs before donning her own.

Ezren: Less jumping, more falling. Wait until the track straightens out.

Together, they moved on to the window frame. He held out his hand, and Ezren grabbed his wrist, Carmella still raving as she jerked spasmodically against the restraints.

"I am the Crow. I-i-immortal."

"Well, you can talk about that with Calderon and York when you see them," Foster said, not bothering with a backward glance.

The train pulled out of its turn, and Ezren squeezed his wrist.

Ezren: Now, Foster!

The tunnel rushed by Foster's helmet as he came within an inch of the siding, his body still moving at somewhere close to

150 mph, only to be yanked back by Ezren. She wrapped her arms around his waist as the jetchutes auto-adjusted to slow their fall and their forward motion in turns.

"Suns, why don't they build these things into topsuits?" Foster breathed, the train still rumbling through the tunnel as it continued its final sprint away from the finish.

His goggs marked their speed decreasing from one hundred miles per hour to fifty down to twenty, and Ezren cut the power to their jetchutes. They dropped to the floor running. Pain stabbed through Foster's body with the minor impact, and he groaned, resisting as Ezren tugged him along after the train.

"Aren't we going in the wrong direction?"

EZREN: WE NEED TO TAKE THE EMERGENCY EXIT UP HERE.

Foster frowned, his mind clogged with pain and a tentative relief.

Ezren shook her head, her voice hoarse. "That blast is going to come down this tunnel, and we're still in the destructive radius."

"Oh fod." So they had escaped a sadistic serial murderer, only to burn alive in a fire blast of terranium. "How far is the safety zone?"

Ezren winced as she reached the ladder, climbing up with fast hands.

EZREN: 1.2 MILES.

Fodding chaff. Foster climbed after her, trying to use his throbbing hands as little as possible. And if Carmella realized that she was about to lose this game, what were the odds that she would somehow trigger the bomb manually? If it blew now, it would turn her loss into a draw. One dead body into three, and a chess board wiped clean for whichever players came next.

The thought drove the breath from his lungs, and he sent

up a wordless prayer that the virus would hold as Ezren whipped open the hatch to the whirling maelstrom above. She pulled herself up, the lightning cracking the sky as she reached down and grabbed his wrist. Leaping out of the tunnel, he slammed the hatch door behind them.

The storm algorithm chirped in his goggs, but he didn't even look at it as Ezren grabbed the retractable tether from the chest of his topsuit and attached it to hers. His gaze caught on her huge dark eyes, and his jaw flexed. As much as he wanted to hold on to her, they would move faster apart.

FOSTER: I'LL FOLLOW YOU ANYWHERE.

Ezren nodded, solemn as her attention flicked from her holo to the tornadoes in the distance.

EZREN: THEN WE GO INTO THE CHURN.

As she programmed their route, the survival rate popped up in his goggs: 50%. Unwillingly, his brain extrapolated those odds. *One survives. One doesn't.*

And he was going to make fodding sure Ezren made it out of here.

FOSTER: INTO THE CHURN.

Together, they sprinted across the jagged mauve rocks, the rain pelting them in droves and turning the stones slick. An ugly gust tore through the air, knocking Ezren to the ground. She scrambled to her feet just as a razor shard of stone sliced into Foster's back. An alarm rang in his helmet, but they ran on as fast as their legs would take them—silent and desperate as the time ticked down in their goggs.

Sixty seconds.

Fifty.

Thirty.

With twenty seconds left, he found himself bargaining as all the doomed do. Maybe it wouldn't go off. Maybe it wasn't as strong as they thought. Surely they were far enough. If they survived this, he swore to Belethea, Casolla, and all of her daughters that he would claim this system as a part of him. That he would protect it like he did his family. That he would make sure they hunted down every single one of the Crow's syndicate murderers.

Ten seconds.

The glow of Ezren's teal topsuit cut through the dark as she nimbly leapt across the jagged terrain, each point as sharp as a knife. *And if I can't survive, just let her be. She has so much more left to give.*

Five.

They'd only come 0.5 miles—not enough. Ezren glanced at him over her shoulder.

Ezren: No matter what happens, I don't regret a single thing. Not a single thing.

Three.

Still running, he closed the distance between them.

Foster: Me neither.

Two.

Grabbing her from behind, he pushed her down into a crevice between the rocks, covering her body with his.

Foster: I love you, Ezren.

One.

"Foster!"

A burning wave blasted over them, lifting them from the ground in a tidal wave of boulders and rock. And Foster was just thankful that the last word to follow him into the abyss would be his name on Ezren's lips.

CHAPTER 26

5.08.44B BRR Day 5

AT ANY OTHER TIME, Ezren would've urged them to slow down over the treacherous terrain. It would've been far too easy to slip and impale themselves on one of the sharp spires jutting up from the ground. But with the time ticking down in her goggs, and her breath burning through her damaged throat, all she could think was, *get out, get out, get out.*

The twisters churned in front of them, beckoning them into the heart of the churn as the clouds raced to follow the unbalanced terranium, the slick ground disappearing beneath their feet as their legs ate through it.

They had more time.

They could make it.

They would survive this.

She could make the seconds stretch.

And then she couldn't.

EZREN: No matter what happens, I don't regret a single thing. Not a single thing.

She glanced at Foster, the mix of hard resolve and tenderness pooling together into something too deep for words.

FOSTER: Me neither.

Then Foster was pushing her down between the rocks—his

body warm and solid as he pressed her protectively into the mud.

FOSTER: I LOVE YOU, EZREN.

Her eyes widened as the clock hit zero, desperation jolting through her. "Foster—"

Heat enveloped them in a merciless blast, and Ezren's jaw clicked shut. Foster's arms tightened around her, but it was too much. They lifted from the ground in the maelstrom of rock and debris, flying through the air even as their jetchutes tried to right them. Sharp projectiles of stone battered against her body, shredding her suit and the skin beneath, cracking against her bones and the shield of Foster behind her.

Then he was ripped away in the torrent of rock and fire.

Ezren cried out, pain and terror flooding every thought from her mind, not sure if it was the storm or the blast taking him. Something cracked against her head, and for a moment, everything went black. She came to again with the jolt of her suit's resuscitation protocol, alarms blaring in her helmet just before she slammed into the ground—the impact only slightly cushioned by her damaged jetchute.

Blackness again, and then another jolt sent her muscles spasming—bringing her to another painful awakening. Everything was agony as she lay on her back, staring up at the relentless storms above. Navy thunderheads curled across mauve peaks, silver lightning laced the sky, white pearls of hail streaked down, and the gray-green of the funnel clouds tore through it all. The same gray-green of Foster's gaze.

Foster.

She clawed at the scrap of snapped tether at her chest, distantly aware that a mayday signal whined through the air. Her mayday signal. No, wait. She listened harder beneath the roar of the wind. There was another one.

EZREN: FOSTER, WHERE ARE YOU?

A mayday didn't mean he was dead, she told herself. If she'd survived, then so had he. She just had to find him.

Groaning, she forced herself to sit up and take stock. Rips littered her suit in a dozen places, blood oozing from wounds both shallow and deep. Hairline fractures ran through her left foot and right shinbone, two bones in her left hand were broken, a concussion clouded her head, and at least one of her ribs was cracked.

For now, it was survivable. With the impossible storm raging toward them, her algorithm blinked with their survival rate in their current location: 3%. The storm would be there in eight minutes, but they were barely a half-mile from the hatch of the train tube where they could take shelter until help arrived. She just had to reach Foster first.

EZREN: FOSTER!

She scanned her surroundings. Jagged stones and boulders littered the ground around her with a steep cliff rising to one side. A wall of rock that had probably saved them from tumbling into the oncoming storm.

And one with the loose remnants of a rockslide stacked against its base. A glint of teal pulsed amid the rubble, and her damaged goggs finally zeroed in on the mayday signal.

"Foster!"

Lurching to her feet, Ezren stumbled toward the rock pile, the pain electrocuting her body only matched by the flames of adrenaline licking through her. Three times the wind threw her to the ground until she was crawling on her hands and knees to reach him.

"Foster!" Her goggs reported a life reading, but her holo was too fritzed to read the particulars, and he was covered in debris. That didn't mean he was dead. It *couldn't* mean it. That wasn't how their story ended. She wouldn't let it end that way.

With shaking hands, she dug furiously through the mud

and rock. Much too slowly, she uncovered one of his arms and then his head.

"Foster!"

His topsuit was attempting to initiate resuscitation protocol but was coming up with some kind of error, leaving Foster unresponsive. For a moment, Ezren stilled—frozen in horror as her goggs refused to register a heartbeat. With a scream, she fell to her knees and began to pump on his chest.

"This isn't happening. It's going to be okay. The mayday call was sent, help is on the way." And Carmella's words echoed in her head. *They resuscitated me for eight hours... history repeats itself.* Suns, no. This couldn't be happening. She refused. She would not let that monstrosity of a human being do this to them. To Foster.

So she continued to pump her hands against his chest while his helmet forced oxygen into his lungs. She could do this—she didn't care how long it took. She would do this until he woke up. Until she got help. Until the world ended.

Tears gathered in her eyes, and her goggs blinked again with a warning of the unnatural storm bearing down on them. The one they wouldn't survive.

"C'mon, Foster." Ezren pumped harder, his ribs cracking beneath her palms. "You can't let her beat you. You always win." Her goggs beeped again, urging her to leave as the wind picked up around her. Seven minutes until impact. "You're the strongest person I know, and you've survived everything Casolla could throw at you." Sweat or blood trickled down Ezren's cheek inside her helmet, thunder cracking overhead. "Belethea..." Another bolt of lightning illuminated the sky, casting a shadow over her hands.

And an idea sparked through her.

Even though his suit's resuscitation protocol wasn't working, hers was... and the nanites could conduct the shocks from her suit to his.

Tensing with hope, Ezren ripped away the glove of her already torn topsuit and laid it across his chest. With her chip-link, she separated it from her own resuscitation protocol before initiating the first shock. Foster convulsed with the jolt, but his eyes didn't open.

One shock.

Two.

Wheezes racked her body as the panic caught in her chest. This had to work.

Three.

And still nothing. No. Ezren slammed her fists down on his chest, screaming so loud she almost missed the chime of his heartbeat in her goggs. With a relieved gasp, she cut the proto-col, collapsing to the ground with her skin still burning beneath her topsuit. Her goggs registered Foster's vital signs—his pulse weak but present and his breathing in normal bounds. She allowed herself the smallest of smiles. *Alive. Thank the suns.* Everything else was fixable.

But she couldn't stop yet; they had to keep moving.

She unearthed the rest of him in a flurry of mud and rock, noting a badly crushed leg, a mangled hand, and a warning in her goggs about internal bleeding. Chaff, she hoped someone had gotten their mayday call. With one eye on the black tempest hurtling in their direction, she pulled him toward the nearest hatch, which was—perhaps in their first lucky break—only three hundred feet away. Ezren counted the steps, not bothering to avoid the jagged rocks as she dragged him toward it.

They just didn't have time.

EZREN: SHIRO... SYLVIA... IF YOU'RE GETTING THIS.

THE BOMB DETONATED, BUT WE'RE STILL OUT HERE, AND WE NEED YOUR HELP. FOSTER'S HURT BAD.

And though her strength was fading fast, stopping was unthinkable.

SHIRO: WE'VE GOT YOUR LOCATION AND WE'RE ON OUR WAY.

SYLVIA: JUST HOLD FOR TEN MORE MINUTES, EZREN!

Ezren could've cried with relief. She and Foster were going to make it through this. She reached the hatch and opened it with a thought. Using the scraps of their broken tethers, she lowered Foster down into the blackness of the tunnel. She was about to drop down herself when a shadow in the haze of rain stopped her.

Someone was walking... no, limping toward her.

Shiro? A royaler?

With another glance at the storm—now only three minutes way, Ezren straightened as best she could. Misgivings slithered through her gut, and she let the hatch slide closed, hoping the newcomer hadn't seen Foster in the low visibility.

"Hello?" Ezren called. "Do you need help?"

A crack of lightning split the ground on the peak not a stone's throw from them, the thunder crashing all around. But Ezren barely noticed as the monster's face lit up in front of her.

Because Carmella had survived.

Holy shaft.

"How did you..."

"Th-the virus was c-c-clever." Carmella looked more android than human with a foot and an arm stripped away by the blast and her shredded face glinting with the metal underneath. "But it wasn't p-perfect."

Ezren reached for the holster at her thigh. Carmella must have managed to get free not long after they jumped. She'd been caught in the blast but had managed to follow them anyway. And honestly the force of pure will that must've taken was terrifying. From the way she was still glitching though, it seemed like the virus was continuing to intermittently affect her system.

And what did that leave Ezren with?

Ezren felt for her gun, but it had been stripped away by the storm. Though damaged, the only things she had left were her jetchute, her goggs, and—

Lightning flashed above so close Ezren could feel it sizzle along her skin, the crash of thunder reverberating almost simultaneously through the air. She could work with that.

"Where's S-S-Sterling?" Carmella asked. The lightning snaked down again, so close it singed the air.

"I'd like to know too." Ezren took a tentative step away from the hatch. She'd get one shot at this.

Carmella scoffed. "And I suppose that makes you the owner of Calderon Industries, his little w-wife?" Another lightning bolt lanced the ground not twenty feet away, the electricity tingling through Ezren's mag-boots.

"It does."

Carmella shook her head, stalking ever closer. "You don't have what it takes to run the system. Calderon saw that from the start. You're too soft. You could never make a life-or-death decision. Never kill."

"Maybe he was right," Ezren said. "But—"

This time, the lightning spiked straight into Carmella's metal skull. Carmella screamed, her jaw opening too wide as all of her sensors short-circuited.

"Then again, maybe not." Ezren raced forward, pulling her jetchute from her back.

Carmella stood frozen as her electronics rebooted, the nanites inside her scrambling to repair the organic damage to her tissues as Ezren grabbed her shoulders. "I like to be kind. To spread hope. To save rather than hurt."

The stone and ice pelted them from above, the lightning coiling to strike once more as Ezren frantically strapped the jetchute onto what was left of the once legendary royaler. "But when you tried to kill Foster, you changed the game." Setting the chute to manual, she pointed it into the heart of the storm. "And since all the legends said you died in the churn"—Ezren's gaze caught on Carmella's green eyes, and she could've sworn a spark of fear flared to life in their depths—"let's make sure they're right."

With that, she pressed launch, and the jetchute rocketed Carmella's cybertronic body up into the spinning supercell. Ezren followed her trajectory, her goggs still registering a heart-beat right up until a cyclone caught her in its vortex, and a lance-like stone shard embedded itself in her skull.

The weak pulse in Ezren's goggs flatlined.

Dead.

The terror of the Casolla system had been snuffed out, and Ezren felt nothing but relief.

Leaning down against the savage wind, Ezren staggered toward the hatch, her battered body protesting every step as the stones cut into her suit again and again, the wind pushing against her with impossible force. Though the hatch was only ten steps away, she couldn't force her legs toward it.

Falling to her knees, she tried to crawl, dragging her body as debris ricocheted off her goggs and helmet, her holo screaming for her to find shelter. But she was so close. Something smashed against her helmet, and her vision went dark again. Electricity crackled through her, jolting her back to painful consciousness, but Ezren couldn't tell if it was from her suit or the storm itself.

And the twisters were barreling relentlessly toward her. She had thirty seconds to cross the last four feet, but it could've been miles for all Ezren's body was responding—her topsuit too shredded to compensate for the debris cutting into her. Something stabbed into her leg and her fingers scrambled for purchase on the rocky ground as the storm threatened to rip her from the surface to join Carmella.

History repeating itself.

EZREN: FOSTER, I'M SORRY—I DON'T KNOW IF I—

The hatch slid open, and a tether sailed out, the wind whipping it toward her. She barely had a moment to grab hold of it before someone pulled on the other end. With three strong tugs, Ezren was at the hatch, and she could do nothing but fall as it opened beneath her. She grunted as her already broken body impacted the hard floor, but it was nothing compared to the death blender she'd just escaped. Above, the hatch sliced shut, leaving them in darkness.

"Ezren?" Foster dragged himself to her, pulling off her helmet, his eyes wild. "What happened?"

Ezren's vision blurred, barely able to register as he checked her wounds. "You got me."

The curve of his pale lips was too weak to be called a smile. "I always come to get you."

"Always." Ezren tried to smile, but couldn't manage it for some reason.

"Chaff, you're bleeding bad," Foster rasped. "It'll be all right. Help's on the way."

"I'm supposed to be telling you that," she whispered, a heavy exhaustion coming over her that she'd felt before. A coldness. She pressed closer to him. "Your heart stopped beating."

"It couldn't have," Foster murmured, trembling beside her with what Ezren knew had to be shock. "My heart's right here." He ran a hand across her cheek, his lashes drooping as his words slurred. "Just stay with me. Stay with..." His voice faded as his hand went limp against her, his eyes rolling back in his head once more.

Ezren wished she could have done something more for him in that moment, but her eyelids were so heavy. The pain was everywhere, and if she just let sleep take her, it would all slip away. So in the end, the only thing she could do was honor his request to stay with him. As she lost consciousness, her last consolation was that they were together.

But no sooner had her lashes fallen closed than a hand roughly jerked her shoulder.

"Ezren!"

Ezren groaned, but couldn't lift her heavy eyelids. "Mm."

"You have to wake up." Something sharp jabbed into her neck.

Fire burned through Ezren's veins as consciousness hit her like a magtrain. "Suns, what did you do to me?"

"It's a stimulant. It'll keep you alive until we can get you back to the finish line." Though the voice was familiar, Ezren couldn't quite place it. "How's Foster?"

"Bad." The second voice was familiar too, though Ezren still couldn't find the names through her pain-clouded thoughts.

"Someone take him!"

Foster was bad? Someone take him? Ezren cracked her eyelids just wide enough to see a blurry swarm of people surrounding them. And all she could think was they were supposed to stay together. "Don't move him!" She bucked as an uncontrollable panic born of pain and fear spread through her. Were these syndicate people? Were they still not safe? "Who are you? What are you doing to him?"

"Ezren." Soft hands cupped her cheeks, forcing her to look into a warm, brown gaze. "It's okay. It's Sylvia and Shiro. We've got you."

Ezren relaxed just a touch, the unbridled panic still rampaging through her. "But... you said he's hurt bad."

"I know," Sylvia said, her voice smooth and sure—almost commanding. "But he's going to make it."

"Get the airstretcher, now!" Shiro barked from somewhere in the darkness. "He's lost a ton of blood and looks ready to code any second."

"But you don't know," Ezren said, her voice fading as the full force of the stim began to fade.

"It's all right." Shiro knelt beside her. "Don't worry, Ezren. We're going to take good care of him."

Distantly, Ezren was aware of Foster rising on a stretcher, and a scream escaped her mouth before she could stop it. "No! Let me stay with him! He asked me to stay with him!"

"It's okay, Ezren, you're going to the same place," Sylvia said, her voice soothing as someone wrapped something tight around Ezren's leg.

Shiro chuckled. "Yeah, did you notice that you're also slowly bleeding out?"

"I'm f-fine," Ezren slurred as they rolled her onto the stretcher. "I can donate blood to Foster. We're... the same."

Shiro and Sylvia shared a look, and then Sylvia offered Ezren a warm smile. "Ezren, dearest, you have a foot-long metal bar sticking through your calf."

"What?" Ezren lifted her head, but as soon as she laid eyes on the shard of steel in her leg, there were no stims in the 'verse that could save her from blacking out, and the pain finally faded away.

CHAPTER 27

5.08.44B BRR Day 5

FOSTER WOKE IN A HAZE, his body numb and his thoughts scrambled. Where was he? He searched back for his last memory... something from the finish line. The BRR? He turned his stiff neck, taking in the state-of-the-art recovery equipment sitting next to the med tank where he was currently immersed up to his neck in frothing nanite water. He distantly recalled he'd been in this room after they won the BRR. It was the medical wing the racers reported to after the race on one of the lower levels of the finisher's outpost.

But they weren't supposed to run the BRR again. He flexed his fingers and toes, pain radiating from his every pore. At least all his appendages were accounted for, though his left leg didn't seem to be responding. Stretching his neck to one side, he racked his memory for the origin of his injuries as unfamiliar voices drifted to him from across a curtain.

"How many did we lose?"

"So far, we have over two hundred bodies. Twenty-four are royalers, with another sixteen still missing."

"And that was just from the storm... can you imagine if that bomb detonated here?"

"I really can't. This is already the biggest loss of life in BRR history."

Bodies. Bomb. It all came back to him in a painful blast. The syndicates. The Crow. The train. The explosion.

Ezren.

Rising from the water in only his shorts, he reached out and yanked the curtain to one side, fixing the doctors with a steely glare. "Where's Ezren." It was more demand than question.

The white-coated doctors moved to push him back down with twin expressions of concern. "Executive Sterling, please sit down. We need to heal your—"

"I said"—Foster flung off their hands as he climbed out of the tub, balancing on his good leg—"where is my *wife?*"

"Please just stay calm, she's—"

Shouting echoed from outside the door in a voice he recognized immediately as Ezren's.

"Ezren!"

"You need at least another hour in the tub!" one of the doctors called.

Using the wall to brace himself, Foster limped to the door and threw it open. Following the shouting, he hobbled into the hallway where he found Ezren, also dripping wet—a robe thrown over her sports bra and shorts as she leaned heavily on a crutch and maneuvered around yet another protesting doctor. "Which room is he in?"

She was alive. And he was alive. They'd made it.

"Ezren." His voice was soft, but somehow she heard it, her head jerking up. Her eyes filled as soon as they met his.

"Foster."

He made a staggering step, and she hobbled toward him, dropping the crutch as she threw herself into his arms.

"You're okay, you're okay, you're okay," she sobbed, her face buried in his chest. "Suns, Foster, after the explosion, your heart wasn't beating, and I wasn't sure I could get you to come back. Chaff, it was a nightmare."

"Shh, I'm all right." He pressed his lips to her hair as he rubbed her back in soothing circles. "And besides, I'm pretty sure you're the one that almost got swept up in the storm... and for some reason I thought I heard Carmella up there. But I couldn't have. She should've died on the train."

"She didn't, but the storms got her in the end." Ezren smiled up at him, tears streaking down her cheeks. "It's finally over, Foster. The Crow, Carmella, Calderon, York... they're all gone."

He nodded, his own throat thickening. "Because of you."

"And you."

An exhausted smile creased his face. "No more fear."

"Hey! You can't go back there!" a doctor yelled over another commotion coming down the hall. "This hallway's for the severe cases. They need rest."

"Fod off, kin. I just came eighteen hundred miles, and I'm not stopping here."

"Touch him again, and I'll make you heal yourself, Doctor."

Foster couldn't suppress a laugh as Grady and Bex's voices echoed down the hall. His gaze met Ezren's and this time, he quickly wiped away the tear spilling from his cheek. It was a fear he hadn't let himself acknowledge until that moment.

"They made it," he whispered, voice hoarse.

Ezren nodded, scrubbing her own tears away as she turned in his arms. Grady and Bex rounded the corner in teal robes like two battered prize fighters on a grim mission. But as soon as they noticed Ezren and Foster, they stopped dead in the hall. Grady looked fit to faint on the spot. Slapping a hand to his chest, he slumped against the wall. "Thank the suns. Shaft, when that bomb detonated, and your maydays went off, we thought you were *dead*."

Bex ran down the corridor, her strong arms encompassing both of them and—fod—were those *tears*?

"Bex..." he whispered. "We're all right."

"You don't have any idea, Sterling." Bex straightened, her voice thick as she drank them in like a girl starved, her bandaged hands lingering on them like she was afraid to let go. "They played the dirge for you."

"Worst seven minutes of my life," Grady said. "Your goggs even reported your heart was stopped." He staggered toward them and tugged Foster into a hug. "Don't do that to me again, Sterling. I'm serious." Giving him a strong squeeze, he moved to scoop Ezren into a hug next, and Foster didn't miss his tear-stained cheeks.

"What about Dean and Kit?" he whispered.

"They..." Bex's voice faltered. "They didn't make it."

Ezren gasped, and Foster's heart sank, his legs going weak beneath him as he leaned against the wall.

"The storm took them." Grady shook his head, jaw tight as his hazel eyes shone. "And so many others."

"But I thought they were supposed to stop the royalers at the brawl," Foster whispered, his mind still uncomprehending. Kit and Dean, the scrappy, spirited speed demons he and Ezren had trained for the last nine months. Had eaten with. Lived with. Celebrated with. They were gone.

"The storm was so big, many of the royalers died trying to make it to the arena," Bex said. "There was nothing anyone could've done."

"And Sylvia has already contacted their family," Grady added.

Memories of training the two bickering siblings flashed through Foster's thoughts. How Kit and Dean had looked up to him and Ezren as if they were their own personal heroes. How hard they worked. How excited they'd been.

"You're sure?" Ezren said, tears still silently streaming down her cheeks. "Maybe—"

Bex squeezed her shoulder. "They recovered the bodies."

"What about everyone else?" Foster said, his voice rough. "There were so many here in the dome."

"All the rest of ours are accounted for." Grady leaned against the wall beside him. "Sylvia, Micah, Shiro, your mom... they're all okay."

"They're helping to find the missing," Bex said.

Ezren wound her arms around both Bex and Grady again. "I can't believe you made it—you were right in the heart of the storm, and the maydays started going off in the channel." Ezren's eyes rounded with wonder. "How did you survive?"

"It was your algorithm, E." Grady's mouth tugged up in a bittersweet quirk. "It kept saying to stay in place; I think the others must've thought it stopped working."

"But we trusted it," Bex said. "So we dug out a hole and sat in the channel for over an hour. Then when the bomb left, the storm receded, and we were able to move again."

Foster's brows knitted, but before he could say anything else, his legs crumpled beneath him.

Grady and Bex caught him on either side. "Whoa, Sterling," Grady said as they shifted him back toward his open door. "I think you need to sit the fod down."

"You too, Hart," Bex called over her shoulder.

"Hey, Dr. J," Ezren called as she hobbled along the wall. "I'm moving into Foster's room."

"Are there still royalers out there?" Foster asked, his head spinning.

"Yeah," Grady said as they lowered him onto the edge of the med tub. "And they're refusing help until they finish." A rueful grin twisted his full lips. "You know how insane royalers are."

"Chaff yeah, they're racing." Bex crossed her arms, her hard blue eyes flashing. "We're not going to let some terrorist take the BRR from us."

"Oh!" Ezren ran a hand over her hair as if just realizing her goggs were missing. "I need to let my family know we're okay."

"Ha." Grady snorted. "That's one thing you don't have to worry about. I think the whole 'verse knows you're okay. They actually had to release a proof of life holo to keep people from storming the churn to find you."

Bex nodded. "Micah's been working with *The Royaler Review* and some of the other holologgers to release the whole story. She wanted to wait for you to wake up, but there were too many panicked rumors flying. They had to set the record straight before Casolla rioted."

So their story was already out. Foster shared a glance with Ezren. Who knew what Micah had put out there? Their story was so wild, he wasn't even sure if *he* believed it. Would people understand the choices they made? Or would they blame them for the lives lost? For their mistakes and missteps? Perhaps they should.

"How... uh..." Foster rubbed his damp hair where it started to curl at the ends. "How're they taking it?"

Grady shared a sly glance with an expressionless Bex. "Let's just say," he said, "if you were heroes before, you're fodding legends now."

"As you should be. We don't even know how many lives you saved today." Bex lifted her chin. "But you saved our hope too. Our future." She reached out and took both of their hands. "You're more than royalers now, and we're chaffing proud to know you."

Foster's heart squeezed as he thought of Davis hurtling somewhere through the blackness. Ezren sat on the tub next to him, and he put his arm around her—tugging her close as he kissed her hair. Despite their victories, the losses still weighed heavy on his chest.

"Lives saved, lives lost," Ezren whispered. "It's a hard day."

"And so we sing them to the storms," Bex whispered, touching two fingers to her lips. "Belethea accepts her children into her heart with open arms."

For a second, the words hung between them, before the clicking of two pairs of boots punctuated the quiet. Ambassador Villegas strode into the room, her weathered face creased with sorrow and fatigue, and her burly security guard following close behind her. But when she saw them, her lips bent in a weary smile.

"Oh thank the suns." She leaned against the doorframe, her floor-length ambassador's coat wrinkled and stained. "I thought the two of you told me you weren't going back into the churn. Did you lie to your lead ambassador? You may be a force to be reckoned with now, but I'm still your boss." The words were friendly, almost teasing, and though Villegas still wasn't Foster's favorite person, his estimation of her grew just a little more.

Ezren's lips tilted in an almost-grin as she bobbed her head. "It wasn't in the plan, Ambassador."

"Indeed." Villegas scuffed the floor with one of her heeled boots and sighed. "Well, I know you're in pain, so I'm truly sorry to say this, but we're still in chaos, and we need you to make a statement." She winced with an apologetic frown, a lock of her black hair falling from its tight coil. "Please know I wouldn't ask if it weren't truly necessary."

Ezren looked at Foster, a silent question in the tilt of her head. Even while exhaustion and pain haunted her every breath, she would rise to this occasion and each one after. The girl was unstoppable. And as much as he wanted to say no, there was no ignoring that this was what Belethea—no, what *Casolla* needed from them. Rest would have to come later.

With a sigh of resignation, Foster took Ezren's hand. Her shoulders relaxed, and she smiled up at him with an unmistakable gleam of pride he'd never get enough of.

"Okay." Foster rose on one leg, helping Ezren to her feet. "Upstairs?"

"Fod that." Grady stepped in front of them, his shoulders tense. "You're in no shape to go anywhere." Tossing a glare at Villegas, he gently pressed them both back down. "If anyone needs a statement, they can take it right here."

"But..." Ezren looked from her robe to Foster's shirtless chest—both of them wrapped in too many bandages to count. "Our clothes... our faces."

Bex grabbed another robe from a hook on the wall and tossed it to Foster. "So what? Let them see what real life looks like. It'll be good for them. Besides, you've come so far." Her gaze softened. "Let them come to you for once."

Grady fished two hovercams from the pockets of his robe as he raised a challenging brow at Villegas. "How about it, Ambassador?"

Villegas rolled her eyes, waving him off. "Fine. Fine. Just as long as we get it."

Grady flashed a victorious grin and sent the hovercams spinning in the air. Ezren turned quickly to Foster as she folded her robe around herself.

"Chaff, do I look okay?" She grimaced, her skin still littered with bruises and cuts. "I don't want to have survived all of that just for Micah and Sylvia to kill us later."

Foster reached out and tucked a magenta strand of hair behind her ear. "You look beautiful."

Bex and Grady backed away while Villegas watched them from the doorway, her expression somber. Foster grappled for words as he realized he had no idea what the state of the system was now. Were they blaming Belethea for killing the royalers?

Were people calling for the BRR to end? Blaming him and Ezren? Were Obrone and Dreitis threatening a terranium war? He had no idea. In fact...

"Wait." Foster held up a hand. "Who won the BRR?"

Bex and Grady gave him matching worn smiles—the bitter-sweetness waylaid by loss and suffering. "We did, Sterling," Bex said, her voice unbearably soft.

Grady's grin was almost indulgent. "And you're live, kin."

Foster cleared his throat, trying to master his shock while Ezren sat beside him in a similar state. Suns, they had to make this quick—there were too many emotions careening through him to be live on a holo in front of the 'verse.

"Casolla," he began, his voice surprisingly steady despite the maelstrom of his thoughts. "On behalf of the Belethea Race Royale council, we'd like to offer our sincerest condolences for the lives lost in the record-breaking storm here in the churn. We share in the sorrow of all Casollans as we mourn for friends, teammates, and family..."

His voice trailed off as Kit and Dean's faces flashed through his mind once again. How they would've loved to see Grady/Guns win. How much they'd wanted to cross the finish themselves. How they should be celebrating with them right now.

Ezren took over where he left off, drawing herself up straight. "Of course, the BRR and its churn belt are inherently dangerous, and we salute those who brave the challenge every year. So we also must congratulate Team Grady/Guns"—her soft gaze swiveled from the hovercam to where they stood beyond it—"on their win during a year of extraordinary circum-stances."

Ezren looked to Foster, the unspoken question in her eyes. How much were they going to say? Two weeks ago, he would've cut the feed and called it good. But his death bargain with Belethea's storms echoed through him. If he was going to truly take responsibility for his planet—his system—and enable change, he had to speak. He had to step up to be the voice to follow. To lead. Not because he had to.

But because he wanted to.

The Crow had used fear to control the masses, and in the wake of her destruction, he only wanted them to feel safe.

And, as much as he was loath to admit it, he'd been well prepared for this, by his parents, Sylvia, Ezren, the ambassadors... as if they'd known this moment was coming. So he knew, in no uncertain terms, that in order to instill confidence into the fearful hearts watching him right now, he had to be confident himself. For his voice to carry, it had to be powerful. And for people to feel his words in their bones, he had to mean it.

For the third time, they had the eye of the whole 'verse. But this time it felt right. Like this was where he was supposed to be. A grand role, but one he could grow into. A place he could do actual good for actual people.

And, suns, he wanted that.

So he squared his shoulders and his voice deepened with a reverberating certainty.

"That's not the only news we want to deliver. As many of you know, the finish line was endangered by a mass terrorist threat. Thanks to the efforts of many, including the CIF, the race organizers, and so many others, the threat was neutralized, and a syndicate kingpin responsible for a web of terror and devastation that resulted in decades of murders has finally been eradicated."

Foster squeezed Ezren's hand, and she nodded in silent encouragement.

"Ezren and I were also victims of the syndicate's machinations to control the wider governance and commerce of Casolla.

And I know there's been a lot of confusion during the last week over the fate of Calderon Industries, but you can rest assured now that it's in our hands. With the syndicates crumbling, this is our time—*Casolla's* time to construct how our still-new world will be. And we look forward to building it with you for the good of all."

Foster looked to Ezren, and her brows drew low even as she gave a fierce smile. "There will be hard decisions ahead, but Casolla has wonderful leaders and mentors we're excited to work with as the BRR Council begins a new era." Ezren folded his hand in both of hers. "Because we're committed to making the right decisions, every time."

"This is our world," Foster said, "and we're here to protect it."

With a nod from Grady, the red light on the cam blinked out, and Ezren collapsed into Foster with a long sigh. "That was so good, Foster," she said. "Micah and Sylvia are totally going to fritz when they see it."

"Chaff, Sterling." Grady let out a low whistle. "That was like you were a different person. I almost thought you were really important there for a second."

Bex's pale cheeks glowed with pride as she regarded them. "That's because they *are,* Grady."

From the doorway, Villegas clapped with the fulfilled smile of a grandmother regarding her progeny. "Today, all of Casolla is proud of you."

Foster tensed as a rumble echoed through the hall, his eyes going wide. Another explosion? The storms? But Ezren's smile widened beside him, and as he listened, he slowly realized it was coming from the floor above them.

Cheers.

CHAPTER 28

8.10.44B T-minus 264 days until the BRR

EZREN BOUNCED in place beside Foster, her feet light as she hopped off the elevator and toward their door, a geometric design carving into the synwood that she had picked out herself. Though the holopro had looked amazing, it looked even better in person. "Oh suns, I love it already," she squealed, placing her hand on the scanner for entry.

"Welcome, Ezren Hart," the scanner chimed.

"Why thank you, nameless scanning machine." She laughed, but when she tried to open the door, it wouldn't move.

She turned to Foster, his hands in the pockets of his long ambassador's coat as he leaned against the wall. A soft, satisfied smile played on his lips beneath his gray-green eyes, unsurprised and quite obviously up to something.

She cocked a brow at him. "It's manually hard-locked?"

He held up a flat mag-key. "Just an extra layer of security in case."

"Well, c'mon, let me see it already!" She held out her hand, but he moved it just out of reach.

"And what kind of husband would I be if I didn't open the door for my wife?" He started toward the door with painfully unhurried steps, almost as if he were moving in slow motion.

"No! You're taking forever!" Ezren protested as she tried to snatch the key from him.

He fended her off with one arm. "Don't you want to soak the moment in?"

"I've already soaked, and now I want to see our new apartment." She reached around him, only to flinch when he tickled her side. "You're playing dirty!"

With a huge leap, Ezren managed to snag the key. Whooping triumphantly, she turned and pressed the badge to the lock. This time the door slid obediently open, and her heart swelled. For a moment, she stared into the foyer with its sleek synwood floors and inviting furniture. Though they'd planned it out together with Sylvia, the sheer size of it still floored her.

And it was *theirs.*

Foster's arms folded around her from behind, his low voice rumbling in her ear. "Well, do you like it?"

Tears budded in Ezren's eyes. After bunking with three other girls for the past year, it was hard to believe. They were standing in their first real home just for them. "I love it."

"Well then let's go inside." Foster swept her into his arms, carrying her across the threshold just like he'd done on their honeymoon. She giggled as he turned her in a complete circle, giving her a view of the stretching kitchen to one side, the wall of windows offering an open view of Petraskis's east garden, the spiral stairs that led up to the roof, and the hall that led off to the rest of their apartment—somehow big and cozy all at the same time.

Foster grinned in the way he reserved only for her as he set her on the ground, his styled brown hair falling onto his forehead. "Ambassador Hart, I present to you our new home."

"It's absolutely perfect." Ezren covered her gaping mouth as she took it in. "I can't believe we actually get to live here."

Foster laughed, the rumble deep in his chest. "Technically the whole building is ours."

"Right. I still think Shiro was overreacting a bit with that one."

Ezren moved to the window, peering down onto the garden below and the newly renamed Amaral Hall beside it. After the CIF had found Carmella's remains and put together the rest of the grisly story with testimonies from captured Talons, Belethean support for renaming the hall had been unanimous.

Foster put his arm around her, and together, they drifted through the apartment in comfortable silence, lost in thought.

While Jabari had stepped away from the BRR after his girl-friend's death, Ezren and Foster had waded deeper with their VSoc cred higher than ever. It didn't hurt that after the BRR incident, the CIF had officially recognized them with Casollan medals for their "courageous acts that saved countless lives." With cross-system favor and no knives lurking in the shadows, Ezren and Foster had officially been promoted to full Belethean ambassadors and, with help from Villegas and Calderon Indus-tries' army of advisors, they'd slipped into their roles as Casollan leaders with an ease she could've never predicted. Amidst the sorrow of the services for Kit, Dean, and the other royalers, it had been a pleasant surprise.

She smiled at the narrow staircase spiraling through the ceiling, and Foster led her up.

Though both the Obronians and Dreitians had submitted complaints about their status, they'd been drowned out by over-whelming public opinion. With the full force of VSoc behind him, Foster had cut down their conceited ambassadors with cold truths of the deadly history of the BRR they were honor-ing. It helped that the BRR of 44B had been the most univer-sally watched race in the history of the event. With Micah and

The Royaler Review's quick and masterful spin of the narrative, Obrone and Dreitis were fighting a losing battle from the start.

But now, Ezren could see a sheen of respect in their eyes when they shook her and Foster's hands. A precedent of peace and unity she could only hope would last.

They emerged into a rooftop garden, the holo of a bright blue sky radiant above them and the flat space filled with small trees blooming in a rainbow of colors. She turned to Foster with a smile. "Suns, it's better than I could've imagined."

"Really?" Foster stuffed his hands into the pockets of his coat. "I kind of thought it was missing something."

Ezren wrinkled her nose with a confused frown. "It was exactly how we planned it though." The trace of a secret tucked into the corner of Foster's mouth, and Ezren closed in on him, narrowing her gaze even as she grinned wide. "Why does it feel like you're hiding something?"

His stormy irises glinted with knowing. "Well, I may have gotten you—or rather, us—a homewarming gift."

"A gift?" Ezren's brows shot up as she looked around the garden, excitement tingling through her fingers as she tried to rack her brain for what it could be. "What is it? Where is it? What is it?"

"Okay, okay, wait." He put his hands on her shoulders. "Just stay here and close your eyes."

Ezren clapped her hands to her face. "I'm ready."

"No peeking."

"Oh, c'mon, Foster, hurry. I'm already dying to know." His retreating footsteps tickled her ears as she waited, the anticipation prickling her skin. "You'd better not leave me out here."

"Since Turnip's going to be living in the building and all," Foster said, "I figured she might appreciate a friend."

A click snapped through the air followed by the patter of

small footsteps. Ezren frowned, trying to parse the sounds together until the scrabble of tiny paws pressed against her leg.

With a gasp, she tore her hands from her face to see a tiny, cream-colored capybog pup staring up at her with two shrewd black eyes. It trilled its pleasure, and Ezren shrieked, falling to her knees to gather the puppy in her arms. It snuffled at her hair, its nubby tail wagging as it squeaked again in contentment.

Ezren looked up at Foster through a glaze of joyful tears. "Ours?"

He nodded from where he leaned against the exterior doorway, his grin bigger than she'd ever seen it. "He is. Just waiting for you to name him."

"Oh Foster. How did you get him? He must have cost a fortune."

"I have my ways."

The tiny creature curled up in her lap with the signature capybog resting-expression of complete boredom, and Ezren couldn't stifle a giggle. "Let's call him Bagel."

A laugh chuffed out of Foster as he crossed the garden to them, kneeling beside her as he scratched Bagel's half-flopped ears. "Perfect. Bagel it is."

Still cuddling Bagel with one arm, Ezren curled her other around Foster's neck, pulling him in for a kiss. "Thank you," she whispered. "He's like the first member of our little family."

"A perfect start." He grinned down at her, his gray-green eyes full and warm as he pressed another kiss to her lips. "And one I don't think I've ever been more grateful for."

Bagel chirped between them—only to be answered by a soft mew.

Together, Ezren and Foster looked up to see Turnip peeking her head out of the doorway.

"Hey, are you two up here?" Sylvia said from somewhere down the stairs. "We're coming up."

"Now we just have one problem," Foster said, raising his voice.

Ezren cocked her head at him. "What's that?"

His eyes glinted. "The neighbors."

Sylvia walked out onto the roof beside Turnip and planted her fists on her hips. "I know you're not talking about me, Foster Sterling."

"Look, Sylvia! Meet Bagel!" Ezren called.

Sylvia smiled as Bagel scrambled out of Ezren's arms and ran over to Turnip, pausing to snuffle the cat over. Turnip's tails flicked as she sniffed the pup in turn. Then with a satisfied purr, she nuzzled her head against Bagel's neck.

Sylvia crossed her arms. "Okay, I'll give it to you, that *is* the cutest thing ever. Micah will have VSoc content for days."

"That's why I really got him," Foster deadpanned.

Shiro poked his head out after Sylvia, scratching at his wild dark hair. "I'm a little surprised you didn't name him Cake."

"Which we left in your kitchen to celebrate," Sylvia added.

Ezren smiled as she leaned into Foster, the perfection of it almost overwhelming her. "See, Foster, how bad can the neighbors be if they brought *cake?*"

"Yeah, it's *so* hard living with your very own built-in security and management team," Shiro said with a smirk.

"Right." Foster rolled to his feet, brushing off his coat. "Because you're not here to remind us about the season kickoff meeting this afternoon or anything."

"Aw, look, we don't have to remind them of their obligations anymore." Shiro smiled as he crouched to pet Bagel. "They're all grown up now, Vi."

"Seriously though." Sylvia walked around the flowers and small trees decorating the roof, her fingers fidgeting with her oversized purse. "Is it what you wanted? We can change anything you don't like."

Ezren rose and wrapped her in a huge hug. "We love it. Thank you, Sylvia."

Ezren knew Sylvia had spent the better part of the last two months putting this together, along with her usual million other things. Though since she'd passed off the coaching job to Greta Sterling and VSoc management to Micah, it seemed like she was finally getting some time for herself.

"Thank you for helping us find our home," Ezren said.

"It's okay, everyone, the party has arrived!" Simon announced as he stepped into the garden with a massive box in his arms and Bex behind him.

"Hey, security, who let these guys in?" Foster called as Simon gave him a rough hug. "He's mugging me."

Bex feinted a punch to his gut. "Um, you forget, I *am* security now."

Foster feigned a flinch, and Simon clapped him on the back before moving to hug Ezren. "Good thing too, he's already gone soft."

A rap of the door drew their attention to the stairs again, where Micah stepped into the garden. "Hey, we're here for the homewarming part—" Her voice devolved into an unintelligible flurry of squeals as she swooped Bagel from the ground like an eagle. "HOLY CHAFF HE'S EVEN CUTER IN PERSON." She turned toward the door, mashing her face into his fur as she bounced up and down. "LOWELL, LOOK! WE NEED ONE!"

Lowell ran a hand over his jaw before waving with a rueful grin. "Hey, everyone, happy homewarming." Ever since the BRR, Micah and Lowell had become inseparable. And while Ezren hadn't actually witnessed the moment *The Royaler Review* had officially infiltrated their ranks, Sylvia's reaction had apparently gone much better than Micah expected. Though he was still a muddle of blushes around them, after his work in the post-BRR chaos, Ezren would almost hazard to say Lowell was at the top of Sylvia's good list.

"Hi, Lowell." Ezren wrapped her arms around Micah. "Don't you worry, you can be Bagel's godmother."

The homewarming party continued through the afternoon as Ezren's mom and Sam arrived along with Greta and Gerard. Drinks (garnished with tiny teal umbrellas, of course), music, and laughter flowed aplenty, and by the end, Ezren had never felt so full. So at home. Then all too soon, Sylvia was shooing out the guests as she reminded them that Foster and Ezren did indeed have an afternoon ambassador meeting.

Bolstered with joy, Ezren reluctantly left Bagel in Sylvia's capable hands as she and Foster crossed the city to the Calderon building that was now their official place of work. The very place they used to hate was now in many ways their bastion of strength. Although the name would always remind her of a powerful man who fell to darkness in the name of ideals, she would also remember that he was a man who always put Belethea first.

And even with the darkness of his memory, that was something she could get behind.

Foster held her hand as they walked through the doors, security and employees bobbing their heads and tipping their hats as they strode by, flanked by Bex and Shiro on either side as their long ambassador coats billowed behind them.

Together they rose in the elevator to the top floor. Though they were five minutes early, the meeting was fully staffed when they walked in—all ten Belethean council members in person. As they entered, the council members stood and bobbed their heads, a small smile on Villegas's thin lips. With the beginning of the season kicking off in the next week, they had a list of topics as long as her arm to discuss... which also made a perfect time for a little secret reveal.

Foster sat down at his place at the round table with Villegas on his left and Ezren at his right. "Okay then, let's get started."

"But before we do," Ezren cut in, butterflies churning in her belly as she met Villegas's gaze. Foster arched a brow at her, obviously unprepared for a second surprise today. "Casolla would like to say hello."

She sent the mental command in her chip, and with a chime, the domed ceiling above them turned translucent, and the blue sky holo on the Petraskis dome flickered out. Then, for the first time in its history, the metal storm shield of Petraskis began to roll down from the clear dome, revealing a pale teal Belethean sky strafed with navy clouds, and Casolla's huge face peering down on them from above.

Gasps and murmurs echoed around the room, and from the street holo in her goggs, they could hear people cheering from around the city. She projected it onto the table for the other ambassadors to see as people flooded into the street to witness the sight. The ambassadors broke out into their own laughter, rising and pressing themselves to the glass to get a better view of Belethea's peaceful teal skies.

"Of course, our thanks to the terraforming teams," Ezren said. "For making this a reality."

Foster turned to her with unabashed awe parting his lips.

FOSTER: YOU DID THIS.

Ezren shook her head.

EZREN: NO, WE ALL DID.

Villegas gave her a silent round of applause, and Ezren settled back into her seat in blissful contentment as she watched a flock of school children whooping at their brand-new sky. Because the next generation would have more possibilities stretching before them, and that was what their work was really about. She glanced at Calderon's seat, now filled with a new, hopeful face. They were all learning from the last generation and giving to the next, and with many small steps, they would walk into the future.

Under the table, Ezren threaded her fingers with Foster's, and he squeezed her hand. Though they'd started off as backwater, underdog royalers, they'd become pawns that had crossed the board and turned the tables. And yet, as far as they'd come, they still had so much life to enjoy. So much love to give. And though perhaps this was never a future they could've imagined, they could make it a great one.

But it wasn't until hours later, when she and Foster stood outside on Belethea's mossy surface, that it all really began to sink in. That this was only the beginning of everything. Though it certainly wasn't all perfect, and it would never be all perfect, it was an imperfect life that she loved.

She drank in the petrichor of the rain-washed air. "We have to do this one fast so we can get back to Bagel." Pressing her lips together, she poked Foster lightly in the chest. "And also because technically you can no longer wear a topsuit indefinitely."

"No need to rub it in." He captured her finger and kissed it before releasing her once more. "So what are you thinking?"

Ezren stretched her arms above her head, the sun setting in a sky that had never looked so huge. "I'm thinking, I want to stand on top of a mountain."

The corner of Foster's mouth kicked up. "I think you're already on top of one."

"True." Ezren hugged one knee to her chest and then the other, stretching out her muscles. "But one's never enough."

"Okay, then, to the first mountain." Foster held out her helmet. "Are you going to cheat this time?"

"No." Ezren sugared her voice with feigned innocence. "I want to go together."

Foster's gaze narrowed. "Well, isn't that swe—"

"Just kidding." Ezren took off running with a wild laugh. "I'm going to cheat."

"Ezren!" Foster yelled. "Put on your helmet!"

She only made it a half dozen steps before Foster had tackled her to the ground in the growing meadow of soft moss and belweed. Ezren laughed so hard she could barely breathe as he pushed himself up onto his elbows and looked down on her with his own grin.

"Are you going to run off without me now?" he said, his voice light with joy and fresh air.

Safe in the circle of his arms, Ezren stroked a hand down his cheek. "Never."

Foster leaned down and pressed his lips to hers. She knotted her hands around his neck, and he deepened the kiss, their mouths and heat swirling together in a well-practiced dance that flipped her stomach. No matter how much he kissed her, touched her, held her—she would never have enough of him. Not ever.

They kissed until she was breathless and all heat, his stare dark and swirling as he looked down on her, his voice rough. "Remind me to pick up where we left off when we get home." He tucked a strand of hair behind her ear, and the word home vibrated through her like the sonorous toll of a bell. The teal sky swirled above him, and Ezren's eyes rounded with realization, her jaw going slack.

"What?" he whispered as he traced her swollen lips with his fingers.

Ezren looked at the face of her love against the backdrop of the clear teal sky, the grass soft against her back. Open skies. New life. And the deepest of love.

"I think," she whispered, "that this moment is everything I've ever wanted."

He pressed another kiss to her lips, soft and gentle. "I think I know exactly what you mean." Rising, he tugged her to her feet and retrieved their helmets. "But you still have to wear this." With one last peck, he slid the helmet on her head before donning his own. "And then you'll have to catch up."

Turning, Foster ran off toward the distant mauve peaks.

"Foster!" Ezren yelled in mock outrage as she ran after him.

"Last one to the mountain has to do Micah's next VSoc interview."

Ezren just managed to jump onto his back, sending them both tumbling again. This time, they rose together, jostling and laughing as they ran on.

Legs stretching across grassy ground, the horizon beckoning them with fair winds, and Foster smiling beside her, Ezren was as light as the air itself. Though they'd faced plenty of darkness and pain over the last two years, here—side-by-side and running free—it all slid away. For Foster. For Belethea. It had all been worth it.

Ezren breathed in the sweet floral scent of the meadow as she looked ahead at the wonder of Belethea stretching before them, waiting for them, beckoning them with a new future of joy and hope.

And together, they raced toward it.

EPILOGUE

6.23.17C Day 0 in the Redincia System

DAVIS EMERGED from the blackness of a dreamless sleep in slow motion. First there was only awareness that he was, in fact, asleep. Or possibly awake. Or maybe just the returning awareness that he was alive. Maybe. His limbs floated weightless around him, each of his muscles twitching in sequence from his toes to his scalp as if to remind him that they were indeed there. He wasn't sure how long he floated like that, his mind as sluggish as his body as it refused to form any thought other than: *I am.*

Finally a soft voice trickled in his ear—smooth and gentle.

"Welcome back, Davis Banda. You have been in cryosleep for the last seventy-three years, and we appreciate your patience as we complete your awakening protocol. Your ship has just emerged from the wormgate into system XE-937, colloquially known as the Redincia System, and is waiting for your next instruction. Please remember, though we are releasing you from the cryochamber, your body will take some time to regain full functionality."

With that, the muted hiss of a door opening echoed through the slowly receding liquid around him. As soon as it passed his eyes, he squinted in the dim light, his vision blurry as he breathed in the sterilized air. Putting one hand on each side of the pod, Davis lifted himself to sitting as his brain began processing again.

What had happened?

He took in the small space of the cryochamber, his gaze flicking to the one glowing next to him with its own awakening protocols and the navy-haired girl within it. Then everything came back in a rush.

Blood all over the deck. Shooting. Screaming. The Crow and Foster and Sam and the wormgate.

It had all really happened.

And then seventy-three years had passed.

Asdef.

He ran a hand through his dripping hair with a disbelieving laugh.

With his chip, he accessed the ship's computer, displaying the system's welcome info on the wall. There was a part of him that still couldn't believe the cryochambers had been working—that, after everything, he'd actually survived.

"Well," he said to himself. "This is what I studied for, even if I am a few years early." Beside him on the red-stained floor, a small hummingbot lay on the floor like a sleeping dog. "But I guess we'll need to find a charger for Giles."

The door on the cryochamber next to him hissed open, and the girl—Thread, if he remembered right—sat up with a gasp, her sea-green eyes rolling with panic.

"It's okay," Davis said. "You're all right." He checked her over as he said it, but the bullet holes that had soaked the deck had been healed by the cryochamber. Suns, it had been a close thing though. Probably better that he didn't mention how close she'd come to actually dying.

Thread's gaze whipped toward him, and ever so slowly, the fear faded from her tense expression—replaced by the heavy memories of what had come before. Her fingers found the holes in the chest of her drenched spacer's jumpsuit before she lifted her legs. Though her clothing was still ragged, at least the tank had sterilized the blood from her clothes. She blinked at him for a second, and Davis realized that the cryochamber hadn't been able to heal her tongue or the scars down her face. That would require regen, if she ever wanted it. He was about to reach out to the table to grab her visor, when her words projected from the room's holo.

I... She glanced at the system map projected onto the chamber walls. *Where are we, again?*

"We're in system XE-937." Davis smiled at her as he scrolled through the ship's freshly downloaded information from the system's welcome transmitter. "Freshly colonized a hundred and seventy years ago, but with one livable planet and a handful of space stations." They'd actually been quite lucky. There were dozens of systems with various states of human presence, but only a handful had habitable planets. He'd actually even studied this one in school when he was trying to decide which system he wanted to visit first. Not that he'd actually gotten to pick—but all things considered, this wasn't a bad roll of the dice.

So that means... we can't return.

Davis cocked his head. "Well technically, we should have enough fuel to get back. That's standard operating procedures for missions like these. But..." He weighed his words carefully. After all, he still knew so little about her. Had she left behind friends? Family? Was she worried what the Crow would do to them? No, he corrected himself. That was seventy-three years ago. What the Crow had *done* to them. "By the time we returned, 146 years would've passed."

Enough time for the great-great-grandchildren of anyone they knew to out-age them.

Will they come after us?

Davis chewed the inside of his cheek as he thought about it. While there would be a record of where they'd gone, he couldn't really imagine the Crow going so far as to come after them. After all, to anyone in Casolla, going through the wormgate was as good as dead anyway. Sorrow swept through him as he thought of his parents. Though they'd always been rather distant, and absolutely work-obsessed, he still regretted that he hadn't been able to say goodbye. To Dr. Evangeline as well.

"I don't think so."

Thread's shoulders curved, the tension falling away from her face, and a knot in his chest unraveled as well. Of course, left between the options of letting her bleed out on the deck and stuffing her into the cryochamber, he hadn't really had a choice. But an unexpected trip through the wormgate was tough for anyone to handle.

For some, it felt like a death, and there were plenty of instances where it had driven travelers mad. Thread drew her knees to her chest, resting her cheek on them, and finally in a well-lit room without anyone trying to torture or kill him, Davis realized just how beautiful she was. And he couldn't help but wonder about the path that had brought her here. How had she ended up as a Talon? Where had she been before that? But there would be plenty of time for those questions later.

So what do we do?

"Well." Davis rolled his neck around in a slow circle and flexed his legs—it seemed like they'd bounced back from cryosleep relatively quickly. That just left... what came next. He drew in a shuddering breath—the enormity of it threatening to overwhelm him. *Small steps.* "First I suggest we both shower and get some real food. Then we can figure out where to go from there."

Thread nodded, and they both managed to crawl out of their chambers on their ridiculously clumsy limbs. Okay, maybe they weren't in as great a form yet as he thought. Davis leaned against the wall as the ship's computer helpfully directed them to the showers, fresh space jumpsuits, and post-cryo meals.

But he and Thread didn't exchange another word until they were both seated at one of the tables in the common area. The common area which Davis was trying very hard not to remember dragging bodies from and tossing them out the airlock before they went into cryo. So lost was he in his own thoughts, he missed that Thread was speaking to him until she tapped on his shoulder.

Are you sad? Would you prefer to go back?

Davis's lips twisted. "I don't really think there is a going back. The spacers call going through the wormgate the final out for a reason. So yeah, I enjoyed my old life, and I loved my friends and family. I'll definitely miss all of them, and I'll probably have to mourn that for a while."

He chewed the tasteless, but not unpleasant food labeled *Post-Cryo Meal One.* He wasn't even sure the others had known the cryochambers had been functioning. But he desperately hoped that, somehow, the others knew he and Thread had survived. He didn't even want to consider the alternative.

"But it was also my dream to explore other systems," he continued. "Not just one, but many. I wanted to start an exploration team to find new planets and see how much of the 'verse I could cover. So in that way, this is exciting." He grinned at her. "And sometimes we just have to roll with what the stars give us."

Thread nodded, but her expression fell.

I suppose you're not pleased that the universe gave you an ex-Talon as a companion.

Davis started. "No, I wasn't—"

I want you to know. It wasn't my choice. The last year with the Talons was the worst of my life.

She bowed her head low over her plate as if to hide her face.

Davis regarded her, carefully choosing his words as they trod over the tender ground. "What did you do before that?"

Her green eyes shone with a wistful gleam.

After Calderon rejected me the first time, the Crow gave me to an old spacer couple to care for me. Though they didn't have a choice in the matter, they were kind. And with them, I could be kind as well.

A shadow crossed her features.

It wasn't until Calderon rejected me the second time that the Crow made me a monster in revenge.

"Thread..." Davis laid a hand over hers. "You saved my life. And Foster's. If you think I'm going to forget that, you're straight wrong."

Thread ran a finger along her scar from her forehead to her throat.

She took my voice to remind me that I had none and scarred my body to mark me as hers—a grotesque salute to the scars she once bore. So I suppose in a way, I'll never escape her.

Davis's gut tightened at the pain in Thread's face, and he could only hope that many decades ago, the Crow had gotten the ending she deserved. He gestured out the cockpit at the brand-new constellations stretching before them. "No matter what came before, this is our fresh start. I know you'll never forget what happened, but know that it doesn't define you. Here, you can be whoever you want."

For a moment, they sat there, the tension of the moment stretching between them. Her expression grew thoughtful, and then she poked at her plate, her downcast gaze almost shy.

I'd like a name. A real one.

"Anything." Davis smiled, the budding hope of the simple request pulsing through him. "Do you have one in mind?"

The girl's holo flicked out from the spacer's visor as she consulted the ship's internal computer.

I think... Lily feels right. It's an old-world flower that symbolizes new beginnings.

Davis nodded, reaching across the table and squeezing her hand. "Lily." The name felt right on his tongue, and she actually blushed, her face lighting up with the first real smile he'd seen since he'd woken. "It suits you, and, Lily, I'm glad to have you here with me."

She drew her hand away, picking up her fork as she blushed furiously into her bowl.

Thank you for bringing me through the wormgate. You didn't have to do that, and this is truly a better fresh start than I could've dreamed of. Her eyes grew distant. *I only hope that Foster and Ezren are also well.*

Davis thought of the last time he'd seen them—crying, wounded, but together. And if the two of them were together, he was certain they could do anything. He smiled through another bite of the mush. "I'm sure they went on to do legendary things, and they're probably ninety years old now with their grandchildren running the BRR."

I wish there was some way we could know.

"There actually is," Davis said. "They could get an update to us in the next ship to this system, but they usually come every three years." His smile fell again as he realized that if Ezren and Foster thought they were dead, there would be no message. But he didn't voice the fear aloud. "Of course, they'll never know what happened to us... but sometimes we have to believe the best."

Lily's face softened. *I want to believe the best.*

"Me too." Davis finished the last bit of his meal, took both of their empty bowls, and stuck them in the recycler chute to be broken down for future raw materials. "Now to decide what to do next."

Lily looked up at him with her huge green eyes. *Did... did you have a plan?*

"I do." He inclined his head to the cockpit at the star map projected there. "Because I figure, we've got a ship, flying credentials, a very nearly completed degree in wormgate navigation, and some on-the-job experience." His smile grew as he worked through the details.

"I'm thinking I'd like to stick around here until the next update from Casolla comes in." *Just in case.* "Maybe work as a transport captain while I finish my degree, and then I might sign up to be a wormgate tech myself, hopping from system to system delivering updates and repairing the gates where needed. Then eventually we could upgrade the ship to an explorer class and apply to the discovery corps."

He gave her a sheepish shrug, his cheeks heating as he realized she probably didn't care about all the steps he'd been plotting since he was six years old. "Honestly it's really the same plan I always had... I just kind of want to see if there's an update from my friends in Casolla first." He scratched at the back of his head as he leaned against the table beside her. "But it also depends on what you want to do since this ship is half yours."

Realizing he was babbling, Davis had to force himself to close his mouth. There was just something about the intense way she looked at him that sent his senses all into a buzz and made it hard to stop talking.

Lily smiled at him as she looked out at the star map again.

No one's ever asked me what I wanted to do before, but I think the stars are calling to me as well.

Something warm in Davis's belly fluttered to life. That's

exactly how he'd described it ever since he was small. A tug from the stars on his chest, as if there was something else out there he had to find. And never once had he heard someone share anything remotely similar. There weren't many system hoppers in the 'verse because most people didn't like the thought of leaving behind a life over and over.

But this girl... could she really have a wanderer's spirit too? Or perhaps she was only lost and needed time to find what really spoke to her. Either way, they had the opportunity to find out.

She turned her huge gaze to him, hopeful and beseeching at the same time.

I like your plan, Davis. And if you don't mind, I think I'd like to stay with you for a while, if you'll have me.

Davis let out a relieved breath, the tension in his shoulders unraveling. "I was hoping you'd say that."

And then Lily smiled for real, her whole face lighting up as she threw her arms around him. The force was so huge that Davis had to stumble back a few steps, laughing as he caught her. For a second, she just hung there, and Davis let her cling to him, sensing something bigger growing between them. The rightness of her in his arms. The feeling of a kindred heart pounding against his.

The dampness of tears seeped into his shirt, and her words projected from the cockpit holo.

I'm sorry... I just... I haven't hugged anyone in almost two years.

"Don't be sorry," Davis whispered, squeezing her tighter. He'd wager that she hadn't even had a kind touch in that time, much less a hug, and he was more than willing to make up for it now. "I'll hold on for as long as you need me. We have all the time in the 'verse." He wasn't sure how long they stayed like that, her wet face buried against his neck as he swayed her back and forth. But at last, she tentatively drew away, wiping her eyes with her palms.

Okay then, where do we go first?

He grinned at her. "Want to see a brand-new world?"

Lily brightened like a sun finally appearing from behind the clouds. She nodded.

Yes. I really do.

"Then let's go."

He offered her his hand, and with a broadening grin, she wove her fingers with his.

Together, they walked into the cockpit, the new, unfamiliar solar system lighting up in front of them. And as she leaned against him, smiling in wonder...

He felt the start of something extraordinary.